ARCANE ADVENTURESS

I0663807

THE RAIL SPECTER

VENNESSA ROBERTSON

GREEN
GRIFFIN
PRESS

BY THE AUTHOR

S§S

THE RAIL SPECTER

Cover art by Deranged Doctor Design http://www.derangeddoctordesign.com/

A Green Griffin Press release.
www.greengriffinpress.com

ISBN: 978-0-9995724-3-6

CONTENTS

For my wonderful, supportive husband and my two amazing children.
I could not have done this without you.

§§§

TO MY READERS

STORYTELLERS bear a responsibility to their readers—not only to entertain and move them, but also to do no harm. This is especially the case when writing tales that cross cultures and continents, as Arcane Adventuress does. In telling the tale of a young woman who discovers, while coming into her own power, that all lands and people are united and that we are all one, this series follows her from London to China to the American West. In this third novel, I wanted to touch on the inequality of sharecropping and to shine a harsh light on what was being done to indigenous cultures. I know this is a risky thing for an author to do; too many times, stories about those in history whose voices have been silenced or marginalized include damaging tropes that do injustice to their living descendants. Though in this story I have taken much creative license with the tale of a family of Cheyenne in search of refuge after atrocities, I hope any missteps I have made may be forgiven, and I would encourage any readers who enjoy the story they find in these pages to also seek out the stories told by our Cheyenne neighbors, in their own voices, today. Just as Vivian would. Thank you for reading.

VENNESSA ROBERTSON

CHAPTER ONE

THE RAIN FELL from the darkened sky, splashing and adding to the gathered puddles on the already sodden ground. Though well into summer, we had not had a break from the spring rains and the land was suffering for it. My dear Nate would be home soon. I rose from my seat in the solar and rang for Mrs. Simms.

Our cook appeared, like magic, a few moments later in her starched white apron. "Yes, Mrs. Valentine?"

Mrs. Valentine. I still got a little flutter beneath my breastbone hearing my married name. As wonderful as marriage was, my life was woefully incomplete. I had married, I had established a home. Now I needed a family, a babe to rock in my arms and bring us joy, rather than the moody gloom of the dark estate beset by rain and wild moors. I swallowed hard. "Mr. Valentine will need something warm to drink when he returns with Mr. Crossdale. See to it that refreshments are laid for them both."

She nodded and left.

Lady Vivian Valentine. Yes, that is who I am now. We are the landholders of a small estate in the countryside, outside of London, where the land is slowly being drowned by bad fortune and ceaseless, unseasonable rain.

In all this space, with all this land and all this beauty, I was suffocating.

When we lived in London and my papa ran a well-respected apothecary shop, we would treat those who needed our help. Mama read the tarot cards for entertainment and helped babies be born. There was always work

1

to be done. And, just as I thought there was nothing for me but to marry well to provide for their care as they aged, a man unlike any other entered my life: a ruffian who swept me into a life of adventure and magic.

At the very least, I had married well with Nate. Adventure had awarded us an estate in a roundabout way. As soon as we had moved in, we invited my mama and papa to join us, from London, to enjoy a comfortable retirement in the country.

I paced our empty solar. Now wealthy and married a year, our grand adventures had degenerated to desperately trying to puzzle out how to feed the souls in our care.

Ironically, the solar was supposed to be the sunniest room of the house. But there were no sunny days anymore. With Queen Victoria's death, England herself was in mourning, and her tears were infinite. It was the end of an age.

The rain made the ground too soft for travel by carriage, so Nate and Mr. Crossdale were out on horseback. Several months ago, Nate would never have attempted this, but he had gained comfort in the saddle over the last year as both an adventurer of the land and an esquire. Now, there was nothing to do but wait for his return while staring brokenly at either the fire or the rain dripping down the window. I did what a good daughter should: I married well. Now, I longed for adventure again, be it a family to raise or a journey back into the unknown.

Our maid, Helen, spoke from the doorway: "Mrs. Valentine, Mr. Goslan and his wife are here to see you."

I turned to her. "Please bring out some hot tea and cake, and…have Hiram stoke the fire. They will be cold and wet. Also, please inform Papa that we have guests." It was only proper that my father help me receive the guests. The proper running of the house was mind-numbing, but the routine of it all was a welcome distraction from my ennui.

"At once." She gave a small curtsy and ran off as quickly as she had come. I smoothed my burgundy skirts and plastered a smile to my face. A lady should never appear miserable.

The Goslans were not the first family of tenants to come visiting in the last month, nor would they be the last. Each of the tenants had come, one at a time, begging our forgiveness, promising they would pay their overdue rents if only we would allow them time, or to offer something they hoped we might take in trade. Two of the tenant families disappeared in the night, leaving abandoned farms of flooded fields and rotting roots.

According to the records the previous landowners had left behind, the Goslans had a reputation for being loyal, hardworking tenants. Now, Mr. Goslan stood twisting his cap in his hands, covered in a farm coat of wet wool over a dark suit with worn cuffs.

"Mr. Goslan, please, make yourself comfortable."

He remained standing. He looked anything but comfortable, dabbing at his nose with his handkerchief.

"Please," I repeated, motioning. The collar of his suit was wet from the rain. His wife curtsied quickly, then sat on the corner of our sofa as though she did not want to dirty it. Her braided hair had been carefully tucked up under her cap. They wore their Sunday best.

Helen brought in a tea tray with milk from our cow and small ginger biscuits. It was far from a grand treat, but the least I could offer, given the circumstances. They were chilled to the bone.

Papa came in and muffled a cough in his handkerchief. "Excuse me. I was in the conservatory. It took me a moment longer than I thought."

"Sir." Mr. Goslan bobbed his head nervously and cleared his throat.

"How can I help you today?" I poured four cups of tea and served everyone a ginger biscuit. I usually let Helen serve, but I needed something to do with my hands.

"Well, you see, it's like this—" Mr. Goslan trailed off then flushed, worrying his hat again. "We owe on our rent." He looked up at me nervously. "And I know we owe," he added quickly.

"We plan to pay," Mrs. Goslan interjected.

"We just need a little more time to pay the full quarter's rent," Mr. Goslan said quickly. "We have part of it." He dug into his pocket for a few coins. "Coal has been so expensive, and we've had no money for meat. We eat what our garden provides."

The front door opened and Hiram hurried from his corner of the solar to attend to the master of the house's needs. A moment later, Nate strode into the solar, clomping in wet boots, rubbing a linen towel through his hair. His collar was soaked, and he had already exchanged his waistcoat for a dry one as Hiram had been ready with fresh clothing.

He greeted them warmly. "Good afternoon Mr. Goslan. Mrs. Goslan, you look lovely as always."

She rose and curtsied. Pleasantries observed, I poured him tea.

"Mr. Crossdale is having hot soup in the kitchen." Nate combed his hair back with his fingers. The fact that an esquire never needed to make excuses to his tenants was lost on Nate. Again.

"Darling, Mr. Goslan was explaining that the price of coal was straining his finances this quarter." I handed Nate his tea. No need to cause Mr. Goslan more embarrassment. "But he just needs more time, and he brought a partial payment."

Nate added milk to his tea and stirred it. It was a show. Men needed to be stern, or they lost respect for one another. Mr. Goslan needed to know his landlord respected him and expected him to honor his commitment. It was an odd game men played. Mrs. Goslan's hand shook as she stirred her tea. They were the third tenant family this quarter. Our people were starving, or freezing, or both. Their crops were failing. They were flooded out. It was the same all throughout the countryside.

"Mr. Goslan, how many children do you have?"

"Four." He wiped his nose again.

"Do you have any staff?"

"We hired a girl to help with the children. She also helps with laundry and cooking," Mr. Goslan said. "She sleeps in the attic. She used to live in the city, but she is orphaned now. She is a smart girl."

"Annie is like a daughter," Mrs. Goslan added tensely.

"I believe we can come to some sort of arrangement. We shall roll the rent due into the next quarter, that portion which is not paid shall roll to the next bill and so forth until your entire debt is paid. That shall keep us from the strain of having to secure new tenants this late in the season. I hope these terms are acceptable?" Nate said. "Hiram, according to the books, the Goslan family have been good tenants and Mr. Goslan is a man of his word, correct?"

"Yes, sir." Hiram confirmed. "I can verify with Mr. Crossdale, he is the land steward, but I familiarized myself with the workings and finances of the property when I was brought on."

Of course he had. Hiram was a wonderful head of staff.

Nate nodded, "Mr. Goslan, Mrs. Goslan, in light of our understanding, I do hope you will be our guests for dinner tonight. It is only proper to seal our new arrangement over a meal. We are not eating lavishly, but it will be a warm dinner to fill your bellies before you set off back home."

Mr. Goslan broke into a smile. With a single action, Nate had placed himself upon equal footing with his tenant and, yet, remained the lord of our land. He had allowed Mr. Goslan to keep his dignity. He demonstrated that we don't eat like kings while our tenants starve. How I love that man.

I drew Mrs. Goslan aside. Her shawl was threadbare and the hem was unraveling. I remember what it was to struggle through lean times. I wrapped her in mine. Made of fine wool and a tight, even knit, it would keep her warm. Most importantly, it was dry. I insisted she keep it.

Mrs. Simms had made more than enough soup and hot bread to feed our entire household, so adding two more was an easy task. Papa and Mama ate on one side of the table in the little dining room. Papa coughed from time to time, wheezing into his handkerchief. Tonight, I would make sure he received treatment for his cough before I went to bed. Mr. and Mrs. Goslan sat across from them, enjoying the beef and barley soup with a hearty wheat bread, filled with the little nuts and bits of cheese Mrs. Simms always baked into the loaves. Our second course was two roast rabbits with bacon and mashed potatoes, and there was a plum pudding for dessert.

I would have to tell Nate there would be no baby this month. Again. I hated to add to our worries: no children, no income, and now our tenants were starving. Every investment we had made was failing. It was as though everything I had touched in the past year had been cursed with utter ruin.

And, yet, I carried a hidden fortune in my pocket, one I dared not share with anyone, especially my husband. As long as it was still a secret, we were safe.

CHAPTER TWO

THE MID-MORNING SUN burned through the clouds, clearing the haze, and promising the day would warm and allow the sodden land to dry, somewhat. Everyone in the household wanted to take advantage of the break in the wet weather to work at either hanging laundry or airing out the home. Several birds took wing across the field. Peace and joy had come to us at last. I hoped the long mourning of the land was done, and England would come to life again and, with it, our tenants' fortunes would change for the better.

Mr. Crossdale, our land steward, met with me and Nate over breakfast in the solar. Ordinarily, Jane would be attending us, but the maids were taking advantage of the sunshine. Even our butler was attending to the house.

"You see, sir," Crossdale began, "you asked me to inform you of the traditions the tenants expect."

My husband nodded, but his attention was on the warming land and the beautiful great fog rising outside the large picture windows. The land fought to warm herself, giving the hills an ethereal quality.

"Every year the Rothechild family held a harvest festival for the tenants and friends of the family, following the harvest moon," Mr. Crossdale said, sipping coffee.

"Of course," Nate said absently. He stood at the window, the sunlight illuminating his ragged ear, torn by Prince Qixiang's spear during our last adventure.

When we first met, my husband had been a dashing airship pirate suffering from a magical curse that forced him to spend half his time as a human, and half his time as a dog. He helped me become an adventuress in my own right. Then, our journey led to an awakening of my Tarot powers, which allowed me to manipulate the world around us, using Tarot symbols buried deeply under my skin. It was on that adventure that he achieved mastery over the dual sides of his nature, finding a third form, a potent mixture of man and beast that was both powerful and protective, sharing the best features of man and dog. We called it his *canithrope* form.

A year later, the explorers' society sent us to China to recover an ancient artifact before the nation erupted in civil war over the Opium Wars. We battled a royal dynasty in chaos, crippled by insanity and rage. We journeyed into the mists to find the grave of a dragon and there, in his canithrope form, he was scarred by the mad Prince's spear.

It was also there that I experienced a horrific premonition. If we recovered the artifact from the grave of a long-dead dragon, the powerful Xihuan-Lung, she would reanimate to wreak deadly vengeance upon the world. The premonition showed her starting with us, for disrupting her grave. I recovered one of her stolen teeth and shattered the key to her eternal resting place, taking the keystone away with me, a ruby the size of a robin's egg, which rested safely now in my pocket.

It was my secret and, as long as I had it, Nate and the world were safe.

After everything we had overcome, it was odd that running an estate and getting pregnant, the most mundane tasks a husband and wife might undertake, were beyond our abilities.

Nate returned to the table, where his eggs and coffee were cooling. "If that is what the tenants expect, then it would not do to disappoint."

Forever the adventurer, he was drawn to the land outside the window. With a heavy sigh, he took his seat, shifted around a stiff hip and resigned himself to discussing the estate.

"Excuse me, please," I said, and left the solar. I simply could not bear to be at the table any longer and watch my Nate struggle with pedestrian matters.

SOS

I found Papa and Mama in the conservatory, enjoying the orchids while they had tea and crumpets with marmalade. Papa would occasionally offer a corner of his crumpet to the beloved finches that lived in a huge, brass cage. He had hand-tamed them to eat from his fingers. They would hop from his fingers to the plants and not give him any trouble when it was time to return to their cage. The room remained warm and humid, thanks to the tight-fitting glass windows. It was the only room in the home that the cold and damp couldn't penetrate.

This was the only bright spot of having an estate. It nearly made it worthwhile. Papa had spent his entire life as an apothecary in London. We had lived above a storefront on Exeter Street, where he devoted himself to the care of others. Now, in his gray years, he had a place to sit, and rest, and drink tea while enjoying crumpets and marmalade. He sat for hours, here in the conservatory, enjoying the wonders of a glass-walled room, as well as an indoor garden of herbs, flowers, and birds.

This morning, he sat by his cage full of tiny, beautiful finches, beside Mama at a little table set for breakfast, trying to catch his breath. "He-hello there darling. Just a bit winded this morning."

"Papa."

His rubbed his favorite bird, perched on his hand, with a blunt finger. Papa had always been a gentle soul. Now, he was free of the worries of feeding his family and running a business, he was truly happy.

Mama motioned for me to join them. Since the maids were busy, I poured. "How are things, my darling?"

"Fine. We are planning a harvest festival celebration for later this month. It is tradition." For a moment, I worried they would make me explain how we could successfully pull off a harvest festival when harvests had been so meager.

Mama sipped her tea. "That's a wonderful idea. A celebration will remind people to be grateful for the blessings in their lives, even in these hard times. You will be inviting your social friends and your tenants, I hope?"

"Of course." I smiled. What was I worried about? Mama always understood. She tipped the crumbs off her plate into the finch cage. The little birds happily picked the bits up and gulped them down. I had half a mind to offer them tea as well. They were British, after all.

"It will be quite warm today." I finished my cup and set it down. "Would you both like to go for a short walk?"

"I would love to, darling." Papa put his favorite finch back into its cage. "But I cannot seem to walk very far nowadays."

"How is your cough, Papa?"

"Better."

I nodded, though we both knew he was lying. "Papa, I made a fresh tincture, will you take some?"

"I am fine, Vivian, it is merely this damp air."

"Papa, I believe I heard that cough before the air grew so damp." When I was a girl, he would use this exact tone with me, reminding me that he saw more than I wished he did and inviting my honesty. He had never accused me, out loud, of being dishonest with him.

"Perhaps you are right." He turned back to his birds.

I searched for words of comfort for Mama. She looked over to where her husband of the past three decades sat gently stroking a fern, murmuring its name in Latin. She allowed an indulgent smile. He had a certain love affair with plants; Papa admired their ability to hurt and heal and avidly kept the secrets the plants held. Mama's smile faded. She turned ashen. "I don't need foresight to know what his future holds."

I stood. Though the mistress of my home, I felt out of place here, too. My vision felt spotty and, for a moment, I feared I had stood too quickly. Then I recognized the feeling for what it was, a Tarot vision. My readings could come when I commanded them or they could come on their own, too strong to ignore. This one was a warning. It was akin to being suffocated with a velvet cord. Gentle at first, but it would strangle the life from me just the same. A Tarot vision could not be ignored.

I grabbed the frame of the French doors. The conservatory was beautiful, nearly overgrown like a jungle painting. The flowers cast uneven shadows in the room, and the red-brown tiles were nearly lost in the shadows. All the windows had fogged over from the long weeks of rain and the sunlight that came through the windows was distorted and wavy, making the shadows dance.

They swirled and moved and the plants formed into a large ring of beautiful, vibrant green that crept around the room. The large branches became spokes of a wheel, slowly rotating as the sun danced in and out of the gathered moisture. My mouth went dry. It was a wheel, and I knew exactly which one it was. *The Wheel of Fortune.* But it had been constructed incorrectly. When oriented properly, the serpent is always on the left. The conservatory had a rare snake flower from the Himalayas that only bloomed in very wet weather; it was on the wrong side, the right one. On the right side of the wheel should be Anubis, the Egyptian jackal god of death but, in this room, a small belladonna plant I kept for pain medicine and when I needed a powerful muscle relaxant was on the left. Instead of eagles, we had a cage of birds and, though we lacked a bull and a sphinx, we did have a small clock topped with an angelic figure.

Despite the missing animals, there was no mistaking the symbols. The sun and the moisture on the windows cast the symbols onto the tile floor. It was *The Wheel of Fortune* reversed; great upheaval, disruption, an unwelcome turn of fortune was coming. More things were about to spin out of our control.

The only trouble was that our fortunes had not been good lately. I dreaded thinking that they were going to take a turn for the worse.

$$S\Omega S$$

In the weeks that came, I did my best for forget the reversed Wheel of Fortune in order to focus on the upcoming autumnal celebration.

We decided that it would be more cheerful to hold the celebration in September, before the harvest at the end of October, and Nate would meet with each of the tenants in turn, in his study, to inform them we would not be collecting rents this quarter. The tenants would be encouraged to spend their income on food and coal, taking advantage of the lower prices of both grain and coal before the weather turned even colder.

The cook's nephew, Rory Simms, returned from posting the invitations and I sent him to the kitchen for a glass of warm cider and a plate of bread and cheese. I found Nate muttering over the ledgers and the week's post in the study like a cranky hound.

I recognized the look on my husband's face. He ran his hand through his hair, a nervous gesture that made him look chronically untidy, a habit uniquely his and charming in its own way. His fingers absently found the scarred and torn ear and he worried at the torn flesh before pulling his hand away. Poor man, adventuring had been so hard on him, but fulfilling the daily responsibilities of being an esquire seemed to elude him.

A nagging feeling that I was missing something consumed me. There was something drastically wrong, more so than my husband's frustration. I took a breath, centered myself and, when I breathed out, I pushed energy out into the world around me like little seeking spirit tendrils. The readings were becoming easier. I hardly had to concentrate anymore to invoke the Tarot. And the ruby in my pocket, the one from the Chinese dragon's key, suddenly felt very much alive. It weighed me down, pulling me toward the earth, from my hip to my breast bone. I shivered at the pull, but as long as I had the ruby, the dragon was locked away forever. I had taken it to protect it, so it had become my responsibility. I took a deep breath to try to clear away the dizziness, but it was no good. I grabbed the back of the chair for support.

Another Tarot vision. This time, it was the *Ten of Pentacles*, inverted. When upright, it is a happy event: a father sits in his home attended by his sons and his dogs, enjoying his grey years, surrounded by ten pentacles, or coins, symbolizing his wealth, providing comfort in his autumn years. It symbolizes a happy, comfortable life with no financial worries. I shuddered, because nothing was as it should be. The pile of mail on Nate's desk would contain bad news for our finances, such as a horrid bill, or more likely bad news about our investments in America.

I forced myself to swallow what felt like a nest of snakes worming its way through my insides. "Whatever is wrong, my love?"

He said nothing, instead handing me a letter. It was the statement of our investment in the Pennsylvania Railroad. There was to be no investment income, again, this quarter. Something had gone wrong with their latest project, involving westward expansion and their anticipated earnings had become, instead, a crippling loss. Every investor had lost money and several of their backers were demanding payment upon the loss. There was no request for additional funding to expand west of St. Louis, Missouri but, should the losses continue, they would have no choice but to request additional funds. The alternative would be to abandon the project entirely.

I blinked hard.

No income from the tenants. That was our own doing, of course. The tenants were stretched to the point of breaking. If we took their rental payments, they would be unable to feed their families and heat their homes this coming winter. Now, there would be no income from our carefully chosen investments either.

I looked over Nate's shoulder. It was too late to cancel the celebration. The grocer was coming tomorrow with items to fill the larder. We had both fish and fowl ready to cook. The menu was planned. We had arranged for temporary help and the families of those servants were counting on the income. The vintner was due within the hour to bring us more wine and sherry for the party. Our cash on hand could support the party, and we could doubtlessly survive the next few years, as long as we avoided any unforeseen expenses, but without incomes from either the investment or our tenants, we could not last indefinitely.

The thought of running out of coal and food, no matter how far down the road it might be, made me shiver. How would I feed my parents without money?

"I am sure this is only temporary," Nate said, more to himself than to me. "The harvest celebration will continue as planned." He patted my hand. "Don't fret. I will keep you fed, even if I have to battle more dragons."

He was joking, but my mouth went dry. A dragon? "No dragons. Promise me."

"Viv, your hands are like ice, and you've gone pale." Nate stood and plunked me down into his chair. "No dragons. I promise." He knelt beside me. "Don't worry. There will be money. We can always pull the investment from the railroad and place it somewhere else. I know you're no fan of airships, but as a mode of travel they do show great promise and have proven to be safe. An airship can go anywhere."

"An airship can also fall from the sky," I said, pointedly.

"And there we go. Now I know you are feeling better, since you're griping about airships." Nate laughed. "It is a ship in the sky. It's freedom, like a ship on the water. It's sailing into the horizon."

"You miss it." I laughed. He had hunted lightning once on the decks of one of those great airships, though it seemed a lifetime ago.

"I do," he admitted. "But I would not trade this life for that one." He caught my look, "Most days, anyway." He rang for Helen.

She appeared in moments.

"A stiff drink for Mrs. Valentine. She is feeling indisposed."

"Is Mrs. Valentine expecting?" she asked.

I could not ignore the look of elation that crossed Nate's face before he masked it. He longed for a baby nearly as much as I did. "A stiff drink, please." It was Nate's lord voice. None of the servants dared disobey him when he used it.

Helen gave a quick curtsy and rushed off.

I bit my lip. "Nate."

"Hmm?"

"Nate, there is no baby this month." I went numb all over. Saying it aloud made it all too real.

He nodded. "Perhaps next time." He swallowed and looked away. His shoulders sagged. He combed his fingers through his hair again. I smiled. I could dress him in a gentleman's finery, but his quirky habits never changed.

$$S\S S$$

What a feast lay before us! It was no wonder the wealthy tended to grow heavier in their later years. It was far from a bountiful harvest but, in honor of the season, we served several courses to our guests, including a rich game soup made with venison and red wine, braised ham, grouse pies, hare with mushrooms, and roasted vegetables. Pudding was Mrs. Simms's marvelous apple tarts.

My dress was nearly new, a silvery-mauve, silk poplin number with bows and muted gray buttons, finished off with a soft delaine wrap draped across my shoulders. I would wear it until the bodies gathered in the great room made it too warm and toasty for a wrap.

Hiram welcomed everyone, and Helen, Jane, and Olive floated like shadows between our guests and tenants, delivering small cups of warmed cider, sherry, and wine to stave off the chill. I watched Nate subtly invite the heads of each of our tenant families into his study for a quiet discussion. They entered stiffly, like men awaiting execution, expecting to be thrown out of their homes, damning their families to starvation and beggary, or even worse, death.

It was my role to be the hostess and ensure that all our guests felt welcome and entertained with good conversation. I made polite talk, inquired of families and farms, and expressed my delight at their attendance. I handed out sweets to the children. Eventually, Nate led us into the dining room; it was his responsibility, as the head of the household, to lead the transitions.

Nate stood at the head of the table and ran a hand through his hair to steady himself. "It is in the sight of God, our family, and friends that we gather here to remember we are blessed. Heading into the harvest is a time of hard work." There were murmurs of agreement. "And this has been a hard year indeed." There were more murmurs. "But this is also a time to count our blessings. A time to remember that seasons come and seasons pass, and we should be grateful for the blessings in our lives." Nate raised his glass. A flush had risen to his collar. "Let us raise a glass to honor our family and our friends. We remember our late, great Queen Victoria, and toast King Edward, long may he reign."

"Long may he reign," our guests echoed. Everyone drank deeply. The festival seemed to be the harbinger of a reversal of our fortunes, a promise of good times ahead.

But, like all good things, it didn't last. Over the next few weeks, Papa's cough grew steadily worse, his edema swelled greater and, on yet another rainy night of many I kissed him goodnight.

I sent him to bed with a warm fire and a dose of laudanum syrup to ease his cough and help him rest.

The next morning, Papa didn't wake up.

CHAPTER THREE

THE RAIN CONTINUED turning the country into a keening land of sorrow where the tears of the nation flooded the land, making the crops weak and soft as a black fungus caused them to rot in the fields. The coal mines filled with water, making coal expensive, leaving houses dark and cold. That was nothing compared to the misery in our home.

We placed Papa's casket in the conservatory, his favorite place in the house. The mourners would arrive soon for the funeral. Ironically, with all the clocks stopped, the mirrors turned away and the house wreathed in black, only the conservatory showed signs of life. Papa's birds twittered and the plants continued to grow lush and green amidst all the rain.

In my pocket, I had put the dragon's tooth I brought back from China. I had reclaimed it from the possession of a mystical creature that had traveled with us for a time. I took the dragon's tooth and placed it in Papa's vest pocket, where his watch had always been. A gentleman always carried a fine watch, but Papa had willed his watch to Nate. It was only fitting, since he had bequeathed Nate with something precious, that I return the honor.

"Papa, I am grateful I was able to have you spend your last months here in peace and comfort. I wish it had been longer." My throat was hot and tight. I sniffed, wiping my nose on the back of my hand in a most unlady-like fashion. "Papa, I love you. I miss you. I wish"—I swallowed hard—"I wish I'd had the time to ask you how else to have a baby."

"The traditional way is usually best," Mama said from behind me.

I smiled, and turned. She had been keeping her vigil over Papa.

Jane attempted to improve the quality of the air in the grand room by adding potpourri to the wood fire, for the sake of aesthetics, as it burned off the chill. Mama's mourning gown helped her blend in with the shadows. The black damask, fabric-covered buttons, and the loss of Papa had worn her down into a shade of herself.

Despite how numb I felt, I had to smile, for her sake. "Yes, I know." That would have been Papa's answer as well: practical and honest.

She patted the chaise beside her. "Come, sit with me." She pulled me close, letting me lay my head on her shoulder. She stared at Papa, lying in his casket. We sat in silence for a long moment. Then finally she spoke. "Do not despair. Children will come."

The finches chirped, flitting from one perch to another. They sipped water from their bowl and cocked their heads back and forth. They could see Papa, but he would not come over and offer them treats or let them out to fly about the conservatory and land on his fingers. They sang and he would not whistle back. Poor things.

Guests began to arrive in the parlor for the memorial. All our remaining tenants would arrive in their Sunday best, and his apprentice that took over his apothecary ship in London would too, along with many of the people whose lives he had touched with a gentle, healing hand. I closed my eyes. They would be given warm cider as they shared their condolences. I could not hide here forever, but I would, at that moment, have traded my entire estate to have Papa back for one more day.

Madame Theodora Bowden, and her husband Isaac, arrived dressed in the finest black velvet I had seen in a long time. Theodora immediately wentto my mother to console her. I had to tend to our guests. It was what was expected of me.

They said kind things that fell upon my deaf ears. I was numb and alone, in a roaring sea of well-wishers, people who pressed my hand and told me Papa had gone to a better place. They were wrong. He belonged with a daughter that needed him and a wife that welcomed his love.

Would it be that way for me, some day, when Nate was gone? I shivered and searched the room for him. He stood, dressed in black mourning attire, talking to a friend. I could not hear what they were saying.

I made my way over to Nate and took his hand. He did not look at me, but gave me a gentle squeeze. I glanced at my husband. It would come to this for us. One day, we, too, would be separated by death.

I was so distracted, I did not feel the pull of the Tarot symbol where it was located on my body until I was consumed by it. There was a chill on the back of my neck, like an icy hand pressing me forward. The symbol beneath my skin there was *The Hermit.*

The room was thrown into darkness; the world shrank to a small point of light. The chill of it made me gasp. All the light, all the warmth of the world had been sucked from the room in an instant. I blinked hard, but the light didn't return. All I had, everything I was, had been reduced to a pinprick of light. I shuddered. The back of the chaise longue had been next to me a moment ago. I fumbled in the dark. My hand brushed the polished wooden frame. I latched onto it, my stiff fingers digging into it.

Here I stood, a woman grown, able to do all sorts of things women did not do—I rode horses, shot guns, flew in airships, used wooden and fiber wings, I bottled lightning, and I fought demons. I am a powerful woman and, yet, all I wanted in that moment was to be held by my Papa and told everything will be right in the world. I wanted to return from adventure and have tea and cake by the fire, and share stories of my adventures with him, to have him stroke my hair and call me his brave, brave girl.

And I want to return to my world of adventure, knowing that he would be right here where I left him, enjoying the world I provided, with orchids and birds and healthy tenants with rich bountiful harvests and sunlight and joy. And I wanted my husband to be unharmed.

My breath came in gasps, my mouth was dry, my gown too tight around my shoulders. I longed to flex and stretch until the seams burst and I could strip it off the way Nate tore his human skin when his canithrope form burst from within his body. He was a man of raw adventure that flowed from him. Running an estate was smothering him.

I understood, then, why he tore at his own flesh when transfiguring as though it suffocated him like a too-tight suit. There was a pain between my shoulders, a deep pain, a knife digging into my spine, tearing its way between the bones to burrow its way through me. I longed to tear it free and run screaming until my lungs burst and I bled.

"Vivian?"

A strong hand touched my back. The light returned and, with it, the sound and smells and a thousand other things I hadn't realized I had been missing.

Nate's hand guided me though the chaos. "This will all be over soon," he said quietly. "Your papa was a good man. Everyone just wants to pay their respects."

Of course. How did he bear it? Nate was so strong. I looked into his warm brown eyes, then at his scarred ear, and leaned against his arm. The pain between my shoulders receded, along with the crushing darkness though, for the first time, I could see the space the darkness had left behind, the light compressed into a single lantern with an oil wick. The lantern was being carried by an old man, his face barely illuminated as he shuffled along, swathed in gray robes, staff in hand.

This specter, *The Hermit* did not look at me. He existed outside the room, beyond it, as though he was both a part of this world and, at the same time, not of this world. He was Tarot, and I could feel where the Tarot symbol existed beneath my skin, along my torso with the rest of the major arcana. He was *The Hermit*, the guardian of introspection. The symbol of soul-searching. The very personification of isolation.

I needed some peace in this ocean of loss. I reached deep within myself and, with all the will I could muster, summoned a card. Within the Tarot, the Cups were, among other things, our emotions and our connections to others. I longed to feel the weight of a great, overflowing chalice, spilling healing waters over my hand, dripping down my arm, down my body, pooling around my feet. Aces symbolized newness, the beginning of a cycle, but the *Ace of Cups* was like a baptism, either by the church or the soul of earth itself, the promise that grief is not forever.

It reminded me of the purifying waters that flowed in the river beyond the hooded figure of Death. Even as a child, when I was too young to understand that choosing The *Death* card didn't mean an actual death, the card yet gave me a chill. The card meant change: all things must eventually change to make way for the new. I was drawn to it and what it could mean as the hooded reaper rode through the land, striking down kings and peasants alike: clearing the old away to make room for the new.

There was finality in the air. I shut my eyes to the cards. It was a grief and loss I was not sure I could weather right now. I had learned to manipulate the Fates themselves with the cards but, I wondered, with the right application of fate, why couldn't I buy Papa more time?

Mr. Ward looked at Nate. He must have given an agreed-upon signal, for we then moved to the large room where Father Barbary would hold a prayer before Papa's coffin was taken to the cemetery. I heard the hammers, muffled by wool batting, driving home the nails in the lid of the coffin. Mama flinched with every strike.

Father Barbury intoned a prayer amid sniffles and coughs.

"Almighty God, Father of all mercies and giver of all comfort: deal graciously, we pray, with those who mourn, that, casting all their care on you, they may know the consolation of your love, through Jesus Christ, our Lord. Amen."

Our guests echoed the "Amen", whispered their words of comfort and left us to our grief. We accompanied Papa to his grave, where Father Barbury gave more prayers for the safekeeping of Papa's soul before the rain came down to help the workers fill in the grave.

Try as I might, I could not make myself pay attention to the funeral service. I swallowed hard. Papa was gone. Mama sat still and silent beside me, staring ahead like a woman struck mute and dumb. Tonight, for the first time in decades, she would go to bed alone.

CHAPTER FOUR

AS THE WEEKS passed, I became a wraith with mourning. The light and joy of our home washed away with the renewed rains. The land would tease us with moments of peace and sunshine, only to dash our hopes with returned bad weather and no news of hope from America about our precious investments.

I could not remain on the estate doing nothing. I could not look at the walls where I had become a prisoner of pain and loss, as what had been a home of joy and peace became rooms of cold darkness warmed only by Lum Baxter's children as they flitted about like tiny, lost butterflies moving through the meadow. We needed hope, and I needed change. But, more than that, I needed the quickening of my blood that came with adventure. I needed to know why our promising investments were performing so poorly. I needed to get away from being trapped where there was nothing to do but feel like ill luck was a great pack of wolves circling our doors.

Though a part of me felt like I should stay with Mama and continue to mourn Papa, I could not remain any longer. We had a responsibility to the people who called our land home. And just as importantly, the president of the railroad, Mr. Cassatt, to whom we had entrusted a great deal of money, owed us an explanation about what exactly was happening with our money. We would be much more difficult to ignore if we, rather than our letters, were sitting upon his desk.

Madame Theodora came to keep Mama company during her mourning, and the two of them sat in the conservatory, dressed in black. Mama stared into the fire, with a dark blanket over her lap to ward off the chill. She held one of Papa's journals, where he detailed not only his personal life, but also the professional exploits of his apothecary business. She ran her fingers over them—touching them to reconnect with him.

She wore the *Three of Swords* within her and around her. It was her cloak, her gown, her crown, and her soul. Three swords pierced her heart, their razor-sharp blades slicing into the core of her being, her life-blood dripping from her. She loved him deeply. Mama was a strong woman, she would weather this storm. In the *Three of Swords*, the sky is heavily clouded over and the rain pours down. It is truly a grim card, the heart is literally pierced, the world is awash with loss.

"Mama?"

She set Papa's journal aside. "Vivian, are all your arrangements made?"

"I should stay," I said for the hundredth time this week.

"There is only one of you, and Nate needs you more than I do," Mama said.

"I want to stay." It was half true. I wanted to stay and go. I couldn't remain here. I needed to get away and feel the land around me again.

"But you also want to go," Mama said. "You have an adventurer's heart. Your soul is restless, like that of your husband."

"I don't want to leave you." I wished I could rip myself in half to remain with both her and Nate.

"Now, that, I do believe," Mama said. "But you cannot be both places. So, clear your mind and draw a card. Let it guide you. You trust me. You have come to trust them. If we both tell you, then you must go."

"I do not want to abandon you," I said. "You would not leave me."

"I am the mother. You are the daughter," Mama said. "Now, do as I say. Fetch your cards."

I brought her the cards that had once been hers, which had once been her mother's cards. They were faded, the edges tattered, the corners dinged. They were smudged from being handled and shuffled. I no longer needed to carry them to know them. I didn't need to touch them to manipulate them and to read them, but they were a familiar comfort in my hand.

I let them fall between my fingers, loving their feel. One wanted to be drawn. No matter how many times I cut past it or shuffled by it, it kept leaping to hand. Finally, I turned it out on the table.

The Five of Cups.

Mama smiled at me. It was her first since Papa died. "Ahh. It is a good message."

On the card was a hooded figure, head bowed, overlooking a river. At his or her feet, three of five cups were overturned, literally spilling out all the emotions into the earth. Behind, two full cups waited.

She took my hand. "When one struggles with grief, one must remember to look beyond the sorrow, the emptiness that is overwhelming. Look, there is goodness in the cups behind, and here, an entire river of goodness lies ahead. Grief is for now, but it will pass. I loved your Papa very much and I will forever miss him. But, I will be able to drink again. My life goes on, not as it did, for I will not be the same without him, but I will not lose sight of all the good we had for the sake of the sorrow now."

I could breathe for the first time since Papa died. He had shared his apothecary wisdom, wide and wonderful as it was, but Mama had another sort of wisdom. She had a courage that I never fully understood until I decided to break my engagement to Byron and become a wild adventuress with Nate.

Mama handed the card back. "I am heartsick, my darling, but I am not broken. We are made of stronger stuff, and as stronger stuff we are tested. Now, you can sit here with me and mourn, or you can travel to the head of the Pennsylvania Railroad and demand to know how he is managing your investment before he harms the people you and Nate look after. You must go. That fellow of yours means well but he finds no end of trouble without you. He plays the part of a gentleman when he sets his mind to it, but he still possesses a temper and forgets what he is supposed to do when his ire is up."

I smiled. Nate was nothing if not impulsive. Papa healed men, Mama read them. It was the way of things.

"I am a widow," she said. "Mourning is an old woman's chore. No one could accuse you of being a daughter who does not care for her father. If anything, Vivian, you care too much. If we still lived on Exeter and we still had Calvin to share the load, or you were wed to Mr. Goodwin, you could bury yourself in mourning and not think twice. But you have too much to think on now." She took both my hands in hers. "How many children live under this roof?"

I blinked hard.

"Oh, dear heart, I know you and Nate are trying for a babe of your own. There was no barb in that, but how many children are you feeding under your own roof?" she said, kissing my cheek.

"Three."

"And how many tenant families do you have on your land?"

"Fifteen."

"Before your Papa died, Nate came to him asking for his advice. Nate wished to know how to spare a man and still make sure he knows it's not charity, that it is kindness and mercy, not pity." Mama paused. "Rowan was good that way. Nate is the same. Good and honorable. A good man. It is a rare thing, to have a good man. Nate is good but he is not practiced at being good *and* in a position to do good with it. He will stumble." Mama swallowed and took a steadying breath. "And that is why he needs you. He is a kind man. He is a smart man. But he is not always a wise man. Smart and wise are not the same thing."

She was right, as always.

"Wisdom will come with time. But, until then, he will make many mistakes. The dog within him is loyal, but dogs are not patient. He needs his mistress. He needs you with him to keep him from doing something foolish."

"I need you." Saying it out loud reminded me how true it was, and I burst into tears. "I miss Papa!"

We grabbed one another as we sat on the settee and held tight, sobbing. "I know, my heart!"

I had learned so much from him: how to treat so many illnesses, how to treat people beyond the illnesses, how to keep a wound from becoming septic, how to love a family, how to love those whom society forgot. My nose was running. I gave an unladylike snort and blew my nose on my handkerchief. We were going to need quite a few more.

How could I have not asked how to help *him*?

Mama took out a handkerchief of her own. "There was nothing you could have done." She always had a knack for reading my mind. She dabbed my eyes. "Everyone dies sometime. There is no helping it. Life does not stop when someone we love dies."

I bent to kiss her. One day, if I am half as strong as she is, then I will have honored her well.

She called to me as I reached the door to the suite. "Your Papa served the people, Vivian. Honor him by serving your tenants."

SS

I left her bedroom both soothed and guilty. I had her blessing to go, but I hated that I needed to be free of mourning. She had needed Papa, and he had needed her. Nate and I needed each other in the same way. We also needed adventure.

But where Mama and Papa had had our tiny household in London to care for, my responsibilities were much greater, and the investment with the railroad was failing. If we wished to safeguard the welfare of our household and our tenants, we needed income. If Nate believed the best way to do this was to speak to the president of the railroad, then we would head to Philadelphia in America. That meant traveling by airship. Again.

Adventuring meant packing for an adventure, and since the household already knew we would be traveling, Jane had taken it upon herself to make sure I was suitably attired. She had laid out my entire wardrobe on every available surface so she could inspect it for suitability for travel.

I pulled out my pack and set my adventuring attire out on the bed. Aside from all the proper clothing, namely sturdy trousers, shirts, a corset, and my heavy jacket, I was at a loss. America was billed as a wild frontier and a land of innovation, refinement, and class. One generally did not find the two descriptions together.

Jane set another day dress upon the bed. This was her fourth attempt. She was doing her best to not be annoyed, but I'm sure, when she was hired, that she had expected a mistress that threw dinner parties and had her hair dressed and acted respectable: a proper lady, not one who enjoyed gallivanting off into the wilds. Jane. Poor lamb.

CHAPTER FIVE

OUR JOURNEY ACROSS the Atlantic by airship was short, only a few days, before Captain Remington's Nomad landed in Buffalo, New York in the middle of the World's Fair to expound the benefits of air travel to the masses. We were minor celebrities for all of three hours as brave explorers who traveled through the sky until we went on our way and retired to the train station to continue our journey to meet with Mr. Cassatt of the Pennsylvania Railroad.

Train travel beats air travel, handily. We climbed aboard a green train car with black walnut, hardwood benches decorated with carved scrollwork and fine velvet-cushioned seats like fine couches. Above the glass windows, decorated mirrors hung in painted frames. This was what travel should look like. I was actually unhappy we would only be taking the train for the afternoon.

The miles raced along steadily, and we made several stops along our route to allow passengers off and on. Though I knew rail travel was slower than air travel, the speed was still exhilarating as I watched the great locomotive engines run along their tracks. Surely, the trouble with the railroad was merely a mistake. The rail cars were full of happy travelers. There was no reason our investments should not be paying off. In fact, I was looking forward to speaking to Mr. Cassatt.

When in our train stopped in Philadelphia, we were greeted with the most terrible news. President McKinley had been shot. He had been greeting people and shaking hands in the Temple of Music when an anarchist by the name of Leon Czolgosz shot him. Czolgosz had lost his job as a result of labor disputes, the sort of disputes that arise when goods become cheaper with trade with other countries. The British Empire was familiar with these issues. America was dealing with the chaos for the very first time—the growing pains of a young nation as they learned this lesson, and President McKinley might very well pay the price.

His doctors were doing what they could to save his life, but even as I stood there, the *Eight of Swords* consumed my thoughts. There were too many things beyond my control. It left me feeling helpless, which I hated with every piece of my soul.

Not long ago, I was a woman like the one bound and hoodwinked in the *Eight of Swords*. She stands blind to her fate, surrounded by swords, paralyzed by fear, consumed by the inability to act. The loss of my papa, the babies that never were, the life of responsibility, it was all something I was not prepared for.

Well, that ended now. Refusing to act was worse than the wrong action.

I was grief-sick for my father, and the recent tragedy here reminded me of all that could go wrong in this beautiful land, but I needed to move forward. I said a silent prayer for President McKinley and turned my attention to our meeting with Mr. Cassatt.

There were a great many hotels in Philadelphia, it being one of the oldest and most prosperous cities in America. Of course, that was not saying much as the city itself was just over two centuries old. But Americans are a canny bunch and the proud city where their great Declaration of Independence was signed before being delivered to the crown just over a century ago was a place of great importance to them, so much so that our London accents were viewed with everything from interest to mistrust.

The Philadelphia station master directed us to a hotel not far from the Pennsylvania Railroad's offices where we could store our belongings and freshen up before heading over to Mr. Cassatt's office.

"Well, I am looking forward to this meeting," I said trying to banish the dark cloud that had suddenly settled over our visit. "Surely when we explain our position, he will be able to make a full accounting of our investment."

"Don't bet on it," Nate said scowling. "Viv, I've lived on both sides and I don't believe there are many men who will easily part with money, even when it is rightfully ours." He charged across the street, and I had to move quickly to catch up. "He may be a business man who makes his money by leveraging deals and using the capital of others to fund projects. We just have to know why they report paying investors every quarter since gaining their charter, but not us."

"You don't expect him to cheat us, do you?"

Nate took my hand and we crossed another street. "This is the reason gentlemen have agreements and businesses require contracts."

"We at least need to be ready to hear him out," I said.

"I know you want to trust him, but trusting people in power to do the right thing is foolishness. We trusted Langston to send us to China for artifacts not into a literal dragon's mouth. We believed Sterling would help London, instead he hired a madman. The only man who hasn't lied to me is Old Captain Morgan. Men who don't sweat for a living are, as a rule, either dishonest or idiots." He was right of course. Aside from the rare exception, it was hard to find a man of worth in high society.

There was no reason for him to be so difficult. He was now a man of means that did not have to sweat for a living. He did, of course, but that was more for the preferred life of an adventurer. He had become a man in power and the fact that he didn't see it was maddening. If we did not use out new position to help others, we were no better than Sir Langston or Lord Sterling. He was so frustrating at times.

I don't know if it was the stress of the journey or the bright sun, but I suddenly had a horrible headache. My blood hammered in my ears. I could not breathe. My dress was too tight. The world was blurry. My jaw ached and my chest hurt, and I felt irrationally angry. My hair fell over my eyes and, through the curtain of it, I saw Nate blinking at me. I felt I wanted to snap at him—more than that, I wanted to bite him.

A change passed over him, and he stared at me, his eyes wide. He stopped what he was saying, his mouth hanging open. He grabbed my arm and the thrumming in my chest grew louder—no, not in my chest, my stomach, maybe my waist. It was a deadly heartbeat that made me feel both hot and cold. The desire to snap at him like a wounded hound was so strong I ground my teeth.

The desperate thrumming of my blood rushing through me was gone. Nate wasn't trying to fight with me. And though he made me terribly frustrated at times, I loved him. I wondered how could I have been so angry before. It wasn't me. I would never want to do him harm. My hand was deep in my pocket, the ruby clutched so tightly in my hand it felt hot.

I still had it. No one could raise the dragon and turn it loose against the world. Nate was safe. I forced myself to let go. My fingers ached.

"Men shouldn't decide the fate of others. It's not natural." He scrubbed his hands through his hair, in his habitual tense, angry motion.

He took my hand and tucked it into the crook of his elbow. Maintaining a struggling estate, the loss of my papa; all these things created a distance between us that filled up with an absence I could not name but in that moment, the image of biting, gnashing fangs filled it and consumed me. I pushed a deep breath out though shaky lips. My breath was hot like fire.

I leaned against my husband's shoulder grateful for his strong frame.

Poor Nate, he wasn't thinking of Mr. Cassatt, or Mr. Langston, or even my papa. He was thinking of himself and all the lives he was suddenly in charge of. Poor decisions could cost them their lives. It wouldn't matter how hard our tenants worked. It would not have mattered how hard he worked. He'd been one of the poor, one of the men living moment to moment, meal-to-meal, trying to figure out how to survive, before he turned to a life of adventure in the sky.

A tall building loomed before us, at least five floors of cut-glass windows, brick and steel, and inside was the man we had come all this way to see. A gentle touch was apology enough for both of us. He smiled at me and I at him.

SOS

Mr. Cassatt's office was a stunning suite with wood paneling and a thick, green carpet. In the anteroom, a gentleman roughly Nate's age stared at a thick ledger through a pair of glasses, an inkpot dangerously close to the edge of the desk as he muttered to himself and motioned in the air with his pen. His shirt must have been purchased off the rack with sleeves that came in the standard length. He wore brown garters to keep his sleeves up and out of his way. This had to be Mr. Cassatt's clerk, and not a well-paid one at that.

The man was so engrossed in his ledger that he paid us no mind. He stared at the ledger, and the remains of a ham sandwich, in a wax paper wrapper, sat on the corner of the desk. A cup of coffee appeared to have been sitting by the remains of his lunch for quite a while—it had developed a little spidery star of separated cream on the top.

I cleared my throat.

The clerk raised his head and set the pen between his teeth, but his eyes remained glued to the page. "Oh, um, Mr. Cassatt isn't seeing anyone today."

Then he glanced up at us, mouth agape as if we had just interrupted a very complicated train of thought.

Nate pulled a calling card from his waistcoat and handed it over. "Mrs. and Mr. Nathaniel Valentine, Esquire from London." Nate gave him a fierce look, the one that accompanied the Nate-the-Lord voice. "He *will* see us."

The clerk took the card. After reading the name, he saw us in a new light. "Of course, sir, madame. I am Mr. Cassatt's clerk, Mr. Burris. I will let him know you are here." He disappeared through the wooden doors to the office beyond.

A moment later, Mr. Burris returned and ushered us through tall heavy doors. "Mr. Valentine, Mrs. Valentine, Mr. Cassatt would be more than happy to speak with you. May I offer you both some tea?"

A balding man sat scowling at a ledger on his desk. His desk had, in addition to a few fine pens, a heavy metal nail, tapered on one end and flat on the other, longer than my hand and as thick as three fingers, and a locomotive made of metal and painted in red and green.

"Mr. Valentine. I am surprised to see you here."

My husband wasted no time. "Mr. Cassatt, this is a very serious matter. We have trusted you to act in good faith with our money and we have not seen a return on our invested funds in nearly a year," Nate said. "We have several families whose health and wellbeing are our responsibility, as well as our personal fortunes. I am surprised that you do not entertain more disgruntled investors."

Mr. Cassatt leaned forward on his desk. "Mr. Valentine, I do understand your concerns. But there are always delays in the expansion of new business. Your patience is appreciated while we deal with these matters. I assure you there was no need to come all the way from London.

Nate was unmoved. "Little good that does to those who invest great sums of money in your project on the empty promise of profitable returns. We were assured this was a lucrative investment. If this is the transportation of the masses and in such high demand why are we not making any money?" Nate asked, cocking an eye at Mr. Cassatt

"There have been...setbacks." Mr. Cassatt twisted his glass in his hand, staring at the whiskey. "We have hundreds of miles of track laid all along the eastern United States where most of the people of wealth and means reside. We are also working on a project to revolutionize the system of propulsion for the trains from a dirty coal-burning, steam-powered locomotive to a model that runs almost entirely on electricity, saving us thousands on coal annually—a savings that shall put money directly into your pocket, I might add."

"That is all well and good, but it does not answer my question for today." Nate had crossed one leg across his lap. "Mr. Cassatt, if you cannot answer my concerns in a satisfactory manner, my wife and I will be forced to move our money elsewhere. Perhaps we will be forced to move our money to the Union Pacific Railroad or the Central Pacific Railroad. If they currently possess the most complete railroad line, they may be the more lucrative investment for the Valentines."

After a long pause, Mr. Cassatt spoke. "The truth, Mr. Valentine, is that there have been complications in our westward expansion project."

I hated when men used that tone. "What kind of complications?" At best it was a half-truth, at worst, an all-out lie.

Mr. Cassatt spared me a glance. "We have had issues with the steel."

"What kind of issues?" Nate said.

"The quality has not met our standards for the safety and well-being of our line and travelers." Mr. Cassatt turned the gold ring on his little finger with his thumb. *Swords*, Mr. Cassatt was surrounded by *Swords*. They were the Tarot suit of intellect but many of them were inverse. He had lost control of the situation and he was using his intellect to be less than truthful with us. And he was even less inclined to be truthful around me. He was one on those men who seemed to believe women had no place anywhere but keeping the home and looking pretty. I realized I had to leave.

"Would you gentlemen excuse me?"

Mr. Cassatt said, "Of course." They both stood. Their conversation resumed as soon as the door was shut. I could not help but smile. Mr. Cassatt was clearly of the mind that business was not for the fairer sex.

The clerk directed me to the water closet, a fancy toilet facility that flushed, with a carved wooden seat, shiny white tile, and fine copper pipes. I washed my hands with powdered soap, then returned to the office. Mr. Burris was nowhere to be found but he had left the ledgers open along with a huge set of books laid out along a table behind his desk. On the desk was a list of names. It appeared to be a list of employees followed by a location and *stn.* or *cty*, probably the station or city where they were employed. The Pennsylvania Railroad must be massive, indeed, to employ so many men.

There was another drawer, open just enough so the corner of several cream-colored folders poked out. It was careless. Just like his ink bottle sitting uncorked at the edge of his table. I couldn't help it, I corked the inkpot.

The coffee cup was old and filthy, the books all open and in disarray. The folder, and its contents, would be damaged. Mr. Burris' caretaking, or his lack thereof, could affect our investment. I opened the drawer the rest of the way. I would fix the folder and close the drawer. Then, when Nate and Mr. Cassatt were at a natural break, I would rejoin them so as not to interrupt their conversation.

I pulled the folder out, holding its place with my little finger and tapped the papers back together, then made to tuck it back into the drawer when my eye caught the title on the folder.

"Geiger, N."

Geiger. Certainly, it couldn't be Newton Geiger.

I set the folder on the desk and pulled it open. There were dozens of drawings on thin paper, schematics for train parts. Knowing Geiger, there was no way it was merely train parts. I shuffled through them for some clue as to what was really going on. If he was willing to bankrupt an English lord to experiment with leymagic and he would lie to the esteemed Explorer's Society for access to their vaults and, I suspect, to get access to an enchanted arrow, I doubted he had found gainful employment with the

Pennsylvania Railroad. He would certainly have something to do with our failing fortunes.

> *Concerning Newton Geiger. Meeting this morning. I was approached with an intriguing new idea. Mr. Geiger assured me he could revolutionize the way our entire fleet of rail engines is powered in order to lower the cost of running our engines. The result, if successful, could mean huge dividends to our investors and unheard-of westward expansion.*

I heard footsteps in the hall. I hastily slammed the drawer closed and stuffed the folder under my dress, against my stomach. I prayed for all I was worth that nothing would fall out.

The clerk returned carrying a tray of cups and a steaming pot. By the smell it was fresh coffee. "Ahh, Mrs. Valentine. Mr. Cassatt and your husband must be missing you. I made coffee."

If he made coffee anything like he kept books, I resolved not to have any.

Mr. Burris juggled the tray as he turned the doorknob. "Mrs. Valentine, you look pale, are you all right?"

"Yes, thank you," I said, going through as he held the door open.

Mr. Cassatt was speaking. He had his back to us and was looking out over the street. "We anticipate dividends to be forthcoming as soon as these little setbacks are resolved."

"A loss of thousands of pounds of steel is hardly what I would call a setback," Nate said.

"Our engineers are now scouting an alternate route for the westbound line that will bypass the problem. By next quarter the losses will be absorbed, I can assure you. If we cannot pay returns upon your investment, Mr. Valentine, I shall cover the loss of revenue myself so you will not lose any more money."

"I can assure you, Mr. Cassatt, if you did not, we would be forced to cash our remaining stock and move it to another railroad, one that is more consistent." Even though I knew he was bluffing, I was nearly fooled.

"Mr. Valentine," Mr. Cassatt said tersely. "I can assure you, the Pennsylvania Railroad has never failed to pay quarterly to senior level investors." He returned to his seat and looked at us from across the massive wooden desk.

Nate's mouth was a thin line of displeasure.

They sat sizing one another up. We had chosen the Pennsylvania Railroad initially because of its excellent record of paying upon investments. Though it didn't always pay spectacularly, it had a record of always paying consistently upon their investments since being granted their charter in 1846. Mr. Cassatt was right, technically. If they always paid *some* investors, then they could claim they had always paid investors. The politics of how the upper class operated was thoroughly obnoxious.

CHAPTER SIX

WE HURRIED TO a bit of privacy, which ended up being the corner of the common room of the hotel that was temporarily in custody of our belongings. I pulled the folder from my dress. If Nate was stunned at my larceny, it was nothing at what the file contained. Mr. Cassatt had aligned himself with Mr. Geiger and was holding our investment without paying out our fair share. Whether his intentions were good or not, we were going to find out how the two were connected.

Clearly Geiger was in the employ of the railroad and promising them wondrous machines. The railroad was losing both money and good steel. Mr. Sterling had lost his fortune as soon as he got involved with Mr. Geiger. He had trusted the inventor to create machines able to create goods inexpensively to sell to the masses but, instead, Geiger created his own machines designed to harness magic. Anywhere Geiger was involved blood would follow. If disaster was at the end of the line, then that was where we had to go.

Nate told Mr. Cassatt we intended to inspect the line for ourselves while I purchased tickets. For good or for ill, we would soon know exactly what was happening at the end of the line and what misfortune was befalling our investment. If Geiger was behind it, then God help him.

We reclaimed our belongings. There was no need to take a room, we would be moving on to the end of the Pennsylvania Railroad's westward line.

Nate threw his pack over his shoulder as we readied ourselves "I cannot say Mr. Cassatt seemed particularly happy."

I paused, my satchel halfway over my head, "Why doesn't he want to know what is happening at the end of the line?"

"He does. He has rail men working there. They have been looking into it for months. He says the problem is with the steel itself. He doesn't believe there is anything we can do there." Nate took my satchel and tossed it over his own shoulder. "He advises against interfering."

I touched my belt making sure my pistol and seax were there. "Clearly, he has no idea who he is dealing with."

"Geiger?" Nate nodded, "The man is a lunatic."

"No, darling, us." I said. "We happen to be champion interferers."

"First London, then China, now America." Nate took up our last piece of luggage. "I am afraid of what Geiger is seeking here."

I touched his back. Whatever Geiger was seeking in the new world, it spelled doom and he must be stopped at all costs. Mr. Cassatt seemed consumed with the railroad so I doubted he was purposefully helping Geiger with whatever mad master plan he had devised, but we could not let it happen.

The rail line had been extended almost to St. Louis before the quality of the steel had degraded. Interfering or not, we were headed to the end of the line. We had our destination.

$$SS$$

We boarded the train for St. Louis, ignoring the stares of the other passengers. Clearly, they were not accustomed to women dressed for adventure and they were not friendly to the British. We ignored them, taking our plush seats near a carbide gas light.

I closed my eyes as the train pulled away from the station, and saw a Tarot card materialize in my mind. It was *The Hermit*, the one I had seen in our parlor before we left home, walking, following his lantern, led onward by the light of understanding as he tried to find his way. *The Hermit* has a strong need to understand not just surface knowledge but why things are. I knew deep inside something was very, very wrong with the whole situation, I knew it in all aspects of my being, but I could not determine exactly what it was. I had closed my eyes to try to make sense of it. What could Mr. Geiger want with a train? They could not leave the track. Trains were not weapons, they were new technology and would not hide some ancient weapon. I touched the ruby in my pocket and the frantic energy in my brain calmed somewhat. As long as I had it, Geiger did not. He could not get to the enchanted arrow. He could not awaken the dragon.

The dragon. Four horns, four eyes; serpentine and vicious, Xihuan-Lung glared and snarled. Her nostrils smoked, her maw let loose a great fount of liquid fire that turned the forest to ash and melted stone and my Nate, my loving Nate, who had been caught between canithrope and man whimpered and burned. He suffered and died. His warm flesh charred and fell from him.

The ruby felt warm against my thigh. My palm was pressing on it like I was trying to force it into my own muscle and hide it within myself forever where it would never leave me and be safe. I would not part with it, and yet, if we wanted to stop whatever he was up to now, we had to go to him. I would not wait him out and let him complete whatever he was plotting now.

Beside me, Nate took my hand and smiled.

§§§

The carbide gas lights used to illuminate the night-darkened rail car corridors burned with a yellow light so bright it made my eyes water. I blinked hard but I could not make my eyes focus. The rocking of the train and the heat from the pot belly stove at the front of the carriage to warm the space made me feel dull and sleepy. The click-clack of the train on the rails made the world zip by but at least during the day there was something to look at. By night, all I had to look at was the reflection in the window beyond Nate and the occasional glimpses of the moon as it peeked out from the canopy of trees. The train was a haven of warmth and light and, yet, also a den of isolation from the world beyond the glass windows.

The lady across the aisle from me slept, her chin resting against her neck. Her husband read a newspaper. He squinted at the page and pulled it closer, then moved it further away. He would have to give up soon.

We retired to our section in the sleeping car and pulled the curtain that separated us from the rest of the passengers. Though airships moved faster than trains, the ship dancing upon the winds was smoother than the train, and the train was more mechanical, more rhythmic in its motion. I stared out the window, letting my eyes fall out of focus. I was not crippled by the terror of being far above the ground as I was in the airships, this was a calm stupor as I watched the land.

Blink. *Click-clack.*

I saw a man, or rather two men. They stood back to back, alternately smiling and sneering. Both men were beautiful, tall and lean, swarthy with dark brown hair that curled just around his ears. On anyone else it would look shaggy, but they looked rather daring, handsome on the image that smiled, menacing on one that sneered.

No, it was not two men, it was a mirror—distorted like the kings in a deck of cards, flipped and inverse to one another.

Kings. This was a *King*. He was dressed in green velvet. Not the cool green of an emerald, but the warm golden-green of peridot stretched tightly across his shoulders. A crown sat in his dark hair like flames of gold.

And, like flame, the King shifted, he smiled, he flirted, he glared, he sneered. Fire was mercurial in this way—beautiful and dangerous. In his hand he held a staff, knotted hardwood blackened with char and soot and dotted with small white flowers that curled around the staff with little green vines of regrowth. Fire manipulated, consumed, and made way for the new.

This was the *King of Wands*; pure fire-energy. Cross him at your peril, for he is a charismatic master, but he could burn you if you displeased him. And fire is a masterful patron when pleased.

The *King of Wands* turned to me, the left half of his face warm and welcoming. Offering me a smile that was suggestive, lewd, though not entirely unwelcome from such a pleasing face. I reminded myself I was a happily married woman. The other half was mocking, sharp, cruel; each half entirely at odds with the other.

He offered me the staff. I did not want to touch it. I could not resist. I reached out to touch it. Before I could, I was distracted, somewhere off in the distance I smelled smoke. Hot like a coke fire and sharp like over-heated metal.

Blink. *Click-clack.* Wheels on rails. Such a hypnotic sound.

The king was gone. I looked around. The train was gone. I could still hear it if I strained my ears, but it was far away. And I was not alone. The *King of Wands* is a man of vision. I stood behind another man, shadowed by a dark brown hat and coat. There was something about him, the odd, off center way he shifted his weight, I knew I had seen him before, but where?

The man stood within a circle, a wheel made of rocks, tiny ones and large ones alike, but all polished smooth by the water.

Long grasses had been gathered and twisted into a long braid, salt poured, a bundle of white, leafy herbs I had never smelled before but were pleasing and sweet sat burning on a wide flat rock. The smoke they gave off was thick but there was nothing noxious about it. Long brown leaves, dried and curled, sat bundled, waiting. Waiting for what?

The man had strips of white fur, cured and soft. He stroked the fur, burying his fingers in it before he set the twists of grass and brown leaves burning. The scent of charred grasses and leaves broke into fierce competition, creating a choking smoke that was both cleaner than the pea-soupers of London and fouler. The man chanted, the words themselves unfamiliar but there was something unmistakably familiar about them. The language was beautiful, foreign, and yet some words were halting and choppy, like Latin. This was a language the man did not speak. He had learned these phrases, but not the language that contained them.

I knew the voice. I know I knew that voice. The hair on my arms stood on end.

Before my eyes the smoke took on a form, hulking, human-like, tall, taller than me, taller than the man, even taller than Nate wearing his canithrope form. It had sharp eyes, round and reflective like the eyes of a fox catching torchlight. The eyes watched me in a hungry sort of way, as a hawk stares at a mouse. Something about the eyes showed no contempt, no respect, not even hate. Even when the *King of Wands* looked at me he saw my humanity, though he may have despised it. Whatever this thing was I was a toy, a plaything, I was prey and nothing more.

I wanted to jump into the stone circle but then I would have to touch the man. I could not make my feet move closer.

"Now, monster! Come!" the man commanded in English. He had a Cockney accent.

The smoke and gleaming predator eyes narrowed with mild irritation at the man who spoke, regarded me for a moment more, then turned toward the man and the wheel of stones and salt.

"Those damn savages are cheap drunks. Hope that won't be a problem." He pulled a leather wrapped bundle from a basket. It dripped something gooey and inky, foul and unsettling. I wanted to turn and run but found myself unable to. I was dimly aware of the train so far away, rocking me, lulling me, keeping me from waking.

Click-clack. Click-clack. Click-clack. Wheels on tracks. The sound was comforting. It was a prayer to cling to.

I sensed the *King of Wands* and the mercurial nature of fire, ever shifting, warming and warning, punishing and purifying. He was showing me something I needed to see. I felt the ruby thrumming in my pocket, a heart in panic beating a desperate tattoo and pulling me toward the ground, keeping me from running back to the train.

The man unwrapped the bundle. Something gleamed. Was it gleaming in fire or moonlight? Did it matter? It gleamed like silver, but it was not from within. It was the hand, the right hand, that gleamed, silver and red as though bloody. I blinked hard. My mouth formed the words, but nothing came out: "Please, no."

I only knew one man with a silver arm. I needed to never see him again.

The bundle he held was meat, oozing, red, raw meat. Though I had no way of knowing how, I knew it was not cow nor venison nor pork nor anything else I would eat. My stomach lurched. I didn't want to know what it was.

"In the end he was more whiskey than man," the man laughed.

Human. The meat was human. I retched. The ruby in my pocket jerked me to my knees. Blood rushed in my ears.

The man's accent was lower-class Cockney, a Londoner's accent, there was no mistaking it now. "But he was a sinner. I made sure of that." He poured a flask over the meat—the human flesh, I corrected myself. Blood, it was blood; viscous, pouring out of the flask in glugs. I tasted bitter bile burning in my throat.

The smoke and eyes drifted over the corpse flesh of that poor person, sinner or no, and the blood and meat melted away before my very eyes. The smoke became more and more dense, a black hulking mass of flesh, shaggy and fierce, crouched over where the blood and flesh had lain.

I wanted to run but I was frozen. My mouth was dry. I tried to swallow back the bile. My tongue was glued to the roof of my mouth. My limbs were cold. I would shake but it might draw the monster's attention.

The hulking black mass raised a shining head white as old, bare bone. It raised the head, in profile a coyote head, a bare wolf head, lupine and fierce with jagged teeth, sharp and overlapping. Horns like a red deer sprouted from its bare skull. It sniffed the air with a nose-less muzzle, tasting it, searching for more meat.

The eyes, white orbs but reflective like fox eyes in lantern light, took in the firelight and it shone back, transforming them into reflective opals. They swept the land and passed harmlessly over me once, then swept back as though it caught my breath or my shadow.

I stopped breathing. Could it see me? Like *The Hermit*, I was here but not here.

I struggled to hear the noise of the train, but it was like a drum too far away to hear clearly.

Click-Clack. There, but only when I strained to hear it. I needed to hear wheels on the track. *Click-Clack.*

The man turned, straining to see what had caught the monster's attention.

My lungs burned. I needed air. I didn't remember how to breathe. It was Geiger. Scowling and snarling. He had cut his hair since I saw him last, cropped it short to his skull, and wore a thin mustache and a tight triangle of beard just below his lower lip. He wore a stiff bowler hat and a dark suit, finer clothes than the last time, but I would never forget the man who wore them. The gleam of silver had not been a trick of the light. His right hand, the entire arm, was gone, missing at the shoulder and replaced with an artificial limb made of silver. It was fiercely strong and as dexterous as a flesh limb.

He was a man of ambition and wicked purpose and under the employ of the railroad. But why he would align himself with a creature such as the one he had summoned was beyond me.

Geiger turned back to his protective circle of stones and smoke. I released the breath I was holding and gulped another breath of air. I felt lightheaded.

Geiger chuckled. "Well, aren't you amazing? My research promised a powerful ally and here you are. I suppose that drunk wasn't as crazy as they said. You sure are ugly. A true horror to look upon. You're perfect."

The monster stared, its fleshless head cocked and staring. Could a monster like that be intrigued by us? But if the monster was moved by this little speech it did not show it. It merely paced and stared, cocking its head, like some sort of awful mix between canine and bird. It bobbed like a vulture, sizing up where to strike, trying to make sense of this man who had summoned it.

That was why Geiger was in America. That is why he was working with the railroad. He could travel across this nation to find and summon another monster of unspeakable evil. His dark ambition was limitless. I could never allow him to get his hands on the ruby now.

"You are immortal, but you are not invincible." Geiger said to it, "I shall grant you a form, one that is resistant to damage. There is magic in this world, ancient magic that a learned man can combine with the new magic of the age. Science can make a new body that cannot be so easily banished even when the evils of man are less.

"I warn you, creature. You will not betray me. If you lay hands upon me, I will destroy your form. I shall never be without my protective charms. But serve me and there will never be another that can offer you what I can."

A body? He was offering this monster a body? One that was indestructible? A body that could not be reduced to smoke and mirror eyes? Would it feed upon sinners? Were we all sinners? If so, such a monster would threaten the entire world. If Geiger was right, and he was able to grant this monster a form that could be nearly indestructible, then I needed to stop him.

The realization was a light, a lantern to guide me. A lantern that suddenly moved with my thoughts, carried by a hermit in gray robes. *The Hermit* was moving ever onward, searching for enlightenment, searching for truth. I had a path. To stop the monster, I had to stop Geiger before he gave the monster a body. I just needed to figure out how.

Click-clack. Wheels on track.

I shook my head sharply.

The files I had stolen from Mr. Cassatt's office's office were in my satchel. I needed to see them again. Geiger may have promised a train to Mr. Cassatt, but he was working on much more. In London, he had built a machine designed to force transformation. He tried to use magic to transform men into something else. Now he was trying to transform something else into something living. I would not be surprised if that was what was ruining the steel.

The file was depressingly thin. I took a deep breath and opened it up. Notes, a drawing for what looked to be a boiler, a train engine dissected into several parts showing what pieces should move, all signed "N. Geiger".

There were diagrams and measurements and figures. I glared at them, daring them to tell me something about the monster he had summoned and the man he had murdered and defiled. Nothing. Worse than nothing, it was a pedestrian promise a man would make in a bid for a job as an inventor employed by the railroad. I flipped through the thin sheaf of papers. Nate peered over my shoulder.

I felt the hot drums of panic beating within me, faster than the wheels against the track, as though it was working in double-time. *Click-clack, click-clack, click-clack.* It was not the train I was feeling, but the racing of my own heart pounding in my chest, the stone thrumming away in my pocket, and me toward the ground.

The train whistle screamed, and I almost echoed it. My head screamed. A flood of images bombarded me all at once, leaving my vision hazy as I tried to make sense of what I was seeing.

The monster, all ragged black fur and a lupine skull of white bone and antlers and soulless white orb eyes, bent over a man with beautiful mahogany skin who moved with the slow reactions of one who was either drugged or drunk. The man only seemed to realize he was in danger as a heavily shadowed figure slashed at him. The mahogany-skinned man was suddenly on fire. The monster was upon him, teeth tearing, flesh rending, his whip thin screams cutting the night.

I closed my eyes. What had I missed? The ruby was warm. Xihuan-Lung, the ancient, long-dead dragon, raised herself from the forest floor where her bones lay. The flesh grew back, covering her bones once again. Tendons and sinew bounded from bone to bone, leaping like trout spawning from point to point, intent on their placement and nothing else. The muscle spread like a red fungus, covering the pale stone bones, a thin layer at first, then spreading in patterns one could predict from a simple knowledge of anatomy. She grew powerful legs, a deep chest, and a well-muscled back; a sleek graceful hunter, both leonine and serpentine in form and function with a long, thin body and four clawed paws. She had four eyes and two sets of horns, one angled forward, like great spears jutting off her forehead, the other curling back like rams horns for slamming and butting into her foes. Her scales were a layer of dark purple-blue that shimmered and rattled like a nest of vipers and, though they were patchy and several of them were missing, it never hinted at a weakness. It was merely a flaw that left her looking deadly and damaged rather than regal. There was nothing noble about this dragon: deranged energy came off her in waves. She opened her mouth and roared a challenge, just like she had when she murdered Nate with fire. My chest burned. My heart ached.

The Hermit walked through our section. He pushed through me as though I was not there. He was always moving, driven onward by whatever he pursued. Knowledge. He sought solitude and, in removing himself from all worldly pursuits, he dedicated himself to introspection and seeking answers from within. The answer was always within.

As the world exploded in a cacophony of noise, *The Hermit* turned to me, as though he saw me for the first time, and blew out the lantern. Its light guttered and failed, leaving me in silence and darkness.

"Viv!" Nate was shaking me.

Maybe the answer wasn't within. But if the monster was waiting for us at the end of the line, and Geiger waited holding its leash…The thought was a horrific one.

"Nate." I wrapped my arms around my husband and held him tight. "I-I—" I couldn't speak.

"What is wrong with you?" My husband said, not unkindly.

How could I tell him what I had seen? Soon, I would have to tell him what I had in my pocket. But I had to tell him of the other monster, the one Geiger had raised from smoke and blood, the one he had promised a body to walk within the world of men so it could hunt and feed. First, Geiger wanted the magic of the earth. Then, he wanted to enslave a dragon. Now, he wanted a terrifying monster he could control. We had to stop him and, this time, for good.

A heavy fatigue settled over me. Nate tucked me into the narrow bed beside him, then he sat up, looking over the pilfered file with the carbide gas light burning, carefully turning the pages, staring at them for a long while. It was a dreadful peace to know the ruby was tucked away in the pockets of my skirt. It wasn't on my body and not at hand, but I just needed a moment to rest and lay this burden down. For the moment, laying my head in my husband's lap was wonderful and peaceful.

Thoughts raced through me, like the train. What did Geiger plan to do with that monster? Every thought I came up with was worse than the last. A man in control of a monster like that could murder countless people. Geiger was heartless and amoral, and it was impossible to guess his motives. Whatever they were, they would not be good.

The file lay on our bed, fanned out as Nate read, while he stroked my hair, trying to understand what he was looking at, hoping to discover something we could use to either save our failing investments or figure out how Geiger fit in.

Geiger's blueprint for an engine had a double boiler. Well, two chambers heavily riveted together with a window, one for fuel to feed a fire and a bellows, or was that steam? It was hard to tell from this angle. In fact, it almost looked familiar. I had seen something like this before.

"Nate, hold this one like this." I sat up and tilted the blueprint off kilter. "Does it look familiar to you?"

He squinted at the blueprint and scowled. "Looks like that chamber in Geiger's lab beneath Sterling's factory in Limehouse."

I chewed my lip. Geiger had been filling batteries with the very magic that bound Nate and his dog into one body and cursed him to be his own form by day and his dog by night before we managed to alter the magic within him with the second leywell on Molten Cay. Geiger had poured the magic from the batteries into his machine, some sort of chamber he then stepped into before the fire broke out. He should have died in the conflagration. I still remember his screams, high and thin, as the fire closed in. The terrible, echoing sound still gave me nightmares. Worse still was when we found he had not died, but was instead seeking admittance to the Explorer's Society via his knowledge of ancient lore. Lore, magic, engineering, and now monsters conjured by flesh and blood and smoke. I shuddered. "What do you think he's up to?"

"Damned if I know," Nate muttered. "Geiger promised Cassatt more power and distance on less fuel, so Cassatt could save on coal. It would save him thousands on fuel costs."

"That is why Cassatt agreed to work with him. He said as much."

Nate scowled at another page. "What I can't figure out is, what else is going on? Why is Geiger working with Cassatt? There's something here about expansion and eminent domain. Geiger's engines are designed to work best across long distances, not when there are short distances between stops. It's an endurance engine. Cassatt authorized him to utilize their licensed eminent domain over their proposed routes, but they are having trouble moving beyond St. Louis."

I poked my head outside the heavy curtain, but none of our carmates had returned to their sleeping sections. We were truly alone. I took both his hands in mine. "Nate, there is something you need to know."

I considered telling him about the ruby but we had more pressing things to worry about at the moment and we could lose our privacy. "Geiger has a new ally. A monster. I've never seen anything like it, a dead thing conjured by dead men. He wants to make a slave of it. He's mad if he thinks he can bend it to his will." I took the plans, "I can't figure out what this has to do with his monster but whatever he wants, it cannot be anything good."

My husband wrapped his arm around me. I leaned against him and told him, all of it, all the details I could recall.

Nate finally nodded. "Geiger started working for Cassatt and Cassatt found a place he can't pass. Those two things are connected. I'd bet our best horse. We're going to find answers at the end of the line, maybe even Geiger himself."

"That's where we are headed." I said, "Did they have this problem before or after Geiger made a promise to that monster?"

Nate set the papers back into the file. "Exactly."

CHAPTER SEVEN

ST. LOUIS, MISSOURI WAS the end of the line for the Pennsylvania Railroad.

I had never realized how long travel by land actually took. I now had new appreciation for two things: the first was knowledge of how large America was and just how vital the railroads were to opening this land to travelers and moving goods from one coast to the other. The second, and perhaps the more surprising, was a grudging appreciation for air travel. In the Aura we would have crossed from Philadelphia to St. Louis in less than a day and it would not have included a truly fascinating study in the stubbornness of the spirit of American men intent on making money as we witnessed upon crossing a river they dubbed "the Mighty Mississippi."

Due to their penchant for overstating things, I was certain this would be a river like our Thames, where ferrymen and porters fought over the best rates but secretly bonded together to keep prices in a range where every traveler would pay about the same. It was the way gentlemen did business, after all, very civilized and proper. It did little to help the common man other than to make sure graft and price gouging were kept manageable, because if one ferryman became too greedy the others would severely undercut him. It kept the prices in check.

For once, the American practice of overstating was groundless. If anything, the Mighty Mississippi was an understatement. Though I could see clearly to the other side, I had no desire to try to swim it; it had to be well over a thousand meters across.

"What is that?" Nate pointed at one of the two bridges standing like sentinels crossing the largest river I had ever seen.

I strained my eyes. As far as I could tell the bridge was a finely erected sculpture of sweeping arches of iron with large abutments sinking into the Mississippi River. It looked to be intact, though we were too far away to have a proper look. They were nearly twins, one in use, the other waiting for a turn.

"That?" The man across from us in the Club Car laughed so hard he had to wipe his eyes. "That was the great Eads Bridge."

"Was?" Nate gave him a sideways look. "Whatever is wrong with it?"

"Nothing is wrong with it, per se." He snorted and had to wipe his eyes. "It is a beauty to be sure, but it was not planned with the consent of the railway owners."

"They didn't approve?" I looked at the bridge again.

"Who knows, Mr. Eads and the Illinois and St. Louis Bridge Company didn't ask them." He had to stop he was laughing too hard. "You s-see nothing happens out here without the railroads. Eads offended them. And now they won't use it."

Nate failed to see the humor in it. "That beautiful bridge and they won't use it?"

"It sits unused because he offended them. The banks that financed it went under and nearly everyone involved with the project lost everything. Don't you people have a system of prickly lords and honor and all that?"

Nate had to concede his point. "I suppose so, but I would have expected some arrangement would have been made."

"They did come to an arrangement: the railroad built a new bridge and made the people play by their rules! Oh, come now, don't you Brits have a sense of humor?" The man gave Nate a hard clap on the shoulder.

"We do when something is funny," Nate said dryly.

I excused myself to stand and watch the bridge as it faded from view. Having an expensive bridge sit without being used all because of an insult was ghastly. Americans were mostly new money. Knowing England's history, the British were probably once that way, and I suppose some of the upper class were, still. And I should not bemoan new money, because Nate and I were as new money as one could get. Nearly as new as those making their fortunes in railway investments, even newer than some. But how did they forget who they were so easily?

The man might have found the fate of Ead's bridge humorous, but it was more telling of the power the railroads wielded over the land and people. To build a bridge over a river as wide and powerful as the Mississippi was a great feat of engineering. The railroads knew this, and refusing to use Ead's bridge because of an offense showed the prickly nature of the railroad owners. Like the lords of England, they would only respect men of strength. Or men they could use. Which was Geiger? Which were we?

SS

We followed the press of passengers leaving the train through a tunnel made of glass and tile. The domed glass above us was lit with great windows, and even though I knew it was late, it was as bright as the afternoon.

There were two staircases, one led up to the street and darkness. The other led to heavy wooden doors and the HeadHouse, a luxurious hotel attached to the train station. Nate and I took the less crowded path, where a great wind met us between the rail station and the HeadHouse. The tile transitioned to wood floor and music wafted to my ears. Crossing the threshold had brought us to another place entirely.

"Good evening, sir. Check-in desk is ahead," the doorman said.

We were in a grand foyer lit with new electric lighting. A wonder of wrought iron had been sculpted into a grand, swirling chandelier lit with hundreds of bulbs, tiny stars twinkling away above the sweeping curves of the immense edifice. The room itself was a sea of glass and crystal, with glass and steel walls overlooking the train platforms but, if you looked carefully, you could see each pane of glass was two panes thick, one set before the other. This must have been horribly complicated, not to mention expensive to create, but the roaring rumble of the trains faded to a mere growl beneath the band that filled the ballroom with sweet, waltz-heavy music.

It was hard not to stare. No matter how often I saw electric lighting, I never got tired of it. It was one modern convenience we would never see in our country estate. London was rapidly joining the modern age, but there was no way to run electrics to our home.

The man behind the desk looked up from his reservation journal. "Welcome to the HeadHouse, the height of comfort of St. Louis Union Station." He wore a fine suit, and his short blond hair was carefully combed and slicked back. He was quite the handsome man. His brilliant blue eyes were lined from smiling, and a warm, healthy tan kissed his skin from working outside. In America, it was a sign of manliness to be tan from hearty work, but back home it was a sign one was too poor to hire others for labor. Or, in the case of my Nate, the mark of an adventurer.

"We would like to rent a room," Nate announced.

"We have several available," the man said. "There are private rooms with a shared bath or there are suites. Those have private toilets and fireplaces rather than being heated by steam."

"A suite, please."

"Very good, sir," he said. "The suites are seventy dollars per month. That includes your meals, of course."

"Of course," Nate said, agreeably.

I flinched inside. It was still less expensive than being home and attending social gatherings where it was proper to provide gifts to the hosts. On the other hand, it was good to have a place to store our possessions while we attempted to figure out exactly what was keeping the railroad from expanding westward.

"You will be billed when you check out. Here is your key. Your beds will be turned down at nine in the evening and fires laid in your hearth." He rang for a bellhop to take our bags to our room.

There was just enough time to unpack and dress for dinner.

The suite was decorated with cream wallpaper dotted with small, red roses with a dark purple stripe and an orange and green run in a sailor's bird motif. Would wonders not cease in this hotel? They had the luxury of hot and cold taps in the private bath that also contained a washing tub large enough for me to sit in for a proper bath. There was also a private toilet and a mirror and sink for our exclusive use.

Despite my earlier distaste for red meat, I found my appetite kindling at the sight of dinner. I resolved to force the awful vision away and enjoy myself.

Our meal was a fine affair. A crystal vase set with flowers sat in the center of the table and our plates had napkins ironed and folded into triangles, then laid flat in the center of our plates like tiny envelopes. Each had several pieces of warm bread tucked within for us to nibble while we waited for dinner to be served.

Our first course was a fine chowder made of fish and sweet corn, followed by a sliced bison roast garnished with potatoes and asparagus. I was quite pleased with the dish. But if I liked it, then Nate was in love with it. He had three helpings and was nearly unable to have more than a bite of dessert, a rhubarb apple tart, decorated with a dusting of finely sifted sugar that made it look like it was covered in snow.

But as wonderful as the meal was, we were not on holiday. We needed to find Geiger as soon as possible. We needed to separate him from his monster and find a way to return the demon to wherever it had come from.

Geiger was cunning, and it was only luck that had helped us defeat him, before. Now, we needed intentional, even ruthless, planning. We returned to our room.

The maid had already been in, so the bed was turned down and a fire laid. Our room was warm and cheery.

Nate sat in the plush chaise, consumed by the thought of a faceless demon. I poured him a drink and squeezed in beside him with the file. Perhaps we could make more headway on the strange machine. Instead, the ruby in my pocket jammed painfully into his thigh and he squirmed away. He demanded to know what was in my pocket.

I surrendered it, my secret treasure that I had kept hidden for nearly a year. I should not have kept it from him. But, now it was too late and there was no worse time. I took a deep breath. He would never understand. I tipped the ruby, the size of a small bird's egg and warm from my body, into his waiting palm.

"What is this?"

I did my best to sound innocent. "What is what?"

"This. What is this?" He was pale now. "Is this the ruby from China?"

I nodded. "Now, Nate, don't be cross—"

"Don't be cross." Nate let out a strange sound I had never heard before, something between choking on dry bread and an airy chuckle. "Is this the ruby from the center of the key from China?"

Every word was measured and slow. For one moment, he was a stranger. I reached out to him, but he batted my hand away. "We told the Explorer's Society we could not find the dragon, that the arrow of Hou Yi was a myth, a fairy tale."

"It's just a trinket," I stammered.

"No, Vivian!" He slammed his glass down, raining the untouched bourbon and shattered glass across the gaudy carpet. "The tiny jade dragon, the coins in my study—those are trinkets. The Explorer's Society would be within their rights to shun us for this. They could use this as proof we are lying about the arrow, and the dragon, and Prince Qixiang. All of it!"

"Nate, I'm sorry."

His voice cracked. He grabbed a towel from the washstand and wrapped it around his fist. The shattered glass had gashed his palm. "We keep secrets from so many people, Viv, why are you keeping them from me?" The awful strain of the journey, so far, had taken its toll. He sat on the edge of the chaise, his hand bleeding into his lap.

"Because you died there," I said.

"What?"

I burst into tears, because saying it had made it true. He died there. It was truth, or what would have been truth if Xihuan-Lung had been raised. It was another horrible turn of the wheel. That damnable *Wheel of Fortune*. It was the only Tarot symbol that consumed all of me. I was bound to it as if I were a parody of the Vitruvian Man —a Vitruvian Vivian—stretched to the wheel as it moved me through my life. Except, all our turns had been awful turns of fate lately: no baby, my father falling ill and dying, our tenants on the verge of starvation as their crops rotted in the field from too much rain. I chose to take the ruby, but I did it to save us from a worse fate. My vision had been unclear, but it had been truthful and even a glimpse of it was enough. I would have died to prevent it. "Y-you died there."

He had to think I was mad. I reached for the ruby, I just wanted to hold it. If it was safe in my hand, then it was not in the key and Xihuan-Lung could not be raised. I would have to settle with it being in Nate's hand for now. He would not give it to me, of that I was certain. The coals in the hearth were nearly the same color, and it soothed me. I turned to them instead.

"We found Xihuan-Lung—all of us, you and me, Lum and Barrett and Charlotte and Mr. Quinn—and they pulled the arrow out of her bones. Hou Yi's enchanted arrow keeps her dead. She is dead but not forever dead. If the arrow is removed, she comes back. We were in her body looking at her and she started to come back, like rotting away but in reverse. And she is so evil, so broken; Hou Yi killed her because he had to. She was hunting us; Xihuan-Lung killed all of us. And you turned into your canithrope form to protect me, but she burned you, Nate, and you were dying. There was nothing I could do.

"So, I had the key and when Prince Qixiang's soldiers caught up with us I shattered it and I kept the ruby. Not to sell it. Never to sell it. But it is a part of the key to the valley where Xihuan-Lung's bones lie. If no one can assemble them, no one can get to her and pull out the arrow and you are safe."

He snatched my hands. "Vivian!"

My face and hands were hot, uncomfortably so. I had nearly reached into the fire where the coals were glowing merrily. I blinked hard. It was beautiful in a way, like fire and blood and life all in one. I had no doubt that was the reason the monks chose the ruby to be the center of the key to the resting place of Xihuan-Lung and the arrow of Hou Yi. She had been there, a creature masquerading as a human woman. I took the dragon's tooth from her. I should have told Nate all of it before now.

Nate pulled me away from the fire and into his lap. I gratefully set my forehead against his. His skin was cool under my fire warmed skin. "Just answer me this." Nate set the ruby into my hand. It fit perfectly into my palm. I squeezed it until my fingers throbbed. "Is it the only piece I don't know about?"

"No," I said quietly, "MeiLin followed me to Xihuan-Lung's resting place. When I was breaking Xihuan-Lung apart and moving the bones just in case we failed, I took one bone of her neck to the river."

Nate nodded, the soul of patience once again.

"MeiLin was kneeling by the dragon's head. At first, I didn't know what she took but in my—" I paused, unsure to call it a vision or a dream or a nightmare.

"She took something?" Nate pressed.

I blinked at him. When Xihuan-Lung came alive, MeiLin promised Xihuan-Lung she could burn the world, she only wanted one thing—now we know she wanted the fox pelt YaMing had stolen given back to her. But, MeiLin promised to destroy the arrow only after she got what she wanted. If Xihuan-Lung did not do what she wanted, then MeiLin promised she would put Hou Yi's arrow back into her and she would be dead for all eternity.

"She took one of Xihuan-Lung's teeth, probably to force the dragon to help her get her fox skin back. I made MeiLin give it to me in exchange for the final piece of her skin."

"Where is it now?"

"In London." I closed my eyes. "Buried with my papa."

Nate turned away. "Vivian."

"I'm sorry Nate, I loved him so much and I wanted to send him with something I valued."

He closed his eyes for a long moment.

"I'm sorry." The words were hollow, I knew it even as I said them. Men are islands. There is little they can rely on, little they can depend upon. If they are lucky, they are matched with good wives who care for them and support them and are their partners in all things. If they are lucky, they have a true, loyal friend. His truest friend, his beloved dog, Ranger, gave his life for him when they disturbed the leywell under London and Nate acquired his canithrope powers. Ranger was killed that night. He lost his best friend. Had he been the only one Nate could really rely on?

No. Nate *could* rely on me.

Then why had I hidden the ruby? Keeping it kept Nate safe, but there was something more. I couldn't bear to be parted from it. There was something about it. I was holding it so tight my arm throbbed all the way to the shoulder. I was only vaguely aware Nate was moving.

He was halfway out the door before I came back to myself.

"Where are you going?" I demanded.

"For a walk." The door closed behind him. I would rather he gave it a spirited slam. The quiet click was more than a door between us, it was a wall, built brick by brick, closing us off from one another.

I fell across our bed and cried, the ruby clenched in my fist.

CHAPTER EIGHT

NATE WAS QUIET the next morning. We dressed in adventuring attire, trousers and heavy vests, mine looking more like a bodice than a waistcoat, but of similar sturdy material, and our leather long coats, seax blades, and pistols. We headed out to see the end of the track. We had arranged to meet the rail line workers after breakfast.

I had no appetite, but Nate did. He ate slowly, tapping a knife back and forth like a metronome. I abhorred when he did that. The *tink-tink-tink* of it was an appalling social habit from his previous life as an adventurer and one that he returned to when deeply distracted. I sipped a bit of tea and toast with jam, wishing for something a bit more British to start my day, like kippers or mushrooms on toast or even sausages and tomatoes. Nate wolfed down fatty bacon and eggs and coffee, and a good portion of thin, sweet biscuits cooked flat in a griddle. He must have enjoyed them. I was impressed by the sheer quantity of food he consumed. I wrapped a few slices of toast in a napkin and shoved them and an apple in my pocket. If anything, maybe it could be a peace offering to Nate later.

Fortified, we left the HeadHouse and set out to meet a young man named Samuel Lane, employed by the railroad. Nate refused to believe there was nothing he could do to assist the railroad in advancing west. Perhaps it was the canithrope in him, or the fact that he had so far battled a mad man, monsters, metal men, and dragons that led him to believe that there was little he could not eventually overcome.

Samuel took us out to a fancy, new metal carriage painted the color of a new straw hat, with red leather seats and a pair of shiny brass lanterns hanging from each front corner. He vigorously turned a crank along the side several times and the engine sputtered and coughed to life.

"This is a gasoline-powered runabout," Samuel explained. "We'll be meeting a carriage and horses down the line because my beauty here only is good on the roads. If you want to go any further down the line, then you're gonna need the horses. The rail workers use them."

Nate was immediately transfixed with the runabout. He ran a loving hand over the side like he was admiring a new horse. I felt sure we were going to be taking one home with us, maybe more. I rolled my eyes. This was the plow Mr. Crossdale had brought home at the beginning of the spring all over again. I patiently waited my turn to be acknowledged.

"Just climb aboard, Mrs. Valentine, and we'll have you and your mister out to the end of the line before you know it—duck soup!" Samuel said.

I let him offer me a hand. "Pardon?"

"Easy deal—duck soup means easy deal. I guess it's because it'd be easy to make soup from a duck."

"And why is that?" I blinked at him.

"Well, I never thought about it, but I suppose because ducks belong in water." He laughed. "You don't have to work too hard to get them in the pot. Fill it with water, they get right in and you just pop the lid right on."

I liked him right away.

"Their new man is a real Wisenheimer," Samuel continued. "Thinks he knows everything about…well, about everything. But if he can deliver, then the Pennsy will be sitting pretty with the biggest monopoly on both sides of the Mississippi. Anyone who has invested a dime in the railroads will be minted millionaires, and anyone who has not will be cursing their misfortune."

"Yes, that is the very reason we are here," Nate said dryly. "So far the 'Pennsy' has paid very poorly as an investment, despite very promising reporting."

Samuel was suddenly very focused on the hard-packed dirt road before us. "Well, we have hit some misfortune."

"So Mr. Cassatt has said, and the reason we are here as his agents." Nate scowled.

"Mr. Lane, what's really going on?" I asked.

"Well, ma'am, it's like this, there's a queer turn on the line." Samuel focused on the road, using the handle to steer the runabout down the hard packed streets.

Nate was watching the world zip by. "Queer how?"

Samuel spared him a glance. "Something's wrong with the ground, I guess. Maybe too many of them Injuns are buried there."

"Injuns?" Nate cocked an eyebrow. "What the hell?"

"The land used to be swarming with them like ticks on a dog, they're almost gone now, and good riddance. But there's still some around, and they're buried everywhere. My granddad said used to be you'd find their bones right out in the open. They didn't have the sense to even bury their dead like good Christian folk, so most of them died off. God did 'em in, or the Army. Or they learned to be good Christians."

Nate gave me a look. "Injuns" must be Indians. I read about them once. I never expected them to be such hated, feared heathens, though.

We traveled as far as the runabout could take us before we had to transfer into the wagon that had beaten us here by a few days, bringing a load of supplies to the work camp.

"Nate, darling", I crooned, "Exactly when did we become an agent of Mr. Cassatt?"

Nate refused to look me in the eye, "When you were still sleeping this morning and I went out to gather some information; money changed hands and I got a few leads."

I stared at my husband, the airship pirate. "What happens if we are caught?"

Nate shrugged, "I have no idea. Maybe we get answers, maybe we get stonewalled. Maybe they find out exactly what a canithrope is and how dangerous one can be when you disrupt his livelihood."

The foreman and his crew had a rail car set up as living space. The front of it they were using as a bunk house, the rear was a small kitchen. We were told it was moved to the end of the track by a hand cart operated by two men taking turns pushing down on a lever to propel the cart along the track. Another flat car held wooden ties and long sections of track ready to be laid as the railroad progressed to the west, as well as bins of tools used to drive the ties and rails into the earth and spikes to hold them there.

Samuel introduced us to the foreman, Mr. Massey, a man with square broad shoulders and an impressive gut that hung over his belt. His cheeks were red with too much drink, and he glared at us with sallow, squinty eyes and a menacing expression. He looked as though he could consume a truly impressive amount of alcohol.

"Who the hell are you?" His eyes traveled up and down my body, intimately, like he was removing every bit of my clothing. At my side, Nate clenched his fist, ready to introduce it to Mr. Massey's jaw.

"I am *Mrs.* Valentine," I said, raising my chin. "We have come to see the line."

"My wife and I are agents of Mr. Cassatt and the board of directors for the railway," Nate said through stiff lips. "We are inspecting the lack of progress. Would you care to explain that, Mr. Massey?"

Mr. Massey pushed his hat back and stared at Nate for a long moment. He shifted his weight from foot to foot, spat then said, "Aye. Line's cursed."

Cups, Swords, and *Wands* were all around, emotions, conflict, passion; there were so many Tarot symbols around it was impossible to identify just one.

"Come on." Samuel gave me a nod with his head. I knew I was doing no good here. Nate was ready to fight. So was Mr. Massey.

I nodded and followed Samuel to the rail car that served as the bunkhouse. In the lee of the car, under an awning made of sailcloth, sat supplies: barrels of rail spikes, long sections of rails, wooden ties, tools, and more. He handed me a rail spike.

The spike was nearly sixteen centimeters long and weighty. "That there is real American steel, Mrs. Valentine," Samuel said with a smile. "Impressive, isn't it?"

"I suppose so." I smiled and handed it back.

"Keep it, they come two hundred to a barrel and, truthfully, without track the spikes aren't much good."

"What do you mean, without track? There's a whole car worth of track right there."

"Just you wait," Samuel said mysteriously.

Nate stood eying the barrier that indicated the end of the line where workers had constructed a pylon of timbers and added a hand-painted sign indicating the same. As far as I could tell, the rails continued much as they had behind us, stretching out across the landscape into the west, toward the far end of America.

"We're gonna have to take the hand carts and horses from here." The foreman pulled a cigarette from his mouth. "The runabout cannot go where there ain't no road, and any further, there ain't no road."

"Show me," Nate commanded.

"You'll wait until I'm done with my break."

Nate's eyes narrowed, he was in no mood to be ordered around by the foreman of the rail project, but he said nothing. We didn't actually have any authority by Mr. Cassatt or any other railroad executive, so it was for the best that Nate managed to hold his tongue.

Finally, Mr. Massey finished his cigarette and washed it down with several swallows from his flask. After tucking it back into his grimy vest, he dusted his hands, shook out his coat, and beat the dirt from his hat. "You're not just agents of the Pennsy, you're also investors from England, aren't you? You think you can get richer off the backs of good, hard working Americans?"

Nate could not hide his accent any more than I could. It would be like expecting this layabout before us to act like a gentleman.

"I look to help unite this great nation," Nate said in his most diplomatic tone. It was softer than the Nate-the-lord voice but was no less impressive. "The railroads are the best way to accomplish this. Your Mr. Cassatt looked for financial backers from all over the world, not just America."

Mr. Massey snorted. "Rich men getting richer." He turned to the army of workers doing what workers do best when there is a lag in production; they were gambling, talking, and generally lazing about. He hawked and spat. "You heard his lordship, boys, get hopping. This limey wants to see the true end of the line."

They exchanged glances, then got to their feet. Most were young men, scarcely out of their twenties, many of them younger than Nate and me. They leapt to the pylon and started taking it apart, sliding the timbers off the track.

Mr. Massey climbed aboard the hand cart. "Come on, yer Lordship! My boys didn't move them heavy timbers for nothing."

Nate climbed up and offered me a hand. I swallowed hard, realizing the safest seat for me would be right between Nate and Mr. Massey on the creaky wooden bench. I was thankful I thought to pack my adventuring clothes; a dress would not have fared well against the rough seats of the hand cart.

Mr. Massey stared at me, making me wish I had more than my coat to cover myself. I did not want the type of attention Mr. Massey wanted to give. He leered at me, staring too intently at the curve of my thigh in my trousers. I turned toward Nate as subtly as I could. I did not need Nate fighting Mr. Massey, at least not before we discovered exactly why the railroad was not able to progress beyond St. Louis, Missouri.

Thirty minutes later, we abruptly reached the true end of the track. Far ahead, the timbers had been laid, all that was left was to lay the metal rails upon the railroad ties and hammer the spikes into place. But the metal rails were twisted and warped, pitted as though acid had eaten away at them. Nate leapt from the cart, his boots crunching on the stone that formed the bed for the wooden ties.

I joined Nate at the furthermost edge of the rails, where they were hot and warped, pitted, and so rusty they looked bloody.

I knelt by the edges of the rail. But it was not the rails I saw. *Death* was change, and change was painful. Was this what the people wanted? Change was not always what people wanted, though it was sometimes what was needed.

Tall grass swayed, growing yellow and brittle before my eyes. I blinked hard and when my eyes cleared, I could see figures walking through the grass. A king with a stately crown; a family, a mother, father, and child and old woman. A bishop in a tall miter. They made their way across the dry, golden grasses. Behind them, on a white horse, a knight in black armor rode up, his banner black as midnight emblazoned with a single white rose.

The black knight overtook them easily and raised his visor, revealing a head reduced to a bare skull. He raised a scythe and cut down the king. He cut down the family. He cut down the priest. Blood splattered across the white rose. The knight turned without haste, without hate, and rode on, the grass turning green in his wake. Through Death, all things change. *Death* was transition. The white rose on his banner was our reminder that death was a pure transition without malice. It came for all.

It was a transition, a transformation. Then the banner tore free of his lance and fluttered on a non-existent wind to fall at my feet. A white rose was a symbol of purity and innocence; an action without passion. Now the rose was blood red—a red rose.

Red roses for love, courage and power. I looked over to my husband. We would need courage and power to overcome Geiger. I hoped the deep red was not literally red blood for what was to come.

I looked up. The black knight was fading from view.

Death rarely means literal death, it generally just means rebirth. But for rebirth to come, the old ways must end. No one is immune to the end of one thing and the beginning of another, not the young, not the old, not the rich or the poor, everyone must change. Something was very wrong here, this rebirth was tainted. It was not the innocent change as the white rose symbolized, this was violent. It left behind a bitter taste, something ashen and hot like copper, or blood.

Nate went ahead, following the rails to their termination, touching the end, then pulling his hand back and staring curiously. He turned his fingers back and forth, first looking at his fingers then the rails.

I went to join him.

Nate glared at the metal. "They're hot."

"They're in the sun."

"I know they're in the sun," he said. "But it's more than that. The rails are *hot.*"

I knelt beside him. He was right. I didn't have to touch them to feel the heat coming off them. The rails were hot right where they abruptly ended, reaching up like splinters of steel. Again, he touched the end of the steel rail and his hand came back rust red. He turned to smack the rust from his hands, but it turned to a smear of blood.

We exchanged a glance. He wiped the blood away with his handkerchief then tucked it away in his pocket. He offered me his clean hand and we started back to the rail cart. Out of curiosity, I reached out occasionally to touch the rails as they sat in the warm sun. The rails got cooler as we got closer to the rail cart.

"What does that mean?"

Nate shook his head, as puzzled as I was.

"Mr. Massey, they're back!"

A worker who had been pumping the rail cart pointed up the hill. We wheeled around and Nate thrust me behind him.

"Don't get too excited, those redskins know they aren't supposed to be here," Mr. Massey called.

"Redskins?" I turned. Anyone with red skin would make America even more wondrous. I stared at the dark-skinned man who had appeared astride a brown and white horse. I almost expected him to fade away like the black knight.

"Indians, ma'am," Samuel explained. "The army will be removing them soon enough. There's a few men that up and married themselves squaw wives and had half-breed children. Being half-white keeps them out of the Christian charity houses and off the reservations, but it's a waste if the mothers teach them the old backward ways."

I couldn't believe what I was hearing. "You mean, if their fathers weren't white, then they would be taken away, even though they have parents who love them and would provide for their welfare? A charity house is well and good when a child has nothing but when they have a family—"

"Well, yes, but it is hardly a life. It's not their fault; those poor children can hardly function in this modern age if they refuse to go to the reservation with the rest of their kind. Going to the Christian charity houses may seem cruel, but it's really a kindness. It teaches them about the word of God, it gives them a good education, and gets them away from all that nonsense the rest of the redskins believe."

I stared at the man on his horse. He wore a tan cowboy hat, his long, black hair curled around his shoulder. He wore a red shirt and a waistcoat with a white front that, as unlikely as it seemed, looked like it was gleaming in the light. He sat like a statue on the hill, watching us. I would not have believed he was real if the horse beneath him, a beautiful brown and white paint, did not shift from time to time as it regarded the scene below the hill to the rails and more importantly, us.

"Do you suppose there are more of them?"

"There's always more of them," Mr. Massey said. "Hey!" He reached under the bench seat and pulled out a rifle and brandished above his head in a most unfriendly manner. "You're not welcome here you dirty, red devil! Get yourself back to where you belong!"

The man did not respond. He stared at us, clearly not impressed by the rifle or Mr. Massey.

I turned. "Where does he belong?"

Mr. Massey scowled at me and spat. "What?"

"Where does he belong?" I repeated. "I mean, where would he be if the railroad wasn't here?"

Mr. Massey ignored me.

I knew the answer. If the railroad was not there, if the Americans were not moving so rapidly across the wide country of theirs, the red Indians would be living there. They would not be forced into Christian charity houses to learn to function in the modern age. They would be living with their families, backward and unenlightened or not, where they were loved. I was no longer sure this progress was good.

But who was I to judge when change was warranted? Plenty of other people were also funding the railroad. It was hardly just us who were trying to benefit from this new era, and the benefits of it were great. It brought people together and moved goods across the nation. Why, it was intended to unite America. So why did it feel like an instrument of evil profiteering?

I looked back to where the black knight had disappeared after losing his banner. The benefits were great, but harm was being done, as well. The cost was too high; children were being stolen away, lives were being ruined, and all in the name of progress. This was not innocent transformation. This was progress born from the lust for gold, the lust for glory, the lust for God. The red rose was proof of that; red, the color of passion. The red ruby in my pocket throbbed.

We may not have wished harm, but harm was being done.

Nate scowled. He watched the man on horseback. Something was passing between them. It was an odd skill men seemed to share, just as men are islands. They could take the measure of another with just a look and understand so much about each other. Nate slowly turned to the rails.

"Wha—?"

He squeezed my hand tightly, silencing me.

When we turned back the Indian was gone.

"Does anyone else live out this way?" Nate asked.

"You mean other than the savages?" Mr. Massey laughed. "Just over that hill is a town that is little more than a quarry, a tavern, and a blacksmith. There is the odd farm or two, I think; its Maddenville for the Maddens."

"And then there's Careys." Another man offered

"And the Tates," said Mr. Lane.

"And of course, the Maddens," one of the men who worked the hand cart added. "My mother is a Madden."

Nate and I exchanged a look. Most of the wooden beams rested on a bed of crushed stone, gray and pink that glittered in places as bits of the rock reflected the sunlight, and the green grasses disappeared into dark pine forests that ran into the hills that rose in the distance.

The warped section of track was different, the stone did not glitter and reflect the sunlight. It did not look pink and gray, it was old and charred. The wooden track looked like old wood, the color of driftwood heavily streaked with dark worm-rot. I moved a stone with my foot. The land below was scorched; the rocks sat on a fine layer of ash. Nate reached down and touched the ground. He gathered several rocks and some of the ash in his hand. He smelled it and scowled. The dog in him had found something.

"It's burnt," he explained to me.

"It's cursed," I said. "Mr. Massey said it himself. But by whom?"

Nate made a noncommittal noise and escorted me back to the pushcart.

Mr. Massey had his rifle across his knees as though he expected the Indian to return at any moment, needing to be convinced to leave us alone. Though I had less experience with Indians on horseback, I felt at this point I would prefer the Indian. He didn't make me feel as though I was on display.

"There was a fire," I announced when we stopped.

The men exchanged glances. Mr. Massey pushed his hat back and scratched his hair. He tried to spit but nothing came out; his mouth was dry. If I didn't know better I would have sworn it was from fear. He stared at us for a long moment, then turned and walked to the sailcloth for something. I really hated the sort of man who believed women knew nothing.

Samuel finally nodded. "Yes," he said slowly, "there was a fire, but it wasn't here. Queer thing, it was about half-mile away. Poor family's house burned down. Why?"

Nate picked up another handful of ash and brought it to Mr. Massey. "There's ash beneath the track."

Mr. Massey scoffed. "That's the foundation for the ties."

Nate's eyes narrowed. Whatever the ash was, it was not the foundation for the railroad ties. He was tired of being lied to by the railroad, and so was I. If it were only our own financial security he was concerned about, I doubt he would be so frustrated, but we had much greater concerns. His loyalties in the matter were wide and deep.

We both knew he was lying but I doubted we could prove it right now. And I wasn't about to let something drastic happen. "Do you have more track ready to lay?"

Mr. Massey gave me a sideways look. "We do."

"Brilliant." I dusted off my hands. "Place it, please."

One of the workers stared. "Excuse me?"

Mr. Massey hawked and spat. "I will not."

Nate stepped forward, towering over him. "I say you will. My wife and I are here to inspect this little project of westward expansion. I will bear responsibility with Mr. Cassatt for what happens with the steel."

Mr. Massey scowled up at him. "I will not have my men lay it."

Nate didn't budge. "You will. Moreover, I saw the money we have invested has bought this steel and more several times over. If you refuse, we shall pull all our funding from Pennsylvania Railroad and Mr. Cassatt will be informed of your unwillingness and inability to do your job."

I didn't say anything. We had no power here but Mr. Massey had no way of knowing that. To sell now would cost us more than our initial investment, but there was no way Mr. Massey would know that either.

Mr. Massey glared.

Nate glared back.

Mr. Massey broke first. "You heard him boys, lay two sections of track. I'm only setting two sections, Mr. Valentine. You may very well own the steel, sir, but there's only six men and I won't break them to prove the rail won't stay."

Nate took the victory. "Fair enough."

Mr. Massey gave him a smile. "And, since I'm short-handed, you'll help."

I was excused from the labor, being a woman, but they needed all the help they could get.

The workers took the push-car back to gather the supplies, leaving me alone at the end of the track with just Nate's revolver for company. If they were going to return with all the required materials, they needed all the available muscle and space they could get.

Nate had smelled fire in the ash by the ties. His wonderful sense of smell was one of the lingering superhuman skills he retained whether he was a dog, a man, or the canithrope form in between, so I would have to trust him that the ties smelled like ash. Living in London had taught me ash can travel far and wide and can get anywhere, so if there had been a fire half a mile away it was not unreasonable to believe the ash could have traveled that far. But there was no reason for the ash to stop at the wooden ties. That part defied logic.

I went and re-examined the section of warped tracks. I again noted how the metal looked like it had been eaten away by acid. The warmth of the steel radiated through the leather of my gloves. I dug into the crushed stone by the track where the steel was lifted and damaged, which was nearly four inches deep before giving way to the dark earth and clay below. The one thing I *did not* find was ash and rust. That began abruptly where the metal track ended.

"The metal burned away, but it didn't."

I wheeled about, my hand touching the butt of Nate's pistol in the pocket of my long coat. It was the same man whom we had seen on horseback. He walked the horse slowly down the hill, letting it pick its way down on a long lead. His other hand was open. His long, straight black hair hung to his shoulder, and several feathers were tucked into the band of his tan hat.

Surrounding him was the *Three of Cups*: three maids with uplifted golden goblets dancing in joy and camaraderie, friendship and community. I could tell this man meant me no harm. He may have been one of the fabled red Indians, but he was nothing to fear, not this one.

Mr. Massey called them dirty red devils. As far as I could tell, there was nothing devilish about this man, nor did he have red skin, just warm, brown skin. I had seen a similar color in some of the Africans in London, if not a touch ruddier. "You're one of those red Indians."

His mouth became a thin, red line. I bit my lip. I realized only then that the rail worker's dubbing of "red Indian" might be just as insulting as Mr. Massey's term "red devil." "I'm sorry. Please pardon my ignorance. I am not from here. What would you like to be called?"

He cocked his head at me, his tan hat bright against his straight black hair. He must have accepted my apology, because a smile split his face, revealing bright, straight teeth. He touched his chest over his heart then raised his hand. "We are all Native Peoples. I am Nacto. I am Cheyenne."

I wasn't sure what to say. "Ah, Vivian Valentine. My husband, Nathaniel Valentine, went with the rail workers. We are English."

Nacto nodded. I was immediately glad I had made a point to identify us as English, to set us apart from the American rail workers. At least we were not to be identified with that lot. "Mr. Nacto, what did you mean just then? The metal burned but it didn't."

"Just Nacto," he said. "The rails will not remain. They burn like the house."

I nodded. The house again. Whatever happened to the rails was tied to the house and the fires. Never mind that steel rails should not be able to burn at all. "What house? Can you show me the house?"

"I can show you the Tate house," he said. "It is hard walking for a woman."

"I am no easily frightened lady, Nacto. I would like to see what happened, but my husband will be returning soon with the other men," I added rather belatedly, realizing it was rather foolish to go wandering off into the woods with a man I didn't know.

"You are safe. I give my word," Nacto assured me.

I looked him over, if he was trying to hide something from me, it remained well-hidden. He was simply Three Cups radiating friendship, if possible, even stronger than before. I was certain I had nothing to fear from him.

I followed him down a hill and then up again, where we finally crossed to a dirt road where the tracks of many horses and wagons had caused it to wash out. Far from an expert in such matters, it seemed to me that it had experienced more traffic lately than it was used to. The grass that would have grown up around the wagon ruts had been trampled by more people than usually traveled the path, or perhaps by those who cared less for the land.

Nacto took me to a hill overlooking a dark mass and stopped. "We go no further."

"What?" His horse nickered and tossed his head. "Why?" I wanted to go further. It was obvious, just like the rail workers said, a fire occurred in the homestead below. It looked to be a barn and a home, but most interesting of all, the fire had not spread.

"No normal fire burns that way," Nacto said, staring out at the farm below us. "But you must see, because you are willing to hear, the Cheyenne did not do this."

"You're Cheyenne?" I clarified, more to remind myself.

He nodded.

"Did others like you, not Cheyenne I mean, but other..." I struggled for a term that would not be offensive, "Did other Natives do this?" I asked. If he was trying to slow-walk me to a conclusion I would rather he just tell me what he wanted me to know.

"No." He turned his horse. "This is not our way."

"Wait." I stumbled over a rock in my haste to catch up with him. I caught the reins of his horse and jerked it to the side. The horse rolled his eyes and snorted. "Whose way is it?"

"The devil. The devil burned nine here. He is gone now...and we need to be," Nacto said. "You must return to your husband now, Vivian."

I trembled uncontrollably. Mr. Massey said the Indians were the devil. Nacto, whom I would trust more than Mr. Massey, said the devil had done this. Being raised Catholic, I was sure the devil existed, though since I had also experienced undead dragons, demons, and otherworldly creatures, I was no longer certain the world could be defined in such simple terms as good and evil.

But old habits and old learning die hard, and when one has been taught to fear the devil from church sermons since before they can walk, one learns to fear the devil like nothing else. And fire and sin are the devil's weapons.

I looked over my shoulder. The burned house disappeared over the edge of the hill. I took a deep breath to organize my thoughts. I needed to quiet the moths beating themselves senseless against the little windows in my mind. No good could came of that.

I followed Nacto, walking past the trampled grasses. Now I knew they had been headed to the farm. Devil or no, I could easily imagine they came with murder in mind. It was the careless tramp of feet burdened with ill intent. I had to see the farmhouse again.

SᴖS

I watched the men finish laying the last of four undamaged rails. The ruined steel had been yanked free of the wooden ties and dragged off to the side. They grunted and sweated in the sun, using long metal rods to lever the rails onto the wooden ties and heavy hammers to align them with the rails that were still in place. Then, they pounded the spikes into the rails to pin them to the ties.

I brought them water and spikes as they worked, to keep the work going smoothly. "Nacto told me the steel rails burn away like the house." I offered casually.

"Who?" Nate straightened and stretched his back.

"The Cheyenne man who was watching us."

Mr. Massey choked and sputtered. "Them dirty devils are the ones that burned the Tate family out."

"He said the devil himself did it. He said burning homes is not the Cheyenne way."

"Begging your pardon, missus," Samuel Lane said gently. "But you can't trust 'em. Lying is in their blood. It's part of who they are. They give and take back. They go back on their word. Why, the United States Government gave them a whole parcel of land—good land, too—in Montana and safe passage to get there where they can practice their heathen ways in peace and they still refused to go. They just skulk about frightening good people. You can't trust 'em."

"Well, I want to see what happens to these rails myself," Nate announced. "We will be staying here tonight to see what happens with our own eyes."

Mr. Massey's mouth narrowed for a moment and he swallowed hard but nodded. "Aye, do as you must. But we're taking the wagon. We'll leave you the handcart."

CHAPTER NINE

THERE WAS NO moon, but the stars winked brightly in the night and made the trees turn to dark shadows. I shivered and wrapped my arms in my coat. I was tempted to make a small ring of stones and get Nate to build us a fire but Nacto warned me the steel rails would burn away. For the moment, I was curious to see how that would occur without even a campfire. Having a fire would feel like I was cheating somewhat.

We sat on the handcart. Its wooden bed kept us off the cold ground.

"The Cheyenne man—"

"Nacto?" Nate interrupted.

"Yes, Nacto," I confirmed. "He told me the burned home belonged to the Tate family. We should head there in the morning. Mr. Massey knows something about it; he went pale when I mentioned the fire."

Nate's voice was thick with fatigue; it had been a long day setting the rails. "Burning is a horrible way to go."

"I suppose it would be."

He put his arm around me. Between his body heat, my long coat, and the work we had done together, I was feeling stupid and sleepy myself. I set my head on his shoulder. Nacto had risked the wrath of the rail workers to show me the site. He must have faith that we were different. He must have faith that we would listen. He had to be desperate, indeed, to trust that we were not like Mr. Massey and his men.

Nate snored. I settled in beside him. He had the right idea. I would close my eyes, for a moment.

There was a sound. A groan, a creak, a crack, the low moan metal makes as it's warping. Geiger was in his machine as the factory burned. The metal was rending, shrieking, warping, melting. Men screamed. The smell of hot metal was like copper and blood strangling me where I stood.

I jerked awake. Something was moving in the trees around us.

No. Not something in the forest, the forest itself was moving. The forest itself was shifting. I swiped blindly for Nate, unable to take my eyes off the forest.

Beside me Nate awoke, grabbing my hand and pinning it to his shoulder.

We were surrounded by a slow-creeping, gray-green vine, choking vines with wide flat leaves that snaked around the edge of the rail cart. One tendril touched the edges of our feet. I jerked my foot free of the gray-green plant. It resisted only slightly.

As we slept the vine had crept over the track, all twenty-four meters of it, gently enveloping it until it was cocooned. I ripped a piece of it off and shoved it into the pocket of my long coat. It was rubbery like seaweed, though warm like flesh.

"Nate, what do you suppose that is?"

He shrugged, dulled by sleep, and stared at the growth. He tore at the vines with his seax, hacking at several pieces until he exposed the steel below. "Kudzu maybe?"

My botanical book mentioned kudzu and its frighteningly fast growth, but this was unnatural. "I can't imagine this is any ordinary growth."

I shook my head, if he expected me to be the plant expert because of my apothecary background, he was sorely mistaken. This was beyond my expertise. The plant was low to the ground and swallowed the light, creating a lush, velvety carpet that led over the rails and in the direction Nacto and I had taken that afternoon.

We followed the vines. The growth led us to the Tate home.

I pulled my seax from my belt and crept along with Nate. The walk was pleasant enough, smooth as we walked along this carpet of green, but it filled me with nameless dread. He led the way fearlessly, determined to protect me, pausing from time to time to sniff the air.

We finally came upon a small building, though calling it a building would be generous. Clearly a building had once stood there, but all that remained was its foundation. The chimney had crumbled and broken, and it sagged to one side. A few timbers remained upright.

There was a barn as well, and it had fared better. The shell of it remained but it had been gutted by the fire. Nate headed off to investigate.

I moved in a small circle. The Tate family had been poor, but they had owned a wagon.. The wagon sat in need of new paint, but its wheels were in serviceable condition. They had clearly cared for and maintained their belongings. It was unlikely carelessness had caused their fire. Perhaps they left their hearth burning and a spark caused the fatal fire. That might explain the guilty chimney. Or an oil lamp fell over…But that just didn't feel right. Nacto had said nine people burned here, the Tate family and possibly hired hands. Nine deaths. Surely, someone would have noticed a fire start. What *had* happened here?

I walked the path from the remains of the house to the barn. The soft green ground was painfully beautiful in this place of death and loss.

The dragon's ruby in my pocket was heavy. I felt it so acutely I stumbled. A man lay before me, not a real man, a card to be sure, hoarding four pentacles. Far behind him was his home; he had traveled far from everything he knew. This was the *Four of Pentacles* but inverse. Greed. Materialism.

I fell to my knees in the rubbery leaves, collapsing on the image of the man, shattering it. The ground should have been dry, parched by the fire. But it was cold and wet, slimy and so, so horrible. The fire was months ago, so the ground should have recovered. New life should have sprouted. Instead, a bubbly covering had formed, like algae on rocks, slick and spongy. My stomach suddenly lurched into my throat. Touching the earth disturbed it, breaking whatever spell had been cast upon the land, releasing a scent of evil and rot—the scent of death. It was days old, weeks old—the scent of decay—like a putrid, gangrenous limb.

It came up in my hand like the leaves that enveloped the rails and crawled over our feet. I shook my hand violently to fling the gray-green coating off, it stung like nettles.

Instead of a man of flesh and blood, there was a pile of bones laying in an untidy heap, thrown aside like a tangle of garbage. I had seen bones in finer shape outside a butcher's shop. These had been dropped, and tossed carelessly about, reflecting in the moonlight in a way that nothing else here did. They were queer in this place of ash, gleaming white and so sad.

I squatted down by the bones. He had been a large person, a man I would guess, by his height and the thickness. A hammer would have broken them upon impact, forming lines where they were crushed. These were cracked and splintered from so many places I could not tell from where the damage started, nor could I guess what caused it. Impossibly, it looked as if the bones shattered from the inside, they were splintered and bowed outward. It must have caused the man such pain. Growing up in the home of a healer, I have seen more horrific wounds than anyone should. I had never seen anything like this. I only hoped he had been dead when whatever caused his bones to erupt from within had struck him.

The ground where he lay was depressed in a large ring. Something had stood there while the earth around it was scorched and the farm burned. The bones had been protected.

I gagged, turning my head away to vomit. I could not wipe my mouth with my hand, I was covered in a thin, greasy layer of what I was certain was what was left of this poor man.

Nate was still in the barn, searching out any signs of survivors. There would be none. This man had not been in the fire, his bones bore no marks of the fire. Those who had been in the fire were dead but charred, and I was not sure the fire was what killed them, either.

I reached for his skull. I needed to look upon him. But I needed to not find dead, lifeless eyeballs or something equally disturbing staring back at me. I couldn't explain why. I felt he deserved a witness to his end, his life, his death, something, anything. And I needed to have the strength not to look away.

I let out a sob of relief, my throat still burning from sick. There was nothing so horrifying. I was almost disappointed I did not find the vacant, milky stare of dead, white eyes, the gray of brain, the red of blood and tissue and fresh injury. The skull had been broken, split across the front from temple to far cheek. The bone bulged. Something had been inside the bones fighting desperately to get out.

"I'm sorry," I whispered to the skull. "I'm so sorry for whatever happened here.

This person had been discarded like slaughtered cattle in a butchers-row. That a human being could be treated so, filled me with a choking sorrow.

My hands were shaking. "These people were murdered."

The moment I said it I was struck by a dizzying sensation. Someone set a fish hook beneath my breastbone and jerked me off my feet. The world faded away to a sepia toned tintype and I was sucked into a world that was more real than the one I had been living in.

I knelt again beside the bones and noticed the moment red-black sludge seeped into my knee as if the earth itself was surrendering up the remains of the dead man. With it, a shade crept up my body, cold at first then warmer as though I was sinking into a bath. I closed my eyes. I searched for something to anchor myself to. A hand; I grasped it tight.

When I opened my eyes, I was kneeling in green grass. I was surrounded by several horses that nickered to one another, twitched their tails, and stamped their feet as they grazed with their soft velvety muzzles. Their riders, several men dressed for hard labor, were gathered around the small porch.

One of them wore his brown hat pushed back on his crown as he scratched at his head, his dark red shirt was worn and stained—Mr. Massey. I immediately recognized his clothes. "You must understand, Mrs. Tate, the law just ain't on your side," he said, not unkindly.

A woman sat shelling peas into a bowl. "It ain't a matter of the railroad's offer. It's our home. We ain't moving." Her cream-colored dress was covered in tiny yellow and green flowers, faded from repeated washings. She paused and tucked a wisp of blond hair that had worked itself free of her braid behind her ear.

"Oh, but you are." The gathered men parted to allow one of their number to pass through. He was not a large man, but he exuded a cloud of fear among his followers.

It is one thing to know someone is alive and to see their name in print, it is an entirely different matter to see that someone stand before you. My blood ran cold.

"The railroad has authorized us to make their final offer," Mr. Massey began.

"Good, these meetings are getting tiring. My husband has told you time and time again, we ain't interested." She ripped peas open with tight, angry motions, tossing the pods into a rough wooden bucket, the peas into a ceramic bowl with a blue painted rim.

"Missus Tate, you do not understand. This will be the *final* offer." The icy tone set a chill racing through me. "You would be well advised to move, now."

"You heard her," a deep voice admonished.

Geiger turned. I could not mistake him for another man, though much about him had changed since last I saw him. He had traded the cap for a stylish brown bowler in bad need of a dusting. He wore brown leather gloves despite the warm day, and a gray tweed suit with a waistcoat beneath that was only a shade lighter. A stylish man would wear color of some kind. He had a thick mustache, but his skin had become pock-marked and craggy as though a long-suffering illness had stolen his vitality and health. I had seen burns before; this was not the look of burns, this was the look of hard living. It was the look of permanent scowling and raw hatred.

He was the man who made deals with demons, the man who created life from circuits and machines. Nate and I saw him burn in the factory beneath Mr. Sterling's Factory. Geiger had cheated death itself.

Geiger turned to the man who had spoken and was now making his way toward them from the field. It was the same look Geiger had given me. The center of this man's attention was a horrible place to be. I very much doubted that had changed. I was also sure time had not mellowed Mr. Geiger at all.

A tall, broad-shouldered farm hand made his way to them. His skin was the color of the perfect cup of hot tea before adding any milk. His clothes and cowboy hat were worn. "The Tates are not selling."

Another woman, dark like the man, was swapping dry laundry on the line for wet laundry in a basket. She watched the scene warily, moving slowly. Her green apron fluttered slightly as she moved, the wind determined to keep her from going unnoticed. She was beautiful, with proud, queenly features, her black hair caught up in a bright green scarf.

Geiger rolled his mouth, tasting the words before nodding to himself.

Finally, he smiled, a thin, unkind smile of fury. "Mr. Massey, round them up."

The riders moved stiffly, with pale faces and wide eyes. Mr. Massey grabbed his gun and jammed it into the dark-skinned man's stomach. He froze mid-stride, his mouth hanging open in shock, the same look as the skull on the ground. I screwed my eyes closed trying to hold the vision, but it was fading. I saw both the man and his bones beneath. I saw the farm and the skeletal remains of the burned-out husk of the farm. The two images swam before my eyes, melded, fading into one another.

Two of Geiger's riders charged at the woman hanging the clothes on the line, took her by the arms, and dragged her to the porch.

Mrs. Tate gasped. The man fought against Mr. Massey to get to her. One of the women screamed. The sound jolted me out of the vision.

Screams. A woman? Yes, but also a child, high pitched and fearful. My pulse throbbed in my ears. I forced myself to look through the burned-out land, the skeletal frame of the farmhouse's blackened timbers.

Geiger stood, his arms folded, watching his riders pummel the farmhand between them. "Mr. Massey," he finally warned, "If your boys kill him, I'll have to use you instead."

Use him? Use him for what? I stared at the bones in my hand, at the skull, at my own vomit. Mr. Geiger murdered them all. I needed to know how. I needed to know what he did to this man. What would cause a man to burst from the inside out? I was sure it had to do with his demon, the creature I'd seen with the lupine bone skull and soulless eyes.

Suddenly the ruby in my pocket was hot. A rush of energy flooded through me in a heady burst. I breathed out, and the remains of the farmhouse became whole again.

Mr. Geiger let himself into the farmhouse. The hand I was holding twitched. For an instant it clenched, grasping at my own hand. I gasped and looked and the vision was lost to me. The skeletal hand had not moved. But I know I felt the life reaching out in despair. He needed a witness to his life. He deserved a witness to his death.

More sharp screams, crying echoed in my ears.

Geiger came from the farmhouse, his heavy boots clomping on the steps. "Burn it down, gentlemen. We are done here."

They did not argue. They pulled torches from their saddles and carefully lit them. There was no joy, no bloodlust in their actions. They were damned men, resigned that their master was the devil and whatever their motivation had been in the beginning, they dared not cross him now. They had thrown their lot in with him long ago.

"You can't!" I leapt to my feet. I knew I was missing something, but there were people here somewhere—Mrs. Tate, the woman, and I heard a child, at least one child—people didn't just disappear. They were here! I stumbled.

My breath caught in my throat. What had he done? I spun to catch him as he moved past, but he was already directing his men to unload a large boiler from a wagon.

The riders grunted and struggled under the weight of it. I couldn't shake the feeling I had seen something like it before.

The farmhouse was quickly engulfed in flames, and beneath the hungry roar of flames tearing ravenously into dry timber I could hear sobbing, the pitiful cries of a child. I stepped forward and reached for Mr. Massey's coat. It moved through my fingers. I could feel it, but I could not grasp it.

Then I remembered, I was not there, I was a ghost, an apparition, out of my time. And, yet, I could smell the acrid scent of his tobacco and the stink of a man who was not overly concerned with washing. He moved through me.

"Please, please don't do this!" I leapt forward but there was nowhere for me to go. The harder I tried to move toward the farmhouse, the more it seemed to retreat. Mr. Massey turned his back on the scene. For a moment, I felt he looked right at me, and he recoiled as though surprised to be caught in this vile deed.

"It answers my call" Mr. Geiger did not turn. "The beast calls me master. Remember that, or it will wear your skin."

But Mr. Massey was not looking at me. The little hairs on the back of my neck were standing up. All the breath fled from my lungs and I was dimly aware that aside from the fire's hungry roar, the rest of the house had fallen silent as a tomb.

I wheeled. The men could not see me, but Mr. Geiger's monster could. Its soulless, cold orbs gleamed out from dark sockets. It stared at me, an amused expression on its fleshless skull. I stumbled backward.

"All the sin and misery of the world calls to you," Geiger said, his voice a deep, soft drone. "I will give you a form strong enough to live in this world that does not depend on the vices of man. I, alone, have that power."

Geiger's men beat the farmhand until he was bloody, then shoved him into the little chamber. I turned from the monster to the boiler chamber. Someone had to do something, anything! Please!

The monster looked at me, its head cocked to one side. I bit the inside of my cheek to keep from screaming. It walked the way birds do, bobbing lightly as it moved. The mouth parted slightly and uttered a shriek that set my teeth on edge. It was both a challenge and an amused cry. We shared a terrible secret. We could see one another.

It raised its canine muzzle to the sky, as if tasting misery, blood, and death in the air. Its head swiveled from the burning farm to Geiger to the giant boiler, then it started moving toward the boiler.

I trembled, sweat snaking down my back.

Geiger slid back a panel on the boiler, revealing vents and large circular windows. I had seen it before. It was a version of the boiler chamber from the laboratory beneath Sterling's Factory, back in London, where Nate and I had first battled Geiger.

It was also the boiler on the plans I had stolen from Mr. Cassatt's office. Geiger tricked him into believing it was a new kind of locomotive. Nate and I were not fooled. We had suspected it was something monstrous.

The farmhand beat his fists on the panel, screaming curses at Geiger and his riders. Then he saw the monster. The cry on his lips gurgled away. "I ain't afraid of you, monster!" the man shrieked, punching the wall of the boiler again. His voice cracked.

Mr. Geiger chewed on a sulfur match. "You will be."

The monster stood before the vents, panting slightly, tasting the air. Then it loomed like a giant black shadow, its skull grew dull, out of focus, like smoke. It flowed through the vents, seeping through the cracks and clouding the glass.

The man's screams pierced the night, high and thin. His fists frantically battered the glass. The boiler rocked manically from side to side, burying the heavy rim into the grass, then the mud, then fell silent.

I whipped my head back.

Geiger stared at the boiler. His dark eyes were wide and joyous with the lust of a madman. "Open it."

Mr. Massey was pale.

"I. Said. Open. It." Every word was a separate command, sharply accented. Geiger closed his eyes and took a deep breath.

Massey nodded and rushed past me. He threw back the bolts.

The man within stumbled from the boiler and staggered forward. Then he straightened and squared his shoulders, suddenly very strong and confident. His dark eyes opened, but they were now pale as the full moon, glassy and white. His strong, wide nose lifted in the air and tasted it.

"As I promised, a body free of the need of human vice." Geiger grinned, oily and terrible as a viper.

The world around me was on fire—a hot, angry fearsome roar; not merely a sound but a consuming growl that rattled me to the core. My ears throbbed, my eyes burned. It was the sound of my blood screaming through me, racing through my veins, leaving me weak and shaking like a raw, exposed nerve. I forced myself to open my eyes.

Then the man beside me fell forward, shaking. His powerful frame contracted in jerky fits. I scrambled to him, at a loss for what to do. I knelt over him, cradled his head in my hand. At first, my hand seemed to slide through his hair and flesh, stopping at his skull. His dark and curly hair had been cropped close to his scalp. He was handsome with a strong, square jaw. Now he was curled up, hissing in agony, his eyes were orbs of cloudy ice, empty and soulless. A cold sweat broke out in beads across his face, and his teeth were clenched so hard I thought they might crack.

I took his hand in mine, lacing our fingers together. His eyes went wide and, within them, I could see *The Tower*. Lightning struck and tore the very place he stood from beneath him and sent him tumbling headfirst toward the earth far below. His very nature was changing, becoming chaotic.

His hand punched through mine, striking the dirt. He gave a gurgle, struggled to exhale. He was drawing in air, ever-expanding, ever-pressing outward as though something within was fighting to get out, willing to do anything to get free.

He clasped his free arm around his chest and a groan, sick and fevered, slipped past his lips. His frantic eyes searched my face. He was begging me for help as he struggled to keep himself together, even as something was tearing him apart.

"I'm sorry," I whispered. Hot tears slipped down my cheeks. The back of my throat burned. I couldn't help him. Why was I seeing this if I couldn't help him?

"God," he breathed.

Geiger gave a snort of derision. "He is not strong enough. My monster will tear him apart in a matter of moments. The only hope now is to place him back into the chamber to see if we can keep him together long enough for the transition to become permanent."

How many times had he done this? How many men had died for this monster's stolen body?

The assembled men stared at one another, sharing frightened glances like cornered game. It was one thing to serve the devil when he is allowing you to harm helpless people, yet another entirely when he wants you to grab hold of a monster.

Mr. Massey tried unsuccessfully to spit off to the side, then wiped his dry mouth on the back of his hand. He motioned a beefy man forward and, together, they hauled the huge black-skinned farmhand to his feet. I leapt out of their way purely on instinct. They did not see me, but passed right through me.

I turned and slipped. I could not get my footing. The world was hot, too hot. I felt faint. My vision grew spotty. My skin prickled and my clothing was too tight. The ground rushed up and slammed into my knees. I gulped in a breath from the pain of it.

I looked back at the man in my arms. He was gone. At least the man's flesh was gone, melted from his bones. I held the bones of his hand in my fingers. His cracked skull looked mournfully up at me. Rejected even in death, his bones would not hold whatever tore him apart, the ground would not offer him rest.

The bones in my hand fell away.

It wasn't his flesh I was feeling, for my touch moved through the echo of his flesh. I was feeling his bones. His very human bones. I tried to stop Mr. Massey and my hand passed through him because he wasn't still here. The farmhand's bones were. And I was sitting in the center of them.

Nate was there, stable and strong as a mountain. He knelt, careful to not step in the puddle of spilt human. I laid my head on his shoulder, feeling both sick and faint. In the charnel sea, he was the island I could break upon.

I turned my head to wipe my face against my shoulder. Whatever the dead man had done in life, he did not deserve this.

The ground was...crushed up. But it wasn't really crushed, but that was the nearest description I could come up with. "Nate, this looks wrong."

"This is all very wrong." Nate said, looking around

"I mean this." I pointed to the circular indentation in the ground where we knelt.

The circle was perhaps a meter around, and the curved portion where the man's bones lay was deeper. "It was very heavy, and there was a lip here, like a barrel." Nate traced the indentation. His eyes glanced over the bones and the dark stain of what was left of a human. "I-it was deeper here because it was tipped here, rocked. He was"—I swallowed hard— "he was poured out."

Nate's mouth was a grim line. "It was here when the fire burned," Nate said. "He was dumped after the fire, and then whatever this thing was that held him was moved or the land below would have burned, the bones, too."

I nodded. I already knew that. It was a cold comfort to have confirmation of such dark knowledge.

"Viv, there's something you may want to see." He paused and rubbed the back of his neck, "Well, not want to see...I mean—"

"I need to see it," I said grimly.

Nate nodded. His face matched how I felt. I carefully set the skull down, alongside the rest of the bones. Nate led me to the house.

"What did you find?"

Nate blinked. The soot from the air gave him the swollen, bloodshot eyes of a drunk. "I found nothing,"

I turned. Nate's hand was inches from my shoulder. "I didn't find anything. I mean no one is alive. With a fire, people try to get out, they try to help each other. I saw enough house fires living in the slums of London. I've even seen fires that have burned entire buildings. Something about this fire is"—he motioned to the shell of the building, searching for the words—"wrong."

I understood completely. I was also at a loss to explain it any better.

I followed him into the farmhouse. The floorboards had burned away, revealing a root cellar off to one side. I squatted in the ashes, shifting bits of charred wood and bits of metal here and there. There was a bone. A long bone. A leg.

"Nate, help me with this."

He scowled at the broken beam. It was charred and split, but larger than I could move, probably larger than he could move. A body was half buried beneath it. As much as I didn't want to know what happened, I needed to know. My husband nodded, more to himself than me. He squatted at the sturdier side of the beam. His shoulders bulged, the flesh shifting beneath his shirt. Consciously, or not, he was calling upon his canithrope strength, transfiguring enough to allow that powerful form free and to use it to employ brute force.

The beam groaned, and ash kicked up into the air, foul and evil. Nate shifted the beam aside with great care, dropping it into the soot, then wiped his blackened hands on his thighs, leaving streaks of soot behind.

I surmised it was a man just due to the size, because the skeleton was taller than Nate, but thinner in the shoulder. He would have been tall and lean. His ribs and spine were clearly crushed, probably from the falling beam. It was so sad.

But sad would not make it feel wrong. It would not make it feel evil. I had learned to trust my intuition in these matters. I took his head in my hands and turned it over.

The skull was broken, caved in on the right side at the temple. The ground around him was soft and ashy. I doubted the skull was shattered by the falling beam. This happened before the fire.

Geiger.

I turned in a circle.

The hearth was shadowed by the sagging chimney. It slouched in a spiritless way, sorry it had failed to contain a fire as a good hearth should. I reached out to touch it. A wooden thimble rested on top, nearly obscured by the soot, covered in tooth marks.

Tooth marks.

It was common to allow babies to cut their first teeth on wooden thimbles. The hard chew was comforting and would not harm them the way a metal or ceramic thimble would, and they were cheap. Nearly every household had a wooden thimble, as every woman could mend.

A *wooden* thimble.

It was *wood*.

I picked it up and turned it in my hand. The thimble was as cold as the stone hearth, and the stone beneath it was unblemished by the fire. It had been sitting here while the house burned.

This was proof it hadn't been a natural fire. If so, the thimble would have burned. If someone came after and left the thimble in memory of a child, the hearth would be stained by smoke and soot.

A child. The thimble fell from my nerveless grip.

Two sets of bones, one very young, one a little smaller than me, lay huddled in the dark corner by the hearth. They had not burned, but they were still dead.

"What killed them?"

Nate's voice was rough. I hoped it was from the ash and soot, but I knew better. "Sometimes the fire can take people without burning them; it's the smoke."

I knew better. There was blood here. I might not be able to see it, but I could sense it. Nate would be able to smell it.

These people had been murdered. The fire had been set to cover the murder.

All around us, the trees wailed.

CHAPTER TEN

GRIEF IS MORE than a feeling. It is palpable, like a heavy blanket that settles upon a place, covering it with a taste and a scent. It consumes and strangles, until all the joy and life in a place is snuffed out, like a single, guttering candle.

We moved through the ruined homestead. Our footsteps were muffled by the ash littering the ground. Cutting through the sadness was a deep foreboding. It was more than death here, it was something near and painful, something menacing that stalked the sorrow. It was a heart-chilling feeling like being slowly submerged into an ice-cold bath. I was shivering, and I struggled to draw a full breath. Something terrible was here, too, more than the memory of what happened to these people.

We eventually left the ruins of the homestead. We decided to return to the tracks and follow them back to the rail camp. As we rounded the corner with the broken chimney, I saw it—the creature loomed before us, a dark shadow with a pale head, a glint of milky-white in the moonlight. It was hunched, the way Nate did while in his canithrope form, in a body not fully designed to walk upright, the body of a predator.

It shifted to taste the air. It had a distinctly canine face, but with antlers extending from the crown of its head.

My heart hammered in my chest. My limbs tingled. The thing, whatever it was, filled my vision. I stepped back, into Nate. My numb hand fumbled for his. His hand was cold in mine.

The creature made a sound, a pitiful mewing, the way a desperate baby begged one last time for his mama to come to his aid before succumbing to some horrific demise. Even as the sound tore at my soul and drew me closer, it repulsed me with a secret dread I could not name. It squeezed my heart so tightly I felt I would choke.

The bony muzzle faced us, and the creature's mouth parted slightly, head cocked to the side, watching me, gauging my reaction. The creature mocked us.

I would have preferred something with rotting flesh, something that would have been sad and would have been deserving of pity. This thing was cold and void of mercy, so far removed from life there was not a glimmer of life left. There was not even a memory of blood, if it had ever had blood.

Its eyes caught the light. No natural creature had eyes like that. It was the color that lamplight forms in spilled grease; eerily beautiful.

It cried out again. It didn't have lips. It did not need to part its mouth. The sound just came from it as though to entice us and taunt us. I released the breath I wasn't aware I was holding.

"Nate," I breathed. "What is it?"

His hand tightened around mine. "Death."

It stepped toward us. The shaggy, tattered pelt, all that was left to show it may have once lived, hung from it the way opera curtains hung off abandoned scaffolding, concealing a world of everything and nothing, waiting for the stage to be set. But where I expected to see something as wholesome as bone behind the torn bits of tatty covering, there was nothing, just a vast, empty hole of nothing, and its completeness stole the breath from my body. It was a thing that should not be.

I forced my eyes closed even though I was sure the moment I did so, the monster would sink those perfect cold fangs into my flesh and spill my scarlet blood across the icy white bone.

The ruby from the dragon's key was still in my pocket. It was weighty, pulling me towards the earth. I pulled the stone from my pocket. I could have left it in the hotel, but I could not bear to be away from it. As long as I had it, it was safe. The stone in my hand gleamed. It called to me, whispering secret power. Promising me a fierce force greater than me. I could feel hot eyes, hot breath bearing down on me.

The Tarot sign for *The Sun* marked my lower back, very nearly at the base of my spine. *The Star* is over my eye, hot and bright. *The Moon* over my chest is warm. Usually one sign, the sign that I was reading or the sign that was guiding me, is stronger. The three together give me courage. Without love, there is no life. I could face down this monster to protect my husband, my love. Death it may be, but it had never seen me before and I was fierce, indeed.

The ruby in my fist grew hot. An unseen force guided my hand before me like a ward.

The creature cocked his head at me. Curious. Amused?

Amused? I thought viciously, Watch this.

My papa's words were suddenly in my ears. *Love is the most powerful force in the world. It loves. It protects. It is fierce, it is powerful, it is beautiful. For all its imperfection, it is perfect.*

I was locked in the moment.
Blink.

> *I don't think; there isn't time. The ruby is in my raised hand. The monster takes a step forward and opens its pitch dark mouth.*
>
> *There is a scream. A sound like a thousand bits of glass shattering at once, and below that, the crack of stone.*
>
> *I am surrounded by a light, something holy and pure, warm and welcoming.*
>
> *For a moment I am sure I have died. But no, I am standing within it. Around me, everything has stopped.*
>
> *The ruby is a tiny glowing orb between my hands, emanating a pillar of light. I can breathe for the first time since Papa died. Nate reaches out for me. The creature—whatever it is—reaches out for me, a snarling, snapping mass of nightmare and terror now entirely neutered. It is now slowed to a crawl.*
>
> *I am outside of myself. There is no fear here, no pain, and I am dimly aware that the power I am channeling is coming from within*

me, from my mind and my heart and my core, feeding through the Sun, the Moon, and the Star. The ruby has amplified it into a bright, tangible scarlet light and the monster of black and ice that was devouring all that was good and light in the world has turned grotesquely, bloody red in the light. The light made it look wounded and vulnerable. If we could wound it, we could kill it.

I smiled.

But no, something was wrong.

My hands were hot, too hot. I couldn't hold it.

Crack!
I fell to the ground.

It hurt too much to breathe. I could not lie on my back. My eye felt as though I had been stabbed. I could not draw a full breath.

The creature! Those teeth. I felt something grab my arm. I tried to fight it. I swiped blindly at the air. I connected, and the shock of it sent pain lancing up my arm.

Nate. His voice was an anchor against the throbbing, angry, red and raw thing that had taken over my being. "Vivian. Look at me."

The panic in his voice was palpable. He was breathing in quickly through his nose, scenting the air using short quick puffs. "Blood, I smell blood." He was beside himself.

"I'm fine." It was mostly true. The ruby was still clenched in my fist. I was afraid to let it go. If I released it, I might lose it among the damp leaves. As long as I had it, I would be fine. I thrust it back into my pocket. Nate took my hands, recoiling when I cried out.

I stared dumbly at my hands. They hurt, a penetrating piercing, nagging pain. I had experienced something similar in China when I forced the Tarot gift to do more than I thought I was able to do. I had separated the magical bond between a twin brother and his sister. But, by severing the magical link, I had damaged something ancient and primal, designed by nature and fate itself. The resulting backlash from disrupting those primal forces caught me like a whip across the throat. It left a divot-like scar that still pained me when it was cold. I had never experienced something so painful.

Until now.

What damage had I done to myself now? Was channeling my internal magic through the ruby something too powerful to be contained?

§§§

It was a moonless night, but the stars provided winking reassurance of soft, sacred light interrupted only by the comforting silhouette of my husband kneeling over me. He wrapped his arm around me, his revolver in the other hand. "Viv, we have to go."

He tasted the air, sniffing, sensing we were not alone. He searched for the monster. I sagged against him, listening to his heart hammering in his chest. His eyes were wide and dark. He smelled like gunpowder and sweat. I scrambled to my feet and, together, we walked away from that place.

After only a short distance, I realized that I could not go on for too much longer. My back ached and my hands throbbed. Every jarring step I took sent fire through my burned palms. The power that could banish a creature of darkness was immortal, sacred, holy power. Mortal, imperfect creatures such as humans are not designed to wield such power. That was startlingly clear. The pain of it set my teeth on edge.

Nate began to drag me. I was shaking so bad, I could hardly walk, and we would not make it back to the handcar before I was unable to continue. Try as I might, I struggled to lift each foot and place it before the other.

Something in the woods moved toward us. I raised my head from Nate's shoulder. My hands hurt too much to grab my revolver, but I felt I could slash the monster with my seax. I refused to be murdered without having given a good accounting of myself.

Nate was hot beneath me, his muscles tense and swollen. He began to transfigure into his canithrope form to protect us.

There was a snort, a whinny, and Nacto came out of the trees. "You should not be here."

"Nacto." Nate lowered his gun. "No one should be here."

Nacto looked around, searching for the monster. "You are right, brother. Quickly now, no one is safe when there is a monster loose."

"You saw it, too?" I asked.

Apparently, Nate was willing to take more on faith than I was. He scooped me up and, like cord wood, threw me up on the horse's back. We rushed away over the soft, carpeted path back down the hill toward the railroad track, following the plants that grew so quickly in the night.

Every sound fell on my hyper-aware ears as I strained to determine if the monster was behind us. The sound of the men huffing and the horse blowing were heavy bellows. Nacto's bone bib rattled and twigs snapped. If the sounds were so loud to my own ears, they must be a full marching brigade to anything hunting us. Nate's leather long coat rustled against the plants was the snapping of flags and sails. And beneath it all, I was nauseated at the thought of running into a monster that was made of rotten bone and mothy pelts again.

But the body cannot remain in that state of high alert. My hands felt as though shards of glass were slowly burrowing through them. I sat heavily in the saddle, letting my hips move and sway with the horse's movement.

SOS

Nacto brought us to a little farm. A two-story house and a large barn, took shape in the dim starlight. Several oil lamps burned in the windows and the chimney puffed invitingly.

The barn dwarfed the two-story house. Several horses peered out at us. One nickered, as if inquiring to know who was interrupting their rest. A cow lowed softly. It was so different from my home, and yet so familiar.

The windows gave off a warm, welcoming glow beyond lace curtains. I sobbed with relief. A tiny woman peered around a corner of the lace, then the door burst open and she stood there, waiting for Nacto to enter.

He pulled his hat from his head as he entered. "Chelan." She rushed to greet him. She had the same long, black hair styled in a braid down her back. She had beautiful doe eyes, soft and kind. She was darker than Nacto and less ruddy, but her features were a fragile copy of his. They spoke to one another quickly, their voices rising and falling in a rush of language I did not speak. It was beautiful, and I wished I knew what they were saying. Nacto paused and motioned to me.

She froze, her expression blank, but her eyes were wide. Whatever Nacto had said frightened her.

"I am Chelan," she said. "Many of the folks around here prefer my white name. You can call me Nannie Carey, if you like."

I would have offered my hand, but it hurt too much. "Vivian Valentine. I will call you whichever you would prefer."

Chelan motioned to the children. "These are my eldest, Karl and Daisy." A teenaged boy, who was busy casting bullets at the hearth with tight, aggressive motions, stared suspiciously at Nate; the bullets would have to be recast. A girl, a year or two younger, washed dishes at the sink.

Karl glared at Nate, his attention barely wavering as he twisted the bullet mold, popping a bullet free to fall against the hearthstone. These children had white names. Daisy stared, as well. She kept throwing glances over her shoulder. There was a tension I could not quite put my finger upon, a tightness in my chest that made me want to say something, anything to them…or leave.

Nacto noticed it, too. Finally, he could stand it no longer. He called Chelan by name. Their language broke the stillness in the room.

Whatever he said made some impression. Karl dropped the bullet mold on the hearthstone. Chelan took my hands, red and blistered. "My brother says you banished the wendigo with fire."

I tried to pull my hands away but, as slight as she was, her grip was iron. "I wouldn't say I banished it."

Her brother. So Nacto was her brother. Had Nannie given her children white names to help them fit in better in St. Louis, or was she married to a white man like her name, Nannie Carey, suggested?

How short-sighted was I being? I had met several African individuals in London who had names as "white" as Harper or Valentine. Perhaps "Carey" was a perfectly common Cheyenne surname.

Nannie stared at me.

"It wasn't really fire, it was light. Well, I mean…I suppose the light did burn that…wendigo did you call it?"

Nacto and Nannie still stared. I was sure I had done something wrong.

"Whatever you did, the light burned you," she said.

She was right. My hands were raw, scraped, and blistered, and the outer layer of my skin was swollen and peeling. No wonder it hurt so bad.

Nannie turned to Daisy. "Serve them dinner."

Karl shot us a very sullen scowl, but didn't argue. Daisy brought us bowls of beans and bacon and a plate of biscuits wrapped in a blue-and-white-checked napkin.

I took a delicate bite of bacon and beans.

"How do we defeat a creature such as that?" Ever practical Nate. He only wanted to know who his enemy was and how to defeat it.

"You don't," she said. "It is the wendigo."

"What is the wendigo?" I had to know.

The room was silent. They looked at one another.

Chelan set the pitcher down on the table. "This is not the same land as your land, but the nature of mankind does not change."

I had to agree with her. Aside from the trappings, the virtues and sins of people were much the same no matter where we were. Greed, hate, and pride seemed to cause the downfall of people no matter where they were, be it London or China. It stood to reason it would be the same in the New World. And, if the nature of humanity did not change, then the nature of their monsters would not change. If a monster was a monster then that monster could be repelled, maybe even destroyed.

"It is *Hestanováhe*," Nannie said, touching her forehead with her fingertips in what appeared to be a blessing, as though she was warding off evil spirits. "It is the life drinker."

"It is a spirit," Nacto clarified. "An evil spirit."

"It is more than that," Nannie said. "The wendigo is the destruction of mankind. It is drawn to mankind when they are at their worst. It feeds upon the evils of man and so will remain as long as the great tribes are broken and have lost their way."

And I knew why it was here. Mr. Geiger called it. If it fed upon the evil of mankind, then so long as mankind was wicked and sinful it would remain feeding upon all that was awful in the world. To defeat it, we would have to heal the world, purge the entire world of evil. It was a wonderful thought, but an impossible one.

God gave his son to purge the world of sin, once. Before that, God tried to wash the earth clean of sinners with the mighty flood. Before that, man and woman lived in a great garden and was tempted by sin. It was the nature of man to sin. There was no way to avoid it, no way to purge the world of sin. It was a world of decadence and excess, where a mother abandoned her son and families were burned alive. A world where one of the most virtuous men I had ever known, my papa, was dead and gone. I forced myself to swallow my food. The bite hurt the whole way down.

Nacto shook his head. "The wendigo is the ravager. The consumer. The cannibal. All the peoples know this."

I shuddered. A cannibal consumed human flesh. I hoped it was merely a metaphor. But the memory of the wendigo's teeth was forever etched in my mind. No, *Hestanováhe*, the wendigo, was a consumer of human flesh.

I remembered the vision I had of the man sacrificed by Geiger. Geiger said the man had been a drunk, a sinner, worse even. Geiger set human flesh and blood before the wendigo and the monster came from the shadows and melted the flesh away. The cannibal spirit consumed him.

I pushed my bowl away. "Give me your hands," Nannie said.

I set my hands, palms up, on the worn, kitchen table.

Her daughter brought a steaming copper kettle that she poured into a blue cup with a twist muslin full of tea in it. Nate held it to my lips for me to sip. I could immediately identify sweet sage and something fruity and slightly bitter. I also thought I could taste a concentrated form of willow bark to help ease the pain.

Chelan set a basin before me and put my hands inside to soak. Whatever was mixed with the water felt slightly greasy, but it was extremely comforting, and it took some of the throbbing pain away.

I nodded my thanks and sucked down the tea as fast as Nate could pour it down my throat. If it was willow bark tincture, I hoped it would take effect quickly.

She took another look at my face. "I have seen a great many marks one would paint on their skin, some permanent, some not. Why would you choose that?"

I looked at the bowl, willing my hands to stop shaking enough so I could catch my reflection. Sure enough, clear as day, a star looked as though it had been burned into my flesh around my eye.

Using the Tarot symbols brought the marks to the surface from under my skin. Using them too much made the mark darker and made it last longer. This one looked like a burn or a fresh tattoo. I wondered how long it would stay. I was certain *The Moon* at the center of my chest, to the right of my heart where *The Lovers* sat, was dark and raised, and *The Sun* on the small of my back, where my back met my pelvis, would be dark as well. At least those were covered by my clothes.

"I didn't. They just happen." I wasn't sure how to explain the magic leywell beneath Molten Cay to Nannie. I wasn't sure there were any leywells in America.

Oddly, she seemed unconcerned by my answer or lack thereof. She nodded and took my hands in hers. She bathed them in the slick water, then bound them with the split, fleshy pads of an unfamiliar plant. "Rest now. You are safe here."

I laid my head on the table. The day's events finally took their toll, and my eyes burned from the effort to keep them open. Every time I closed my eyes the wendigo waited, staring at me with its head cocked to one side. Its hollow, pale eyes cut through me, and the smoke of the burning farmstead filled my mind. But I could no longer remain in the state of a frightened hare. With pained hands and a frazzled mind, I fell into a fitful sleep.

CHAPTER ELEVEN

I WOKE LATER to Nate pulling me upright. It was still dark, and my head and hands throbbed fiercely. Another man had joined them.

"His name is Haimovi," Nate explained. "Mrs. Carey is putting us up for the night. As much as I can gather, Haimovi is Nacto's friend, though he also calls him brother. But, then, Nacto also called me brother, so that might be just a custom."

I nodded sleepily. I only grasped part of what he was saying. More brothers or friends of Nannie and Nacto. We were remaining for the night. At least we were not leaving the house in the black of night to meet that monster on the road. I was grateful for that.

Haimovi wore his hair long, with only the top portion tied back in two small braids and adorned with black and white feathers. He had a small string of tiny, red seed-beads of fine bright glass around his neck that had been looped several times and now rested over the top of his blue shirt. A pair of bright abalone-shell earrings hung from his ears. He was a handsome man, with high cheekbones and a strong jaw, but he scowled at us, waiting for us to do something untrustworthy, or as though our very presence was distasteful.

He spoke to Nacto in their language, staring at Nate pointedly the entire time. Nacto defended us.

Nate ignored them and walked me up the stairs and into a small room with a bed covered with a quilt. A small lamp with hurricane glass sat on a wooden table, and a chair sat beside a hand-carved wardrobe containing four shirts and three pairs of pants. By the size of the clothes, it was Karl's room.

I sat heavily on the bed "Do you suppose Karl is upset he was moved to make way for us?"

"I think he is happy to spend the night with his uncle and Haimovi in the barn," Nate responded as he readied for bed.

The bed was narrow for two, but big enough. We lay down. I settled my head on his shoulder, doing my best to banish the sight of the fleshless wolf-skull of the wendigo and the shaggy, inky-black pelt as it moved soundlessly through the shadows of the burned-out Tate homestead. It was a monster, of that I was sure, but the wendigo was a monster of claws and fangs. What if the Tate family had been attacked and fought back? Had something as innocent as a fallen lantern or a rogue ember from the fireplace been the cause of the farm burning?

My husband settled to sleep easily, as he nearly always did. I envied him. He could move from awake to asleep and then to full awareness again with a speed that made me think that he never actually slept, but watched from some sort of restful wakefulness. It must be related to his dog-like nature. He was always aware of danger, and always able to conserve his energy.

I was not so lucky. I fretted late into the night.

The power of the wendigo was not something man was capable of containing, but Geiger was sure he could give it a body.

The black farmhand from the Tate farm was one of the largest men I had seen in real life. Large, strong men did not seem to be the only key. What else would Geiger try? When we first encountered him in the bowels of Sterling's factory, he was building mechanical men. Would he attempt a mechanical body for the monster? Nate and I had no problem destroying that hulking monstrosity. It was hardly a form resistant to damage.

No, Geiger needed someone stronger, more powerful, more durable. What would be able to contain the power of the wendigo within its bones? What living form could house such a thing?

Nate shifted beside me. *Oh, god no!*

My husband was able to transfigure into two different forms. Transfiguring was painful for him, but his bones and muscles were certainly flexible, and used to the process. If any living being was able to contain the immense power of the wendigo from within, it might be Nate.

The only way to keep Geiger from trying would be to keep Geiger from reaching him. But I knew my Nate well and he would not remove himself from either monster. He sought out battle when people he loved were threatened.

My hands throbbed so badly I nearly cried. I needed help. I needed a healer. I needed my papa. I thought of the neat little rows of bottles on high shelves, nearly reaching the ceiling in my father's old shop. One of them, carbolic acid, mixed with water, would protect against infection and I could soak my damaged hands in the cool waters. Carbolic acid was made from coal tar, a sticky, nasty substance, but it produced an amazing antiseptic.

I stared at my hands again. Whatever magic I had channeled through the ruby had nearly peeled the flesh from my hands. My veins were visible on my forearms, showing as dark lines beneath my pale skin as though my blood itself had gone dark, very nearly the color of the ruby itself.

I pulled the ruby out and held it in my hand. It was comforting. Though only the size of a little bird's egg, it felt like it held all the promise of the world within itself. When I held it, my hands hurt a little less. It was glowing, thrumming, and throbbing. I could hear it, like the beating of my heart. It was waves crashing over me, removing all other sounds. My hands throbbed to its rhythm.

I needed healing. I needed peace. Carbolic acid and my father were out of reach. There were a few cards one could use for healing, but most were for spiritual healing, like guides to help people find their way through mourning, or times of trouble.

I closed my eyes, willing myself to look away from the ruby in my hand. I needed more than medicine, more than wine, more than carbolic acid and laudanum and whiskey. I needed something more.

I extended myself again, sinking into the world of mystical energies and feeling the little lines that connected all things. They were veins and all the world a heart drumming along to a sacred beat. I saw a man in armor. A knight of old laying on a stone slab no…a tomb. Across his breast lay a sword held in his stone hands. Above him, a stained-glass window shone down, bathing him in gentle holy light, watching over him while he lay at rest. Beside the window, three swords hung on the wall.

Knights fought, but they were also seen as protectors of the people, at least symbolically. Here, the knight's battle was done.

In my vision, I turned to get a better look at him. He was not stone, but he may as well have been. He was resting, waiting for his next battle. He was meditating, sleeping, healing.

He was healing.

The *Four of Swords.* Three swords on the wall and one in his hand, so there were four swords. Swords are a tool of battle. It was only logical they could bring peace, as well.

I held the ruby to my breast, my heartbeat matching the thrumming of the stone. A moment later, I was aware of my body and the great heaviness of my own mortal form. How strange, I had never been aware of it before. I made myself translucent and lay down upon the knight, sharing his place upon the stone tomb. I took his sword and laid it upon my breast. I felt my own breath slow. Beneath my damaged palms, the handle of the sword was cold, cooling my burned hands. The window bathed me in healing light. Here, for now, my battle was done.

I took a deep breath and let the pain flow from my body into the cold stone that formed the tomb in the image. It was not difficult to feel myself moving from my own body and into the image itself. In that strange place between sleep and wakefulness, anything is possible. I let the cold stone leach the pain from my battered body.

I made myself forget the man whose bones had shattered from the inside out as he fought the evil of the wendigo. I made myself set aside the hurt look Nate had given me when he realized I had kept the ruby. I pushed away the loss of my papa. Here I was, alone, but I was not lonely.

And, for the first time in so long, I felt peace.

CHAPTER TWELVE

THE NEXT MORNING, I woke to the sound of birds and the rustling of wind gently dancing through the trees. Nate stretched and rolled on his side. Every morning, he stretched like a dog might, every muscle long and lean in one great arch, then sat up, yawned and shook his head. I smiled.

There was a heaviness on my breast. I still held the ruby there in my clasped hands.

I sat up and dropped it from my bosom into my hands. My hands…I gasped. They were pink and tender, but the flesh was perfectly serviceable.

Nate snatched my hand, his mouth hanging open. "How?"

I couldn't explain. Was it the herbs from Nannie, or maybe the ruby? My own meditation on the knight in his tomb?

He nodded mutely. There was nothing either of us could say.

I went to clean myself up for the day. There was a small mirror pinned to the back of the door on Karl's wardrobe. My face was filthy. I got a bit of water and a cloth and started to make myself presentable. But as I washed, there seemed to be more and more filth, like I had been too close to a fire or I was washing with ashy hands. No, my hands were clean. I turned to the mirror again. It was my eye. I scrubbed carefully around my eye and the Tarot mark became visible, dark, almost black like a tattoo…then it started to rub away.

The Tarot mark washed away.

I stared at the dirty water, ashy gray. I touched the flesh around my eye. My skin was clean again, no more ash scrubbed away but that was not all, the mark was gone. It was really, truly gone. *The Star*, the symbol of hope and faith, the renewal of the earth, the symbol of spirituality, was gone. I felt the loss of it as completely as though I was suddenly missing a tooth. It was an empty socket within me.

Tears leaked down my cheeks. I screwed my eyes closed. *The Moon* and *The Sun* would be gone too. Burned away by the ruby or the wendigo, or both. I touched the mirror. In the last few years, the marks had meant more to me than my own blood. Whatever I had done, I was burning away.

I cleaned up my tears. I had battled the wendigo for Nate, for the Tates, for myself. If I told Nate the marks were gone, he would try to stop me from helping him fight the wendigo again. But if Mr. Geiger believed Nate to be strong enough to contain that terrible power, then I might be the only person who could save him. I had to keep this information to myself for now.

As soon as I made my way down the stairs and into the kitchen, Nannie took my hands in hers to examine the wounds. If she thought their healing was unexpected, she didn't comment, though she did look at me queerly.

"Where is Mr. Carey?" Nate asked. "We need to express our gratitude for allowing us to take refuge here.

Nannie's hand holding mine suddenly stiffened. "My husband, Joseph, is out of town."

Her tone gave me pause. She was ashamed. The answer was simple. And yet, with most things, it was also complex. She might not be lying about her husband, but she was not being truthful, either. She did not strike me as one accustomed to lying, and I did not wish to strain Nannie any more than we already had. "Please express our gratitude when he returns."

"I will," she assured me.

§§§

It was not hard to return to the railway. Nate's sense of direction never failed to amaze me, though this time I was sure he was following the path we took last night in the direction of the burned homestead. My stomach quivered at the thought of returning to that place of death and the monster that hunted there.

We walked until I caught the unmistakable scent of fire. A thick carpet of ash moved off into the woods, but the rubbery path of leaves that resembled kudzu was gone. Now and again, in its path, heavily shadowed, lay the whispery outline of leaves made entirely of ash. The wind caressed them and blew them away. For just a moment, the wind smelled of rot and death, but then shifted to the good, clean scent of earth and wood.

I picked up one of the leaves, and it was like a twist of burned paper, the fragile bits evaporated into gray ash, the same ash that was under the rails. The night brought rotting vegetation up from the earth, and the sun burned it away.

Nate ran his hand over it, checking for heat. Satisfied there was none, he touched it. I did too. The ash was as fine as soft sand and sifted through my fingers while, beneath it, the grass was green. It was like someone had poured ash from a huge barrel in order to create a trail. I could have believed that to be plausible if the scent of fresh burning was not heavy in the air.

We followed the trail of soft ash. We kicked fine bits of it into the air until it coated our riding boots and trousers. It led us to the wooden rail ties and the handcart that lay untouched. The steel rails themselves were gone. Where the kudzu grew over the tracks, the steel had been reduced to lines of ash.

I stood on the wooden ties, heavily stained with soot and worm-rot. They appeared to have been there for ages. The railroad spikes which had sat so heavy in my hand, two hundred to a barrel, were gone. I squatted where they would have been driven into the ground. The holes, filled with ash, remained. I shoved two fingers into a hole, which was hot, frightfully so, even through my leather gloves.

"The vines are gone," Nate said.

He was right. Mr. Geiger had come to the land, and both he and the kudzu only left death in their wakes.

CHAPTER THIRTEEN

THE HANDCAR WAS left stranded on the wooden ties, since the rails had burned away. It was a long journey by foot back to the workers' camp. But, in no time at all, we made it to the place where the warped, blistered rails appeared again. They were still hot and twisted, just like before, but remained steel instead of ash. The broken edges reached for the sky, like something good and pure that cried out for salvation. I knew how they felt.

Samuel Lane's gas-powered runabout waited at the worker's camp. We located him easily and, within moments, were headed back to St. Louis. Exactly what I was going to tell the local law enforcement, I had no idea, but we needed to convince them to at least investigate the fire as a murder. If I could find doctors in America half as accomplished as the doctors in England, they would be able to see the bodies on the Tate farm had not expired from a normal fire.

We returned to our room at the HeadHouse. As soon as the maid arrived, we would send out our clothing to be cleaned. I was glad to be rid of the ash and blood.

While Nate bathed, I played out a hunch. I went to the rail office and picked up a set of maps showing the available lines and the planned expansions. I was interested in the not-yet-built rail lines, and Nate was better with maps than I was.

"I have half a mind to return to Mr. Cassatt," Nate announced when I returned to our room.

"Oh?" I sat on the bed.

"He must have hired Mr. Geiger as an inventor, thinking he could make great deal of money for both him and his railroad. He could not have known that Geiger is a madman." Nate said

"I refuse to believe that anyone who has met Mr. Geiger believes him to be sane," I said. "Also, we are not acting as Mr. Cassatt's agent, no matter what you are telling people. You might believe you can appeal to his sense of honor, but he values only money. He won't appreciate our meddling."

Nate scowled at me. "Well, there is an entire world between sane and mad as a hatter. Some eccentrics are odd but not dangerous. Geiger is both mad and dangerous."

He was right, of course. And I needed to see just how dangerous Geiger and his new ally were to me. I sat before the mirror at the dressing table with my clean clothing laid out on the bed. I had been dreading this moment since the Carey home. Nate went through his clothes while I undressed. At the center of my chest, between my breasts, a circle of ash was on my skin and on my blouse. I gulped and touched the mark. Almost perfectly round, radiating rays that were divided by a line that dropped down the middle, creating the silhouette of a man looking out, the man in the moon.

On the Tarot card *The Moon*, he looked out over two towers and flowing waters to represent introspection. It would be like comparing a wolf and a dog. The tamed and untamed aspects of our minds, our hearts, and our souls.

I stared into the mirror, rubbing the ash away with a damp towel. It felt like the deep ache of cleaning infected pus from within an abscess. The ash kept coming out of me like a chalky, black poison, leaving me hollow and consumed with a loneliness that crushed me.

Nate caught sight of me in the mirror sitting naked to the waist. He kissed my cheek. "We could just skip dinner or have something brought up later." He gave me his best enticing smile.

I must not have looked interested.

"That ash gets everywhere, doesn't it?" He took the cloth from me and touched it to my lower back. *The Sun* Tarot mark had been there. Once it had been a round orb of power and light that radiated warmth, success, and vitality. Now it was a burned-out mark, a piece of me that was forever lost and forced from my skin.

It was *The Sun* and *The Moon* I mourned more than the loss of *The Star*. He washed the ash of the lost *Sun* away until the water from my bare back ran clear.

When we had first met, Nate was a man by day and a dog by night. In the Tarot, the wolf, the part of man that is wild and free, mysterious and introspective, looks up to the moon and cries the glory of strength. It is to the moon they sing of their love of men.

And *The Sun* represented man's vitality, his hope, and it is the sun that is truly the source of all life on earth. Nate was the awe-inspiring warmth I went to when I felt lost. He was life, he was hope. And now both symbols that had come to represent my husband, the dog that guarded my heart and the sun watching over me, were gone.

So was the wendigo, I reminded myself. But that was a cold comfort as I dressed. It was a blow against an unholy creature I could not make again.

S8S

We went down for dinner rather than taking a tray in our room. Since we had been seen in the hotel, it would have been strange to not take at least one meal, but I found I had little appetite. I just wanted to lie on the bed and hold the ruby to my chest and cry.

We were served creamy pea soup, a pork roast, and a colorful ratatouille, and finished with bread pudding custard. I picked at dinner while Nate attacked his with gusto.

Afterward, we made our way to the great room and I spread the maps out on the table where the light was better. "Can you find the place where the track was eaten away by those plants that the sun burned away?"

Nate stared at the map for a long moment and stabbed a finger at the map. "Here."

"Are you sure?"

He scrubbed his fingers through his hair, that adorable gesture that was all his own. "Fairly sure, why?"

"What if this is where the Tate property begins?"

Nate gave me a look. "Why would you think that?"

"The home was burned," I said. "But, Nate, there's more." How could I explain? "I had a vision. I saw Mr. Massey and Geiger burn the house and murder the Tate family. They murdered a farmhand, too. They tried to make him a vessel for the monster. Geiger failed."

"Failed how?" His eyes narrowed.

"He was trying to give the wendigo a real human body. But the man—he exploded." I shuddered at the memory.

"The bones you were holding?"

"Yes."

"I'm sorry, Viv." He touched the map again. "I wonder if we could look up land records. Then we would know, for sure."

The records were in the railroad's office in Philadelphia. It was a long way to go for a hunch. And, even if we were right, then what? We needed a plan, a better plan.

We returned to our room. Our clothes lay on the bed, ironed and pinned in neat little stacks. My long coat hung on the hook where we had left it. I reached into the pocket I had placed a cutting of the kudzu into. I felt around, but the plant was gone. I turned the pocket inside out, tipping fine, gray ash out onto the carpet. It was the same ash that had been in the stone beneath the wooden ties, as well as the path from the farmhouse.

"That kudzu was taking us to the site of the murders," Nate said. "But the fire consumes it also."

"It has to be the Tates' revenge," I said. "Geiger came with an offer from the railroad and, when they refused, murdered them. Their spirits are refusing to allow the railroad to pass through their land. The workers lay the track and it gets burned away."

"Why the kudzu?" Nate asked

"Kudzu overtakes all things. Maybe it is the natural world trying to set things right." I glanced at the ash on my fingers. "Do you think it's reduced to ash because of the burned home?"

Nate nodded, the idea appealed to his sense of justice. "Fire for fire, live growth fighting death. Sure, it makes as much sense as anything else here."

He rubbed his hand vigorously through his hair several times. We were thinking the same thing: if the railroad could not continue, they would have to reroute. If they would not reroute then we would lose our investment in the Pennsylvania Railroad.

We would have to return to Mr. Cassatt's office in Philadelphia and appeal to him directly. "Either way, it's too late to do anything tonight."

"Yes, but what if the kudzu destroys more of the rail tonight?" I argued.

"It won't."

"But what if it does?" I turned and opened the window to let the cool air wash over me.

"Viv, we've been losing money for months. This has been the proposed line for nearly a year. I doubt they just reached this point within the last week, they probably reached this point months ago, maybe more. The burn was not fresh. I mean, it was last night, but I don't believe it was advancing." Nate held his hand out for me.

"It was a renewed burn." I said, "I refuse to believe that we were lucky enough to witness the only time those plants consumed the rails."

Nate poured us both a drink. "Whatever happened last night happened again, since we had the workers lay fresh steel."

I tried to keep my voice from shaking. "Is that what lured the-the monster?"

He nodded, "Most likely."

He was right. But there was more, so much more. "The man, the ranch hand, was a very strong man." I set my hairbrush down on the table. What I needed was something to do with my hands. "And he was a large man."

"He had very large bones." Nate had only seen the bones.

I covered my mouth with my hand. "Geiger was furious. The ranch hand was not strong enough to contain the wendigo. The very nature of it shattered the man like shook up beer in a bottle. It was horrible."

Nate caught me up in his arms to comfort me.

I couldn't stop babbling. "He tried more science, more electrics, more of whatever his chamber does, but the body would not hold. He needs someone stronger."

"Then we shall have to keep him from finding someone stronger," Nate said, stroking my hair.

"I know of someone stronger," I said softly.

The hand at the nape of my neck stopped the gentle caress. "What do you mean?"

I pulled back to look at him.

He laughed. "You can't possibly mean me."

"You are a creature of earth and magic. Your bones shift and flex. Nate, if any living creature is strong enough to contain that demon, it is you."

"I shall not let him near me with that chamber then," he said with a smile.

"I'm not joking, Nate!" I struck him for good measure. It was like punching a wall.

But he wasn't joking, either. His smile lasted too long without reaching his eyes. He reached for my hair brush and began to brush out my hair so I could braid it. "The Lamia on Molten Cay told us that magic never leaves. It can be altered, it can be changed, but it never leaves. Geiger will find me a very difficult man to trap. And if he does put his hands on me, or upon you, he will wish he hadn't." The brush rasped through my hair in the low lamplight. "Tell me," he said at last, "did you have a vision of him turning me into a monster? Or of harming you to destroy me?" He swallowed hard. "Of making me harm you?"

I took the brush from him again. "No. No visions of your doom. It was just a horrible thought my brain came up with all on its own."

"Well, then, tell your brain to stop it," he said gruffly. "We face enough dire peril as it is."

CHAPTER FOURTEEN

WE STARTED THE day with a hearty breakfast. Actually, Nate had a hearty breakfast, consisting of eggs, and ham steak, and toast with coffee. I had an egg and a bit of coffee and nibbled some marmalade on toast, mostly to make him happy. He had become quite the nursemaid, lately. I just wanted to hold the ruby in my hand. When he wasn't looking, I would slip my hand in my pocket and touch it, to make sure it was still close.

Finally, fortified and ready to head out to the railroad field office, we left the hotel to hire either a car or a couple of horses. Nate was convinced he would be able to find us suitable transportation.

We headed down the main street only to be greeted by the angry murmurs of a crowd.

"I'm telling you, it was those damn savages!" one man said, his voice carrying over the crowd.

The shouting was coming from the open windows of a pub with a colorful painted sign identifying it as the Riverboat.

They were discussing the natives again. If I were a cat, I would have arched my back and hissed.

"Nannie Carey and her damn brother, West."

There were murmurs of agreement.

"If West and that other fella didn't do it, then they sure know who did!"

I looked up at Nate. Appealing to Mr. Cassatt might have been a long shot before, but now it was impossible. We were needed here.

Mr. Massey stood at the bar. "Those savages were given a reservation, land where they could do whatever they want! That's where they should be!"

Massey. I felt cold anger bubbling up within me. He helped murder the Tates. He lied about the fire. He stared at me like I was a bit of meat for the taking. He treated Nacto as less than human. Now he was rallying a crowd of drunken bar swine into a fervor against Nannie Carey and her brother.

My skin felt red hot, as though I was being consumed by a great fire. And, beneath it all was a drumbeat like a heart echoing in my ears.

The crowd murmured their assent.

"And still they stand in the way of progress!"

"We will settle this land! And those that wish to remain can become good Christian Americans."

The crowd nodded.

"What they cannot do is murder good Christian people!"

The crowd yelled in agreement.

"They cannot burn good, honest people out of their homes!"

The crowd yelled again.

"It's time to make them go!"

"If the children are half-white put them in schools and save their souls!"

The crowd cheered.

I clenched my fists. I was ready to throttle the woman nearest to me. The man, too. I could break that beer glass right over his great ignorant head. They were talking about children!

"Hang those murderous savages!" Mr. Massey yelled back. "And if the rest won't go, arrest them, too! Make them stand trial, move them under guard! They have a place, make them stay there!"

Nate grabbed my wrist. I released the breath I didn't realize I was holding. The thrumming in my ears was gone.

The crowd was frenzied, clapping each other on the back, slamming beer glasses together, calling for blood.

My hand was cold and stiff in Nate's. Massey and Geiger were responsible for Tate's murders, but there was no way this mass of people would hear that.

Nate shouldered his way out of the Riverboat, dragging me through the seething mass of human ugliness. The Tate family would find no justice here. The Carey family would find no help here. The mob was an ugly thing, no different than the vicious rioting hordes I encountered in London from time to time. Adding alcohol to the mix would not improve matters.

The Carey family needed to be warned. Chelan and her brother, Nacto—or West—needed to know the people of St. Louis were turning against them. I was sure they were aware of the attitudes already—Nacto did not approach Mr. Massey or the other rail workers. In Nate and me, he must have sensed something different. I was sure he had been watching us for quite some time, taking our measure and waiting to see if we were like the others. But now, what I had assumed was a general tolerance was rapidly turning to abject hatred.

Returning to Philadelphia to speak with Mr. Cassatt would have to wait.

We moved quickly down the street. There was no place to hire a gasoline-powered runabout like Samuel Lane had, but we could hire horses.

We found a horse dealer and, with a bit of haggling, we managed to find two mounts that would get us back to the Carey house. We trotted down the street, trying to put as much distance between us and the mob as possible.

They were mobilizing and had great violence in mind. We had to get there first.

CHAPTER FIFTEEN

WHILE NATE HANDLED the horses, I rushed back to the hotel for our long coats, weapons, and my satchel of healing herbs. As an afterthought, I grabbed a set of clothing for us both and jammed them into our knapsacks. I had no intention of getting my clothing soiled with the blood of dead or dying men and being forced to wear it until we managed to return to the HeadHouse again.

The crowds were still busy drinking and crying out for blood when we headed out for a nice relaxing ride in the woods with a picnic lunch packed by the company that rented us the horses. It was all we could do to not gallop off to protect the Carey family. Instead we rode off, all smiles and happy jokes, before circling through the woods to follow the rails and head directly to the Carey home.

It was the beautiful, tall farmhouse I remembered from a few hours before. An empty wagon was parked out front. The small paddock of split-log fencing had two horses within, looking anxiously at our approach. On the far side of the barn, only barely visible, a second paddock held a cow and, from the sounds, a few goats. Chickens worried and quietly chuck-chucked to one other under the eaves of the barn.

We were not the first to reach the Carey home. Several horses were hobbled under trees, contentedly cropping grass. The saddles were decorated with feathers and beads, painted with faded, peeling paint in red, black, and yellow.

The door to the house stood open, blown open by a foul and evil wind. From where I stood, I could see a table littered with brown glass bottles.

We dismounted and Nate held up his hand, motioning for me to be quiet. He took our horses and wrapped the reins up around the nearest tree. I crept forward. I saw Nacto standing between his sister and who I thought was Joseph Carey, a tall, weather-beaten man, fair and blond-haired. I could not imagine a man who could have looked anything less like the Carey children.

"Do you think I am *blind?*" Mr. Carey slurred. "Do you think I am stupid? Three children off my squaw wife and not a-one of them look like me!"

I heard a chair scrape across the wooden floor. Nate crept silently up the front steps.

A drunken voice I did not know was speaking, "They all look like them damn Indians! It'd serve you right if I just let them take all them damn young'uns!"

I craned my neck, trying to see into the house. Where were the three children?

Haimovi was there as well. I saw the edge of his blue sleeve and his loose black hair falling around his shoulders.

Karl stood by the fire, glaring at Mr. Carey in the way only teenage boys could, his long hair hanging in his eyes.

"I ought to teach you to respect your elders, boy," Carey snarled. "You, you ain't even mine, none of 'em are." Joseph took an unsteady lurch toward the table. "Just the bastard of some savage whore." He turned to Nannie. Karl leapt forward to block his father's way. Joseph slammed his fist hard into the boy's stomach, knocking him to the ground. Karl crumpled with a grunt.

Nacto and Haimovi burst into a flurry of action. Nate charged into the house, sacrificing stealth for speed. Beyond him, I could see what was happening, but I could not stop it.

Nannie dove for her son. Joseph snatched at her hair and ripped her away, aiming a kick at the downed lad. Nannie screamed. Her shriek made his kick go wide, but he spun and caught his wife in the mouth, knocking her down like a shot pheasant. She gave a choking cry, drooling blood and broken teeth. Mr. Carey disappeared beneath a sea of men; Nacto and

Haimovi, and my Nate, who was never one to allow anyone to be harmed if he could help it.

I leapt upon the porch. If Karl and Nannie were fighting Mr. Carey in the front room, where were Daisy and the baby? I raced across the uneven porch slats, my boots slipping on the sand and silt.

Please let them be safe!

I raced through the lounge and the kitchen, where the chairs stood around the small table. I nearly tripped over the edge of a rug. The stove was lit, the kitchen warm and the scent of bread and beans wafted through the air. Several jars had been brought up from the cellar and were neatly placed on the table along with a jar of flowers.

I ran through the kitchen and into the large dining room, where a table and six wooden chairs all sat neatly pushed in.

The sound of fighting grew more frantic. Strange how my mind could catch details when the only thing I desperately wanted to see was missing. Where was the baby? "Where are you?"

There was a sound. Not quite a cry, not a gurgle. Upstairs.

I took the stairs two at a time, nearly falling again as I ran. The door to the right was where Nate and I had spent the night. I threw it open. It banged loudly against the frame. Nothing.

The second door. A washroom. Nothing.

The third door. A larger bed. It must be the master bedchamber. I ran around the far side of the bed. Nothing.

One door left.

Please. Please let the baby be there!

The bedroom had a quilt of a dozen different fabrics upon a narrow bed and a hope chest that had been hastily shoved away from the wall.

Daisy crouched there in the corner, her pretty, dark face etched with fright but fiercely protective of a bundle wrapped in a knit blanket in her arms.

She recognized me and a great sigh of relief tumbled from her. "Mrs. Valentine, I am so glad you are here. He might kill Mama for sure this time."

I crouched down, taking them both in my arms. "He will not. We won't let him. Nacto and Haimovi are down there right now with my husband."

The little baby in her arms let out a grunt and a grumble. Clearly, this was not how the baby believed he should be spending his time. I tried rocking and patting him.

Below us wood banged upon wood again.

"Mr. Carey!" Nate was trying to make him listen.

"Get outta my house!"

My brain was buzzing, trying to draw to mind a tarot card or cards I could use to protect Daisy and the baby.

Scraping, screaming wood, hammering, the sound of glass shattering. Beside me, Daisy set her thin, little jaw and held the baby tighter.

Nate's voice came up the stairs. "Joseph, be reasonable!"

Chairs scraped across the wood floor, clattered to the ground.

Suddenly, it was all noise and violence. I was afraid it was Mr. Carey trying to come up the stairs after Daisy and the baby. More furniture was slammed around and glass shattered as the men fought. Then there was a sound, a rumble of rolling thunder. A gunshot.

My blood turned to ice. Who had been shot? I desperately wanted to run down the stairs and make sure my Nate was safe. But if Joseph had managed to harm Nate and Nacto and Haimovi, then we would be next.

I tried to swallow past the hot coal in my throat. No matter what, I could not leave Daisy and the baby alone. I jumped up, taking the baby in my arms. There was no reason I could not handle one drunken lummox of a man. The window gave us no easy way down, just a straight drop ten feet down to the patchy grass yard below. I would have to help Daisy down and pass the baby to her.

We needed a shield. I immediately thought of my mother. She always protected me from all harm. Papa taught me, but Mama protected me. We needed my mama. A mother. *The Priestess*, mothering and wise, feminine and fiercely protective of all her children, in some depictions she even bore a shield. The deck I learned from had her painted as a gentler sort; reclined upon a chair with cushions of red velvet, surrounded by the images of Earth and Venus, but yet a mother. And there is nothing more powerful than a mother's love. It is the same love that will make a woman lie about her origins to keep her children safe.

I pushed that thought away. There was no time to waste now.

I took on the power of *The Priestess*. I envisioned her mantle settling upon my shoulders. I felt her heavy crown upon my head. I felt stronger immediately. I was more the shield-wielding matron than the couch-reclining matron anyway. I had both my seax and my revolver. I could not allow Mr. Carey to take my seax away from me and use it upon Daisy and the baby but at this distance, my revolver would not miss.

Daisy did not speak but she didn't shrink away, either. She raised her little chin defiantly. Even if we did not leave the room alive, we intended to leave it fighting.

The room below was now silent. The baby stared up at my face, his dark eyes searching mine for kindness or explanation, or maybe milk, his little fists bunched in the shawl, clinging for dear life.

The hall was quiet. Too quiet. The rooms I had searched before Daisy's stood with their doors hanging half open, lazily creaking on well-made hinges. Orange light spilled from the windows on the west side of the house, flooding the wooden floors with the same red-orange color as the cloak covering the fallen man pierced with swords in the *Ten of Swords*—crisis.

The baby made a squeak and I loosened my grip slightly.

If Nate had been the one shot, I reasoned, Mr. Carey would already be upstairs. If Mr. Carey was alive and Nacto or his friend was shot, Nate would have transfigured to protect the women from further harm, consequences be damned.

I took a shuddering breath and crept down the stairs, my back to a wall to steady me, my weapon in hand, ready to defend the bundle in my arms.

Joseph Carey lay on the kitchen floor of the family home, his left arm twisted beneath him at an impossibly odd angle, his blood spreading across the wooden floor. The blond hair that lay across his forehead was matted with blood. The scent of gunpowder hung heavy in the air.

Nate stared at the body. The two Cheyenne men were arguing in hushed tones, gesturing at Mr. Carey in frantic motions. Nannie heard me approach and took her baby from my arms. I touched Nate's back. He turned and reached out an arm to me. Karl crouched in the corner, one eye nearly swollen shut.

In an instant, the world Chelan had made for herself as Nannie and the white names she gave her children to protect them ceased to offer any protection. Like the *Ten of Swords*, a man lay dead and all that surrounded him was crisis and defeat. But, in times of crisis, a healer focuses on what she can do for the living. Nate and I had offered Nannie and the children our protection, and that was not about to change now, though I was at a loss as to how to move forward.

I turned to my husband. He looked at Mr. Carey's body, the wheels in his head turning, nodding to himself as he worked up a plan.

I knew where to begin. I had living patients.

§§§

If there was sorrow at the loss of her husband, Mrs. Carey didn't show it. Nannie held Daisy, softly crooning to her in the beautiful lilting Cheyenne language.

The children were theirs, hers and Haimovi's. You would have to be blind to miss the looks she gave him.

Mr. Carey must have known.

"Mrs. Carey, why did you marry Joseph?" Nate asked.

I stared at him. How could he ask such a thing of a woman? Especially now that he was dead, with their children looking on.

I took Nate's hand. "Surely the reservation is safer for you and the children. The rail workers told me most of the Indians live on the reservations, and if they don't go—" I couldn't bring myself to say it.

Haimovi glared at Joseph Carey's body. "They will take our children. Place them in church housing. Teach them to be good Christians."

Nacto looked grim. "My sister has duties. I stayed to look after her."

Nate turned to Haimovi. "And you stayed here for love. Men will do a lot for the women they love."

Nannie looked out the window at the trees waved in the wind. "I give up much for my people."

An odd peace lay over the homestead as though a cloud of darkness had suddenly lifted, even though the sky was still cloudless and deep blue. I should have been shocked by the sight of the dead man on the floor, but he had been killed in self-defense. He would have harmed Nannie and the children, as well as anyone else who stood in his way, of that I was certain,.

Despite all the awful destruction Mr. Carey had created, all the fear he had caused, leaving his daughter cowering in the upstairs bedroom, I could not help but feel sorrow for the man lying face down on the floor in a lake of blood.

I was only dimly aware of the flurry of activity behind me, out of place in such an awful moment. Joseph Carey was so like the fallen man in the *Ten of Swords*, slain and betrayed. I could not hate Chelan for it. I could not even hate Haimovi for it.

Nannie had given up the right to marry the man she loved, the one who had fathered her children, the one who now stood beside her, a strong arm wrapped around her as he glared at the dead man with contempt.

Haimovi spoke. "Chameli, Meturato, help your mother."

The moment Haimovi said it I knew he spoke truth, a truth I knew without being able to name it. Her name was not Nannie. Her name was Chelan. Her children—their children—were Chameli and Meturato. I looked at the baby in Chelan's arms. I suddenly wanted to know his name because it surely was not Evan.

I was once engaged to a man who I did not love. He had not loved me. He needed a woman who would marry him and I needed a way to provide for my parents in their old age. It seemed a good idea at the time. Except he was a gambler, a lout, a drinker, and a whoremonger. In short, Byron Goodwin was a horrid man. Yet, I might have married him for the protection his name and estate would have provided. It was only through good fortune that I had realized, before it was too late, that he would never respect me, and that he would never grow to love me.

Then I met Nate: wonderful, loving, adventurous Nate. And, together, we managed to solve the problem of providing for my family.

Chelan had stayed with Joseph Carey to remain here rather than go with her people and the safety they offered her and her children.

I looked around. The flurry of activity was the organized chaos of a family preparing to leave.

Chameli stood at the kitchen shelves, packing glass jars of preserves in a wooden crate, carefully wrapping them in towels and stacking them. Meturato—I was still getting used to the unique feel of their true names—

was tying bags of corn, flour, and beans with bits of twine and setting them by the door, then he marched up the stairs. Haimovi returned from taking a load outside to take the sacks of grain and flour.

Everyone carefully stepped over Joseph Carey's body.

"Wait!" Everyone looked at me like I was mad. "We cannot run, that will make Chelan and her brother look guilty."

The children resumed their packing.

"We are guilty," Nate said reasonably. "A man is dead."

I started to protest. But no, the law would not even protect a woman from abuse in London. Not really. In the home, the man was the law. The law protected the wife and children from outright murder, of course but, short of that, the law rarely got involved.

Nate took my hand and pulled me outside. "The law will not protect these people, Vivian. You know that, as well as I do." He lowered his voice to frantic, hushed tones. "They are not even seen here as people. I don't think it's right they are being forced away from their homes, but they will not find justice here, and Nacto and Haimovi did kill Joseph Carey."

I shivered at the thought.

"Not that he didn't deserve it," Nate continued offhandedly.

I stared at him. The casual way in which he said it was startling. My husband was a lot of things, but I never considered him a bloodthirsty man. "How can you say that?"

"How can I not?" he said, aghast. "Viv, if anyone put their hands on you, I would murder them outright! Any other man would do the same."

"Yes, but the law—" I protested.

Nate interrupted. "The law will do nothing for them. If it did, Chelan wouldn't have had to marry Joseph to stay here. Haimovi wouldn't have to pretend his children were another man's, or risk them being taken away."

He was right. It wasn't fair. How could such a country pretending to be so advanced and so forward in their thinking be so backward? How could they hate a group of people just because their skin was another color or because they believed differently?

Behind us, Haimovi and Nacto grabbed Mr. Carey's body and dragged him out of the house. A new age, indeed. They may have new monsters, but they preyed upon the weaknesses of men just the same as the old world demons did. We could pretend technology and education were the virtues of the new man, but what defined us was what united us. Mankind was defined by the same old prejudices and ignorance.

This family would be punished for Carey's death if they were caught.

Chelan stood at the door. Her face was badly bruised, her lip swollen, several teeth broken. "You hate us."

I realized belatedly I had been crying. "No. It is not you." The truth of it set a fresh tear snaking down my cheek.

Chelan cradled her baby like a talisman. She couldn't have known how it tore my heart. "I know you wish for us to adhere to the law. We cannot. Now we must go to my people. There is no safety here."

Chameli filled a basin of water and shook a bit of powder from a paper carton into it. She began to scrub the blood from the wooden floor.

Chelan was right; there would be no safety here. They needed to move as quickly as they could, but it would be slow going with a baby. They would have to stay off the roads and avoid towns or risk being caught, either as fugitives or for being Natives. And if the children were identified as half-breeds or Indians and the townspeople in St. Louis were right, they would be taken away and placed in Christian charity homes. They needed to get to the safety of their people as soon as possible. That meant traveling on roads or, even better, trains.

Meturato whipped his head shaking the long bangs out of his eyes. "I will help."

Haimovi nodded. "You will help."

I pulled Nate aside. "We need to travel with them. They need to go to their people and if they travel with us, we can take them safely."

Nate nodded. "There is a law here called peonage. I read about it in the paper. We can use it to transport them as..." he trailed off.

"As what?" I could tell this was going nowhere good. I touched the ruby in my pocket. I felt stronger just having it nearby. The last few days were so trying, I just needed a rest.

"As our property," Nate finished.

"As *slaves*?" I stared at him. Did he really just say that?

"It's like a modern indentured servitude. No one would bother an English Esquire and Lady moving their property to a new estate," Nate argued.

"You have lost your mind!" I snapped. "I am not having anyone pretend to be my property, even just in name."

"It is the best protection we can offer them," Nate whispered furiously.

"Tell them that you'd be happy to transport them as your personal property!" I turned away from him. How was this the man I married? I rubbed the ruby in my pocket. I clenched my teeth so hard, my jaw ached.

He put his hand on my shoulder. I jerked away. I wanted to slap him. I wanted to strike him. More than that, I was wounded by his very callous words. I wanted to strike back.

"I'm trying to help," he snapped.

"You're failing!" I cried out.

"Then you come up with a better way!" Nate snarled. It was a dog's snarl, a wounded dog pushed past patience.

How dare he snap at his mistress that way? I was cold and hot all over. All I could see was red, red-hot fire and I felt like I was being pulled into the ground. I was filled with righteous rage. I wanted to hit him, bite him, wound him. My throat ached, throbbing and burning hot. I grabbed the back of a chair for support.

He was mere inches from me. I had tried to be kind, but I had given so much. What did he expect me to give now?

"Brother?" Nacto called.

"I mean it, Vivian." Nate growled. "You have a better way, I'll hear it, but no one will molest a man's property." He turned on his heel.

First, it was an esquire and a lady's property, now it was a man's property. I was weighted to the floor with despair. I could not breathe, my blood rushed through my veins. I couldn't think of anything to say. Breathing alone took all the energy I had left.

I thought of the dragon. She was a dangerous creature, but she had been good and nurturing, and she gave and gave until she had become a shell. I was burning away and losing the Tarot symbols we had both come to rely on. I was becoming a shell. Out of balance, the dragon became a broken-hearted creature of evil, who viciously hated the humans she had once loved and guided. We loved our tenants. We would give them all we had. Would they grow to hate us, and us them? Was that why the upper-class often treated the working classes as beneath them?

My hands ached. The back of the chair was gouged, and my nails had bits of wood beneath them. I blinked hard. They looked like claws, curved and tapered to wicked points. I tucked my fingers into my fists. For a moment, they pricked my palms, then the moment was gone.

The most infuriating part was that Nate was right. If Chelan and her family traveled as our peons, then we could safely transport them wherever we chose to go. Which, really, was the most important thing. But the idea of claiming ownership over another human being, even as a farce, turned my stomach. We paid our servants, and the tenants who worked our land paid rent, but they were also free to move off the land and seek better fortunes.

Nate, Haimovi, and Nacto filed out the door to hide Nannie Carey's lawful husband's body. They were intent on their grim task.

I should hate it. And in a way, I did. I hated that Joseph Carey lay dead and that my husband was now involved in a plot to hide his body in the woods. But, more than that, I hated this new world. It should be a place of wonder and advancement, a huge land of enchantment where a man was only limited by his spirit and his hard work. But not, of course, if he wasn't white, or wasn't a man.

America was huge, it should be more than big enough to share. Why were the Cheyenne being forced onto reservations or into church-run state homes when they had families who loved them?

I could understand why Nate had been handed over to a church-run home for boys. He had had no family to look after him. He had no one to keep him out of trouble, and, as much as I loved the man, I had to admit he needed someone to keep him out of trouble. Chelan should not have had to marry Joseph to keep her children safe, to keep them from being stolen away and placed in church homes "for their own good." Chameli, Meturato, and the baby would have had two loving parents and an uncle who would have looked after them.

I watched the men leave with Mr. Carey's body and, slowly, my breathing returned to normal. My heart no longer rattled in my ears, drowning out all other sounds and driving me into a violent rage. More than violent; I was worried. Whatever I felt, it was intoxicating. What was wrong with me? I loved Nate more than anything in the world. I would die to protect him. I never wanted to see him hurt, nor did I want to harm him.

I set my head against the cool pane of glass. Suddenly, I was so tired. I felt as though I had been nothing but tired lately. I touched the ruby in my pocket and immediately felt better. Now I was strong enough to go on, strong enough to own other people, for as brief a time as possible.

If Mr. Carey's body was found, Chelan, Haimovi, and Nacto would be imprisoned and probably executed. The children would be taken away. They would lose their identities, at the very least. They would cease to be Meturato and Chameli and would, instead, be forced to be Karl and Daisy. The baby, instead of being named on his first birthday, as is the tradition Chelan explained, he would be Evan as Joseph had demanded. The name might bring the baby bad luck and draw evil spirits before the baby's spirit is strong enough to fight them off.

Chelan handed me the baby. He gurgled while trying to shove a handful of my hair into his mouth. He smiled, as always. He stared at me in cross-eyed fascination. I swear he could see the Tarot symbols under my skin.

Chelan fixed her braid. "I can offer you something greater than my gratitude."

I shook my head. The baby was heavy in my arms. I would give anything to hold my own child in my arms. "You don't owe me anything."

Chelan interrupted me. "You do not have a baby."

I looked over her baby's head. Surely, she was not offering me her *own* child?

My panic must have shown. She gave me an indulgent smile with battered lips. "A mother can see the look of longing. You wish to have a child of your own, not mine. I see a striped cat. It hunts after you, stalking your steps. It devours your babies before they can make their way to you from the world of souls."

I squeezed the babe in my arms tightly. He squawked in protest.

Chelan took her infant back. "My mother is a *Ma'heóná'e*, a true medicine woman. I am merely a *Nóává'e*, a medicine woman who still learns. I watch over the bones of my people. Now, I cannot stay here, but must move on and join my people. My mother will help you banish the striped cat. It will stalk you no more."

My mouth fell open. How could she know? Mr. Quinn, one of the treasure hunters we met in China, had warned me that there was a terrible price for disturbing a holy grave site. It would result in terrible luck. A tiger would haunt my shadow. I would never get my heart's desire.

I had disturbed the holiest of grave sites, that of the sacred dragon, the mighty Xihuan-Lung. I had been cursed, and the evidence was all around us. Our investments had soured, my father had died. Nate and I had been married for over a year and we had not yet become pregnant.

Chelan took my hesitation as a refusal. "Would you trade our freedom for that?"

I stared at her. "No. It is not about trading your freedom. Nate and I will help take your family north. No matter what."

The baby closed his eyes and gave a contented sigh before grunting and filling his diaper.

CHAPTER SIXTEEN

THE SUN WAS just setting when the men returned from their gruesome task. They were soaked to the skin despite the dry, sunny day. I hoped that they had washed in a well or a stream before returning.

I wanted to apologize to Nate. I wanted to hold him to me and tell him I knew he was trying to help. He had come up with a good idea. No one would molest the private property of a foreign esquire and his wife. We would need to convince Nacto and Haimovi the plan was sound.

It turned out I didn't need to apologize. Nate could read me well. He walked into the house, his brow arched as he glanced at me. Were we still fighting? I shook my head. My husband was a good man and, though I hated the idea of slaves of any kind—I even treated our hired staff more like trusted employees than servants—his heart was in the right place.

I gave him a smile.

Nacto and Haimovi went to speak to Chelan. Nate must have discussed the idea with the men while they were away. While it was not a popular idea, it was accepted as the best plan for safe travel. Meturato seemed to hate it more than I did. He was even more sullen than during the fight with Mr. Carey, if that was possible.

We decided we would leave in the morning. No one wanted to run into the wendigo in the dark. This was no longer a safe place for Chelan and her children. After a night's sleep, the world would look a bit brighter, and the next day we would help them get as far as we were able to take them. There was nothing else we could do, now.

Chameli turned bread dough out on a board and kneaded it with strong hands, adding a sprinkle of flour here and there while Meturato looked on. He nailed closed the window frames on the far side of the house, sealing them up. I watched him move through the home creating an air of finality. The farmhouse had obviously been built by hand and was lovingly cared for as the home where Chelan raised her children. Though Chelan would not return, she sealed the home with care for the next resident.

Haimovi sharpened a knife, using long, even strokes. Since Nacto had put all the horses in the paddock, there was little to do but wait. We would turn loose the cow before we left, hoping it would find a kind master. The goats would come with us in the wagon, north to the Cheyenne home.

And wait, we did. We waited for the bread to rise. We waited for the morning. We waited for the fire to burn down so we could take turns adding another stick. I placed my hand in my pocket to touch the ruby. It calmed my pounding heart.

I stared into the warm, beautiful fire. The fireplace was in our home outside London. Papa was there with Mama, and we were in the conservatory as he fed his birds. They hopped on his fingers and whistled at him. Nate had his arm around me and we sat together on the sofa. I was pregnant and nibbling biscuits and tea. It would be Christmas soon, and due to well-managed investments and a good harvest, all our tenants were well-fed and healthy. It was my home, but with one thing I had never noticed before. Glaring down at us, weaving her way between the mantle clock, the candlesticks, and several books, Xihuan-Lung watched us. She was the same dragon, only smaller. She raised her head and our eyes met as a fierce heat caught me beneath my breast and at the ruby in my pocket.

Nate suddenly grabbed my wrist. Couldn't he just let me have a moment of peace? I glared. It was almost completely dark outside.

He was slowly rising from the table, staring at the darkened window.

"Wha—?"

He raised his hand to silence me. Haimovi and Nacto also turned to the windows, readying their weapons.

Then I heard them. A dozen men and horses, with lanterns.

"The savages did it!"

Nacto nodded to the men and motioned Meturato back. He opened the door. "Good evening, gentlemen."

"Yer sister! Where is she?" one man demanded.

"Where's Mr. Carey?" another man shouted.

"He is away," Nacto said. "I am visiting my sister while he is gone."

"You're gonna have to come with us to talk to the sheriff," a man said. "Just until he returns."

"How come you're always here when he's gone? You and that other fella?" A man shouted, he sounded familiar. I replayed his voice, trying to place it.

"He and I travel together. We are brothers," Nacto said calmly.

"Come out then, both of you! Before we're forced to come in after you!" a faceless man from the crowd hollered.

Nacto stood at the door, barring entry. "We did nothing."

"They burn the homes of good, hardworking Americans and chase them off of their land. And if they won't move, they burn them, too." That voice again. I knew that voice.

Nacto stood his ground. "It wasn't the Cheyenne. Most of our daughters and sons have long since left our lands."

A man raised a kerosene lantern. "They ain't yours anymore!"

Haimovi appeared at the doorway and raised his chin defiantly. "It was Silver Arm. He burns your people."

Nate could not stay back. He joined the two men at the door. His eyes narrowed as he surveyed the crowd. His jaw was tight and at his side his fist twitched, clenching and unclenching slightly—he expected a fight. Even if the crowd believed in Silver Arm, they were more willing to believe the Cheyenne were responsible for the burned household rather than any other explanation. I wanted to be shocked and horrified, but I was already saddened by the plight of these people and what they had to endure.

How many people had Silver Arm killed? Geiger had murdered people in London, several through his manipulation of the underground waterways to expose the leywell under London, nine at the Tate household. How many lives in China had he carelessly dealt with when he thought he could manipulate the Explorer's Society into giving him unfettered access to their vaults? How many more lives in America? He must have an endgame, but what was it?

We would not find out here. Geiger would have moved on, or so I hoped. But, the crowd was becoming more and more aggressive.

"Carey would want his children raised with good, Christian values."

Chelan tucked her son and daughter behind her own, slight form. It did little to hide them, but no one would doubt her resolve and I was sure they would only take them over her dead body, hers and those of the other Cheyenne men. And Nate's and mine.

Someone in the crowd called out, "Arrest Phillip. He doesn't belong here!"

I blinked, feeling stupid, "Who's Philip?"

Nate motioned with his chin unwilling to split his attention from the two sides. "Haimovi. They all have white names."

One man spoke for the crowd. In the lantern light I recognized him, it was Mr. Massey. I was beyond angry. "Steven West, you're going to have to come with us until we get this cleared up."

I had to ask Nate. "Who?"

Nate half turned to me. "Nacto," he said under his breath.

One of the men jeered, "Where is Carey anyway?"

Nate pushed forward. He was taller than both Nacto and Haimovi, taller than some of the crowd, as well. He made an imposing sight. He cast long shadows in the lantern light. "He's away at the moment."

I wondered how far away. Joseph Carey was probably buried in the woods not far from the farm. I hoped the mob would not stumble upon him tonight.

One of the crowd glared at Nate. "Who the hell are you?"

Nate inhaled sharply through his nose. "A friend of the family."

Another man shouted. "Ha! Unless you're a friend of Carey you ain't no friend!"

The crowd murmured assent. "Go back to where you came from, ya limey Brit!"

It was an angry murmur, like bees; like a growl, far off in the distance and drumbeats on the horizon.

I wanted to hold the ruby in my pocket, just for the strength it gave me. I could not leave Nate to them. I joined them on the porch. I would stand beside him no matter what. I would always fight at his side.

A kerosene lantern was thrown into the wagon we had loaded with food and clothing. The glass shattered, spilling the fuel. Suddenly, a gout of flames erupted across the foodstuffs and blankets. The flames rose high and angry, sending up the heavy, sweet, yeasty smell of burning grain and cotton and wool.

The mob's horses rolled their eyes and snorted, tearing at their lead ropes. Glass bottles shattered, spraying their contents and shards of glass in a deadly burst of boiling fluid that stunk of mingling fruit, vegetables, and meat. Debris hit my clothes, and I brushed it away. It added to the general chaos of the moment.

Suddenly, my world spun and I was removed from the moment and thrust into the world of the mystical and out of the physical. It was like someone set a hook beneath my breastbone and jerked me into the sky. I thrust my gaze upward. Even the stars here were different. No not different, this was a pattern. The stars were making a picture. A man sat on a throne. A king, maybe? No, not a king, a priest. A priest didn't sit on a throne, but a high priest might, *The Hierophant* would. His hand pointed toward the earth, his feet to the sky. He sat in heaven, his hand stretched out to the land itself. It took me a moment to realize this was not his natural orientation. So, *The Hierophant*, reversed; question society, break convention, break the rules, challenge the status quo. Finally, something made sense.

Someone threw a bottle. It hit the side of the house and shattered, sending up new shards of glass to explode around us. There was a new sound, a sound I knew all too well: a low growl. My canithrope was loyal and fearless. The trouble was, he was not the most patient of creatures, especially when someone he loved was threatened.

"Enough!" I screamed.

Everyone stared at me, their cries for blood died away, replaced by angry murmurs.

"How dare you?" My outburst forced them to stop and focus on me. My throat feel like vipers were wrapping their way around my neck, but I could not stop now even if I had wanted to. "How dare you come here and threaten this mother and her children?"

My knees felt weak and sweat dripped down the back of my neck despite the chill in the air. These men came here to do violence. Challenging them would not stop them.

I softened my tone. "Doesn't a mother have the right to protect her children and raise them, no matter what?"

Mr. Massey smiled at me, the kind of smile one gives children or simpletons. "Now look here, ma'am, poor Carey loves his children, but if work takes him away from home then it falls upon his community to keep his family on the path." He pulled me aside as though he was revealing some great truth. "Nannie here is all right, she's a good Christian woman, but her brother, Steven, is never in church and we never see her brother's friend. They're nothing but trouble. It's best for the children that they go where they belong."

I couldn't believe what I was hearing. I longed to slap him. "Where they belong?"

I believe it was the man who threw the glass bottle that had barely missed Nate who took a step toward Haimovi. "Are we going to let these dirty Injuns turn us from our Christian duty?"

The mob spoke as one. "No!"

"We can't save the souls of these demons, but these children are all half-white. It's our duty to look after them."

Mr. Massey pushed back his hat. "We're taking Carey's children. All of them. Nannie, don't interfere. You are free to go back to your people or you can stay with them at the mission school, but they need more structure than a woman can provide. I'll speak with Joseph when he returns. He'll understand."

Haimovi drew his knife. "They're not Carey's children. None of them."

Suddenly, I saw it on the top of the hill watching over us all. The monster. Its black pelt swallowed up most of the light around it and the white skull gleamed in the pale light so the head appeared to float eerily. Its eyes glowed like icy moonlight that had been caught and swallowed up, a dead and glassy light.

It approved of this awful scene. The long, bony muzzle was smiling. The eyes were watching us the way a predator fixes on its prey, enjoying every subtle movement. It drank in the anger, the rage, and the hatred. Its shaggy shoulders swelled in delight.

I don't know who fired the first shot.

The door frame exploded less than a foot from Chameli's head.

The baby had been sobbing, now he was hysterical. The baby's wail drew the thing's attention. It started down the hill. The nightmare moved like a predatory bird, bobbing its fleshless skull as it walked, but I did not believe it actually touched the ground. I thrust my hand into my pocket. The ruby was hot. It was calling to me and I could not ignore its pull. The last time I used it, it burned me, but I would gladly try to do it again to protect Chelan and the children. And I would do anything to protect Nate.

I caught a flash of movement from behind me. Despite being focused on the mob and the monster I did not think the men I was with were capable of doing something stupid. But I forgot one of them was a teenage boy. And the mob was threatening his mother and his sister.

Meturato threw himself at one of the men with a bellow. Both went sprawling into the dirt. Neither of them saw the monster descending the hill. Before I could shout a warning, the mob, galvanized by Meturato's attack, came alive.

One brought the stock of his rifle down upon Meturato. The young man grunted but stayed on top of his target as they rolled, hollering and beating each other, with the hollow, meaty sound of flesh on flesh.

I swallowed my protest. A man screamed.

The front yard of the Carey home was chaos.

Nate transfigured. He didn't bother removing his clothing. He dropped one hand to the ground to support his frame as his shoulders broadened and his hips shifted. His thighs became more massive, the pelvis tilting slightly and tucking forward. His feet shifted so he would prance and walk on his toes. He groaned: changing quickly was painful.

He didn't bother with the smaller, compact form of his dog, Ranger. Instead, he chose the hulking form that was a killing machine of both dog and man, larger and stronger than both.

His hands became claws, tipped with dark, sharp nails capable of rending wood and denting steel. His jaw deformed and jutted forward, the muzzle lengthening, teeth sharpening and extending into fangs capable of gripping and tearing flesh. His ears moved higher on his head to pick up sound—one had been split by a spear a year ago, giving him the look of a battered street cur.

He stretched and arched his back and unleashed a bone-chilling growl that made the men cower in fear.

I beamed. There was my husband. He was a wonderful, masterful man—God and Dog, both noble sides of man in a single, wonderful, protective form.

The Cheyenne behind me stood, mouths agape.

Nate placed himself between us and the mob, creating a raging barrier of fur and flesh, challenging them with a snarl and a gnashing of teeth. *Come forward, I dare you. They are under my protection.*

Meturato and his opponent ceased their mad pugilistic battle, staring at this new development. Meturato recovered first, and slammed his opponent's head into the earth, knocking him out cold.

The flurry of movement started the battle anew.

In the chaos I lost track of Chameli. She returned from inside the house with a pistol. She leveled it, drew back the hammer, and fired.

The pistol went off with an angry, ferocious report. One of the mob fell with a cry.

Chelan took the pistol from her daughter and handed off the baby, shoving them back inside the house. She drew back the hammer herself, ready to shoot the next man to threaten her children.

Haimovi and Nacto were both armed with knives. They were grossly outnumbered if the mob started shooting. The only way they had any chance at all was if the mob refused to shoot for fear of hitting their own friends. Haimovi and Nacto knew this and dove into the crowd. Nacto held his knife so the blade rested against his forearm. Haimovi soon had a man immobilized in his arms.

Nate grabbed one man, dragging him to his feet, and roared in his face before throwing him back and clawing viciously into other men. Nacto slashed wide, connecting with the forearm of a man wielding a broken bottle, trying to stab anyone in range. Haimovi was a less elegant fighter: he grabbed one man, much taller than himself, and threw him over his shoulder, onto the ground, before knocking him out with a single punch.

I needed a Tarot symbol to gain control of the situation, but I could not think of anything capable of moving an entire crowd. Every card I brought to mind dealt with an individual facing a situation, and I could not battle the mob one individual at a time. Or could I? I readied myself. Swords were action and asserting power. I just needed to come up with a good one.

Then I saw the monster again. The wendigo had no fear of the firelight. The monster came down the hill, watching in morbid satisfaction as the thirsty ground lapped up the blood. It moved impossibly fast, gliding rather than running. It passed through the men looking quite pleased.

The demon reached out a skeletal arm. I expected it to be purely bone but, instead, its arm was long, impossibly so, thin, wiry, and tipped with sharp, curved claws.

It touched one of the men in the mob, its touch feathering upon the back of the man's neck. For a brief moment the man went stiff as though he was suffering from catalepsy or some other trance-like state, then he dove for the man nearest to him, one of his neighbors, a man so similar in looks they might have been kin.

His new victim was so stunned he didn't fight back at first. Then the man leaned in and tore a chunk out of his friend with his teeth. The victim screamed, a high pitched, keening cry of shock and pain. Men tried to pull them apart. The monster reached into the fray again, touching a man here, another man there.

I could no longer follow the chaos in the darkness. Only the monster and its skeletal, wolf-like head stood beyond the mob that was frantically ripping itself apart—and Nate, wearing his canithrope skin, stood between them and us, staring, creeping backward, trying to put as much distance between us and them as possible without drawing the thing's attention. Behind him stood the Cheyenne family. I wished they would retreat into their home, but I knew if they did they only risked the mob burning them out.

Before us, the three men the monster touched ripped their friends apart, glutting themselves on blood, and tearing into their friends with their teeth. They'd turned cannibal, turned murderer, turned Cain to Abel, brother murdering brother. The monster was among us. Worse, now it was inside us. I swear, despite the lack of lips, it smiled.

The rest of the mob, untouched and uninfected by the monster's touch, stood in a panicked circle swinging their lanterns around, trying to defend themselves from their friends and neighbors, and also from Nate, now a terrifying monster in his own right, and finally from the Cheyenne they had come to threaten and harm. They had descended into a great seething mass of human misery, crying and fighting each other in a senseless orgy of violence that moved too quickly to follow.

Nacto and Haimovi stood, back to back, weapons in hand, each protecting the other's weaker side. Nacto glared at the grim scene of death as Haimovi squinted into the darkness, his eyes darting to and fro, searching for his enemy as he stood before his beloved and his children, ready to fight to the death to protect those he loved.

I suddenly understood. Not everyone could see this demon of sin that made brother turn against brother. Nate and I could see it. Nacto could, he had proved it the night he found us at the Tate farm. I was sure Chelan could see it. She followed its movement, glancing from it to the mob and back again, but Haimovi and the children stood terrified, staring into the darkness and at the mob, searching for the force that had driven the men mad.

Oh God, if that thing touched my husband, what would it turn him into?

"Nate!"

The monster—the wendigo—ignored me. The monster, who had turned so many men into vicious killers, stalked toward us like some horrid macabre bird, bobbing as it stalked. It strode forward, intent on feasting on the misery it brought. It reached out to touch Nate.

I pulled the ruby from my pocket and thrust it before me.

Star.

Moon.

Sun.

I thought them as frantically as I could. Pain shot across my body where the symbols once resided beneath my skin. I opened my mouth, ready to spout dragon fire at the wendigo—it would not take my husband. But like a ruined circuit they merely sparked uselessly. I cried out at the pain of it. Nothing happened. I didn't know how to activate the ruby, to make it do what it did before. My mind was a battlefield.

The monster grabbed Nate by the throat. I had to help my husband!

Nate fought. He arched his back. The monster glared, his teeth bared, snarling. The change that came so easily with the men was nothing to Nate. Whatever power the wendigo possessed, Nate was fighting it somehow.

Fight, Nate! Fight, love!

Love.

A great strength bloomed in my heart. I *loved* him. More than anything, I *loved him*. Love needed to be enough.

Then I saw it, something I could do that could help. A symbol came to me clear as day. A man and a woman stood nude under the great Archangel

Raphael as he blessed them and watched over them. Trust, confidence, faith, love. *The Lovers*, they were lovers, in this world they had each other and that was all they needed. I felt great heat coming off me in waves, building, burning me, blistering my flesh. I bit back the pain.

Red light slammed into the monster, knocking it free of Nate, across the bloody dirt.

For an instant the whole yard was as bright as noon.

Nate hit the ground. He was a man again, wearing his man-skin, naked and face-down in the moist, healing earth at its feet.

I screamed. Not in helplessness, but a fierce battle cry.

The monster wheeled to face me.

The ground was a slick, wet mess, made so by blood and gore. I struggled to keep my footing.

I was not about to lose to this creature. Two sphinx; one black, one white, drawing *The Chariot* across a field. The charioteer was victorious, wearing a laurel and a crown. This struggle would make me stronger. *The Chariot* is willpower, victory, control, determination. I would win, and quickly. Nate lay naked and motionless. And, in the light, I could briefly see that the mob had not dispersed, but that they had destroyed themselves. They lay moaning, crouched in the grip of mania, bloody and broken.

That would not be me. Nor would it be my Nate, nor would it be the family we swore to protect. I felt power burning through me, coursing through my system. My feet dug into the earth, made soft by blood and struggle. But where the others had fallen, we still stood, strongly. Nothing would stand against love. It was victory, and before that it had been the sun, the moon, the star: hope, peace, and vitality.

The virtues of man. The goodness of man.

There was a *crack* and the weight was gone. I stumbled forward, both exhausted and relieved. The light left me in darkness, but a clean sort of darkness, nothing ominous or frightening, merely calm.

I waited in the eye of the storm.

The land before the Carey house was dark, almost supernaturally so after the red-white light that had poured from me left us all in a state of night-blindness. I jammed the ruby into my cleavage, for in that moment I knew the ruby was a piece of my heart and that was where it belonged, and dove for Nate. I was sure I knew where he lay. I had caused the supernatural light, somehow summoning it from my own body to battle the monster and, as it rushed through me, the details of his exact location had burned into my brain.

The mob lay in piles of human misery of their own making. It had been a mania and bloodlust I had never seen before.

They had turned their violence upon one another. No, the monster made them turn their horrific violence upon each other. There was no stopping it, as even men that appeared to be brothers fought one another to the bloody end.

Haimovi and Nacto resumed their back-to-back positions and readied themselves to face off against the mob should they attack again.

The world went white. The red. Silent.

My chest burned like I had spilled a whole tray of hot grease down my front. The Tarot image of *The Lovers* centered above my heart. It was from my heart that I had called upon love to give me the strength to banish the monster, and to protect Nate before any evil could tear him from me.

My heart pounded in my ears. And Nate shifted, proof my prayers were answered. His hand curled and clawed at the soft earth beneath him. *Thank God.*

I wished I could not hear the low groans from the injured and dying men.

Nate groaned. The yard was as dark as midnight, but the flash of light from the ruby was burned into my mind, and so, despite the dark, I could see him, a pale expanse of nude flesh against the dark earth. At least it wasn't the stark white of the dead bone of the monster.

My head shot up, searching for the monster. I half-expected it to be looming over us, ready to pounce and strike our heads clean off. It was already dead, so I couldn't kill it.

Then an odd thought struck me. Could I kill an undead evil?

Haimovi and Nacto stared at me. Meturato looked torn between wanting to run back into the house with his sister and baby brother, or wanting to stand with the men. Only Chelan looked upon us with the soft look of sympathy and kindness. She ducked past Haimovi and Nacto, untying her shawl as she moved. She draped it over Nate and whispered something.

She stood and switched to English for our benefit. "Haimovi, get them back into the house."

Nacto lifted Nate and, together with Haimovi, they managed to get him to his feet. I cast a look at the yard. My eyes were adjusting again to the near darkness. My breath caught in my throat. The men in the yard were not dead, not all of them. The moon was absent, but the stars cast a little light upon the scene.

The force of the light from the ruby had thrown the horror into the trees. Were I bolder, I could see if shattered bits of bone and charred black flesh and fur lay scattered beneath the trees, or if the monster had survived. But the thought of facing that thing alone was enough to make every part of me quiver. Nothing in the world would make me go hunting for it, alone, in the dark.

The blast from the ruby had made my hearing hollow, causing my breathing to sound too loud in my ears, but my vision was starting to recover. I looked one last time for the monster among the trees.

One of the men was crying, pleading. No...many of them were.

"Mama."

"Help me."

"Please."

"No..."

This last one was a moan, low and sobbing. I choked on a cry.

Haimovi took my arm. There was no demand there, just strength stopping me for a moment, holding me long enough to give me pause. "Do not go to them. If the monster is still there it will drag you down."

"If?" Then I remembered, Haimovi could not see it. Maybe it was still there, and I could not see it now.

There was a resigned sadness in Haimovi's voice. "I will help them pass."

I opened my mouth to protest but he stopped me. "The monster will not see me now. Chelan will be sure."

I longed to ask him how, but my breast was on fire and I was so tired I could hardly stand. I had managed to twice bring fire and light down upon this monster without any clue as to what it was or how to defeat it. I may have driven it off, but I was not any closer to defeating it for good and, every time I fought it, I seemed to be on the losing end. So far, despite Nate's good intentions, his canithrope form had not been helpful.

We all went inside. The home was in disarray; crates and bags on tables and chairs were scattered throughout the rooms. A large red-brown stain that had been Joseph Carey's blood remained in the center of the wood floor. It would never be scrubbed fully away.

I collapsed into a chair, nearly missing it as I did so, painfully slamming my tailbone against the edge of the seat.

Chelan pulled out a set of red stoneware bowls. She painted Haimovi's face white with red and black streaks and dots. She lit herbs and blew them into his face and whispered over him. It was a prayer of some sort, that I knew, but when he took up a long cord from his belt and tied it around his torso, I sat up, transfixed. It was even stranger to watch Nacto also tie a band around his chest. Haimovi took his knife and returned to the yard, where the men lay broken and dying.

I tried to speak. My voice was so hoarse nothing came out. I cleared my throat and tried again. "Chelan, what…?"

She shushed me and brought another bowl of the same poultice she had used to treat my burned hands. "Haimovi and my brother are great warriors. *Hotamétaneo'o.* Dog soldiers. They make vows to not leave a place. They will defend it to their death to protect those they love and to protect their people. The band tied around their chest is their tether. If Haimovi is defeated , my brother will not leave this house, it is the site of his tether. He will fight to the death to give us—you, Nate, the children, and me—a chance to get away from the *hestanováhe.*"

The poultice felt wonderful against my burns, I wished I could lower my entire body into a bath of it. "And the paint?"

"It will protect Haimovi from the wendigo's eyes for a time," she said. "It is made of burned bones. The dead draw less notice."

"Why can't he see it?" I asked. "Nate and I can see it. You can."

"Wendigo is a creature of the spirit world. Only those who are chosen by the spirit world can see it. My mother is a great medicine woman, chosen by the Great Chief to look after her people. My brother was chosen by her to look after me. He can see the shadow the wendigo casts upon the land of Man. The shadow it casts is stronger in the light."

I looked over to Nacto, who was staring out at the yard. "Then why not send Nacto out to help the men in the yard?"

"Haimovi will be safe for a time. If wendigo does kill him as well"— Chelan swallowed hard—"if the wendigo kills him as well, Nacto may be all that can stand against him. We will need one who can see it to fight it."

"I would fight it," I said, a little insulted she didn't consider me in her plan for defense.

"I am sure you would. Nate, too. But it is not my place to decide what you will and will not fight." Chelan dried my hands and wrapped them in soft flannel. "I am not your chief. You are not mine to command."

Nate came down from the upper level of the home, wearing Joseph Carey's clothes. He buttoned a striped, homespun shirt. If he had any concerns about wearing a dead man's clothes, he didn't let it show. "What *exactly* is that thing?" He gripped the banister for support and closed his eyes for a moment. Perhaps he wasn't as unscathed as I had hoped.

Chelan put another log in the wood stove and set the kettle upon it. "*Hestanováhe*, the life drinker. Another name for it is wendigo."

"I get that," Nate said. "What is the wendigo? A spirit of evil? We can't fight it, so how do we get it to go away?"

It was a relevant question. "If it stays as long as people are sinful and wicked, how do we banish it? Man is not going to get better." I had hoped my Tarot magic would be enough. My first blow to the wendigo outside the Tate home had not been enough, and it cost me three symbols. I saved Nate from it tonight, and I was sure I had not killed it this time, either. "If it was somehow summoned, can it be banished?"

"Yes." Nacto stood at the window watching over Haimovi. I could have laughed. Oddly, I felt an immediate sense of relief that at least if the monster had many names, it was not an unknown horror.

Nacto made a sign like he was slashing over his eye. I was surprised they warded off the evil eye here, too. We were not all that different after all. "It is a monster. But like all monsters, it is bound by the law of Maheo."

"He is the god of all things," Chelan explained to me.

"If we stop the one that summoned it, would that banish the wendigo?" I thought about Geiger. Stopping him would probably mean killing him. I was shocked at how easily I accepted that conclusion. He murdered to get what he wanted. Was I any different? My motives were, but was that enough?

We sat in silence as the water heated. Nate expertly worked his jaw as he always did after a fight, checking for cracked teeth, testing his bite, and easing stiffness. I sat with him, in the oppressive silence that only the popping fire occasionally interrupted. I was terrified the monster had done something to him. What if it had? I would not harm him nor allow anyone else to, but, if the wendigo had turned him into a monster that hungered for human flesh, then no one would be able to stop him. As far as I could tell, Nate wasn't a werewolf. And, even if he was, could I hunt him with silver bullets? According to legend, that was the only thing that could kill a werewolf. I dismissed the thought. The wendigo had touched him and had not turned him, so somehow the magic of the leywell protected him. For now, that was comfort enough.

Chameli tended to her brother, bathing a bloody knot the size of a goose egg on his face. He protested, but only half-heartedly. Then she served us tea. It was weak, but I was grateful for something warm to hold and sip.

Nate accepted the cup Chameli handed him. "Why is the wendigo here?"

Chelan offered her breast to the baby. "It comes when it is called."

Nate flushed at the sight of her bare chest and immediately busied himself with his tea. "Who calls it?"

Chelan adjusted her son's latch and closed her eyes, allowing herself to relax into the comfort of the bond between mother and baby. "Man calls it."

I set my cup down. "Which man?" I already knew *which* man. Nate did, too. We weren't asking the right questions, but it was so hard to think clearly after a fight like that.

Chelan motioned for Meturato to move a crate of canned food from a chair so she could sit. "*Hestanováhe* is called when mankind is out of balance. When all is wrong with the world. When we have fallen so far into sin and vice that there is a great sickness in the souls of mankind. The wendigo is a life drinker, it consumes souls, and it consumes flesh. It will consume man for as long as sin and evil are greater than the good in man; for as long as it has a body. It tricks man, poisons us. We consume ourselves."

A life-drinker, a soul-taker. I shuddered. If Geiger thought he could truly control it, he was madder than I thought. "How long will it have a body?"

Chelan looked up from her baby to the darkened windows where her brother watched over Haimovi in the yard. "As long as it can pull together enough evil to form one."

Based upon what I had just seen, there was more than enough evil to keep the wendigo here for a very long time. "How long could someone manipulate it?"

Chelan looked at me, eyes wide. "Only one of true evil, one with a heart heavy with vengeance and hate, can keep it enthralled for a time. Only one with no care for his brother would attempt such a thing. And he would have to offer the wendigo a prize of great value." In her arms, the baby shifted and squawked. She shushed him and held him close. "You would have to be insane to attempt such a thing."

I had to know. "Chelan, have you ever seen a man with a silver arm?"

Nate gave me a look.

Nacto moved from the window and drew his knife. I leapt to my feet. I could see a shadow moving outside, and Haimovi was facing it alone. I wasn't sure I could bring forth another beam of light like I had before. It was love of Nate that helped me channel *The Lovers*, but I had to try. I could not leave anyone to face the monster alone.

I leapt for the door. Nate lunged from his seat and looped his arm around my waist.

"But Haimovi is out there!" I protested.

Nacto nodded. "He is. My brother is being polite. Haimovi is letting us see him."

I stopped struggling. "He what?"

"If he were tainted, he would not wait. He would be consumed by the monster's hunger. My brother is letting us see that he is still himself."

I exchanged a look with Nate. "Polite is all well and good, but while he is being polite, and if the monster is there, Haimovi is as good as dead." There was my reasonable husband.

Chelan nodded "Yes, but if the *Hestanováhe* is still hunting you, then Haimovi cannot stop it."

My blood turned to ice. "What do you mean 'still hunting me'?"

"This is twice you have fought the *Hestanováhe*," he said. "Why else would you encounter it twice?"

Nate shrugged. "Coincidence?" He didn't sound convinced. His hand on my back was heavy as lead.

Nacto opened the door.

Haimovi stood there, knife in hand. His eyes were heavy and black, the black traveling far down from his eyes, toward his mouth, squaring at his lower lip. The rest of his face was pale white.

Nate had not been in the room when Chelan had painted him in the sacred ash paint. Nate shoved me behind him. I tripped over the table leg and handed hard on my backside.

Nacto stood before him and reached up to touch Haimovi's shoulder where the leather strap had been tied. "Is your duty completed?"

"It is. For now my family is safe," Haimovi said.

"Then I remove your picket, my brother." Nacto untied the band. Haimovi expertly caught the rope before it slithered to the ground.

They both coiled up the flat ropes with practiced ease and tucked them away in pouches they wore around their waists.

Dog Soldiers, loyal and ready to defend those they loved. Ready to bind themselves to a certain point and defend it to the death to ensure the safety of their loved ones. I looked over at my husband. A dog is the most loyal of creatures, beloved of those who hold their hearts, and unwavering in their devotion.

CHAPTER SEVENTEEN

THE DEAD MEN lay scattered in the yard. The kerosene lamps burned low. Inside the Carey home, we all stared at one another over more tea and fresh bread. Chameli opened two glass jars that had not been taken outside before the mob arrived and dumped them into a cook pot. The preserved stew warmed and gave off a fine, rich scent that mingled with the choking stink of the kerosene, making my stomach turn flips.

Chameli served the stew in bowls, with large chunks of bread for our supper. I could not even consider eating now. It was a somber meal, as everyone picked and poked at their food, more for something to do than out of actual hunger, other than Meturato. Teenage boys are furnaces, always in need of fuel.

"I know we were going to help them get north to their people," I told Nate quietly. "I'm going all the way with them. I'm going to meet her mother, the medicine woman. She can fix…" I took a deep breath, "…me."

Nate took my hands. "There's nothing wrong with you."

"When we were in China, Mr. Quinn said a tiger would haunt my shadow. Chelan can see a striped cat. She says it devours the spirits of our babies before they can reach us." I swallowed hard, suddenly unable to draw a full breath. "Nate, I—"

"Quinn was an idiot," he said. "Keeping Xihuan-Lung from returning to the world and devouring it is something we should be rewarded for, not punished."

"I have to go. I need you to understand." Even if Nate was right and we deserved to be rewarded, our luck in all things had soured. We needed a way to put things to rights and I would ask anyone who might help us.

"Then we have to go," Nate said. "Where you go, I go. Even if you hate the idea of them being peons, it's just an idea." He looked around the room. "We can go by foot, if you like. I would be honored to protect you, and them."

I was immediately grateful I would not be taking the trip alone. Traveling by train would be swifter, and safer, because the faster we moved, the less time it would mean for the bodies of the missing men to be discovered. If everyone agreed, it would be better for them to travel with us as peons.

Nate took my hand. "Viv, I know what I am." The silence between us was easy again. I looked up at him and he smiled; handsome, friendly, happy. "I've been your dog since the night I followed you home, after you were almost mugged in the alley."

I couldn't help but return the smile, it was infectious. "What?"

"I've always been yours. Your dog, your man; I meant it. I would have laid on your feet every night until the end of my days if I needed to." He gave me a crooked smile. "You came with me to the Molten Cay so we could face a demon and fix the magic, or at least give me some measure of control over it. Maybe this medicine woman can do the same for you." He pulled me against him. "Remember. when we first battled the Lamia she said magic cannot be cured. It can be changed, but it can't be cured."

"You believe her? For God's sake, Nate! She was a demon." I would rather the curse, which I could only suspect was magical in nature, be cured.

"I don't think she was wrong," Nate said. "She was bound by some form of the truth. Remember when she tried to hypnotize us with riddles and that awful bone flute? The truth broke her spells. And when we asked her questions, when we asked them in the right way, she answered them honestly. She wasn't happy about it, but she did it was like she was bound to it. Remember how she growled at us?" Nate's voice cut through the memory, "Vivian, when we traveled to China, you managed to sever the link between that woman and her abusive brother, Prince Qixiang. You were able to wake us from a monster's spell. I still don't get how it works, but I'm glad it does. Now you can banish a monster with holy light you summon through your body. Whatever this is, you're getting stronger. I don't want to cure it, but if you cannot control it, I worry it may control you. I love you." He paused. "I can't let it destroy you. We need to go see her mother, but not for a baby, for you. Something is wrong."

I dismissed it with a wave, but Nate caught my hand in midair. "You stole the ruby, Viv. You hid it from me."

Something in his tone made me pause. I caught an image of three swords piercing a heart, but not just any heart: Nate's heart, and all around him poured rain. I had wounded him. But how could I explain? I swallowed against the sudden lump in my throat. How could I tell him I kept the ruby, the center of the key that lead to the dragon's grave, to prevent the dragon from being set loose upon the world?

"You're right." I whispered. "I kept it."

"Not that I'm not glad, now." Nate turned my hand in his own, stroking it. He probably assumed he was being comforting. "It sure helps against the wendigo. Right now, I need you to eat something."

For his sake, I choked down a few bites. My blood was sluggish, like tar in my veins. I was cold and numb. He was right. We had traded one monster for another. The ruby did give me a focus I had never known before, but now I could not use *The Star, The Moon,* or *The Sun.* When I tried to draw the cards to mind, they were lost to me like before I had awakened my power. I was more likely to summon gold from thin air than I was to call up those cards. Even trying to find their place within myself left me feeling hollow and empty, like someone had torn great pages from a book. Sure, most of the story was still there, but something was missing. It would never be complete again.

The loss of *The Lovers* hurt more. Symbolic or not, it was us I saw, hand in hand, strolling through the garden, watched over by a loving angel as we cared for one another, when I thought of that card. If I could not have a child, then at least I wanted to have The Lovers.

My heart hurt as though a fresh burn had settled over the area. I needed to picture myself in the deep tomb of The *Four of Swords* again. I needed to lay the blade down, for a moment, and let the peace of the earth soothe me. It had helped before. I was sure it would help again.

Nate's lifted me from the chair and walked me upstairs to bed. I was tired, so tired. I just wanted to rest, deep in my dark tomb, where I could heal.

"You wouldn't just go there for a baby?" I wasn't sure if that hurt or not. It was a cold comfort.

Nate shook his head. "I wouldn't go there for a baby. I will go there for you. You are becoming more powerful, but whatever you are touching is also destroying you. You are seeing things I can't see. If I can't see them, I can't help you fight them."

He wasn't just referring to the wendigo. The dragon, the dead one we had left in China, Xihuan-Lung, I could see her in all things; her eye was the moon, her growl was the train's wheels on the tracks, her foul breath was the smoke of the fire. I could see her. Nate could not.

I didn't know where I preferred to lay. The bed was warm and inviting, and Nate was there.

It was cool beneath the earth in the tomb. Only in the knight's tomb, where the four swords were laid to rest, where the four women attended the tomb, was I safe from Xihuan-Lung. I closed my eyes and felt myself sinking back into the tomb, that sacred, quiet place, my tomb. I just needed to gather more strength. I just needed more time.

Nate put his arm around my shoulder. "I don't need a baby, Vivian. I need you."

I opened my eyes. He looked at me with that wonderful, loving gaze. "You are my wife, and a powerful woman. You are amazing. You are mighty. I know what I am. It's easy to be what I am. I'm just your dog. I will keep you safe. I know my job."

"But—"

"You're searching for something, Viv. I just wish I knew what it was."

I wished I did, too. It was buried in my tomb, safe and secret, attended by four women. Today they were queens, regal and sacred. Blonde, Brunette, Scarlet, and Raven-haired, all radiant and resplendent as goddesses, staring at me, waiting for me to see something I could not yet see.

I lay down beside him but as soon as he was asleep, I retreated to my tomb.

CHAPTER EIGHTEEN

IT WAS A long journey from the Carey home to St. Louis. We turned their livestock loose, including the goats, because the wagon was never going to move again.

The bodies in the front yard were too numerous to try to move and hide. We had to create as much distance between the farm and us as possible, before anyone noticed the missing men. There was some discussion of whether or not to set fire to the house but, in the end, we decided the smoke would probably draw too much attention and the dead mob would be discovered sooner.

We gathered the Carey family horses and the horses we had rented and packed up the remaining portable foodstuffs and clothes. The chickens squatted below the porch and in the eaves of the barn, scolding us for all the fuss from the night before. I hoped the rest of the horses would eventually find their way home and the goats and cow would find someone to care for them.

Chelan went inside and knelt beside her hearth. No matter her true feelings for Joseph, it had been her home for a long time. Her children had been born there. The home had probably been built by Mr. Carey, for her, so that they could have a life together.

Haimovi searched for the wendigo. I could have told him he would not find anything. I thought I had destroyed it before, but I was wrong. I was sure it was not gone now, no matter what damage I had done to it last night.

The people of St. Louis must have seen Haimovi and Nacto before, and had probably even seen Chelan and her children, but they did a double take at seeing all of them together at once. They went ahead to the train station, where we would meet them shortly.

We returned the horses and explained that we had gotten lost in the darkness. The stable master laughed at us for being "dumb Brits" and bid us good day. We laughed it off, but Nate muttered insults under his breath.

We walked into the St. Louis Union Station, avoiding the HeadHouse entirely.

When we had arrived in St. Louis the first time, it had been evening. The train station had been illuminated by fancy electric lighting, and the deep shadows had hidden the rest of the lobby from view. Now, in the daylight, we realized the far wall was entirely consumed with a huge painting, a map of the United States of America. I counted forty-five stars on a flag, painted in a corner below an eagle and above a bunch of white flowers that looked a bit like the hawthorn from back home.

Haimovi, Nacto, and Nate pored over the maps I had bought earlier. Meturato stood with them.

"Where are we headed?" I asked Chelan.

Chelan pointed to the map, near the top. "Montana."

I followed her finger. I had been aware America was large, humongous by the standards of England but, until today, the sheer enormity of America had been lost upon me. "And where are we now?"

She pointed again. "Missouri."

I blinked hard. Three endless days on a train, chugging from Pennsylvania to St. Louis with only the occasional stop at a station to allow passengers off and on, had falsely led me to believe we must be nearing the edge of America, the other end of this great land.

I would never see the far side of America, California. To orient myself, I found the Mississippi River on the map. If that was still so far east, how much of the land was left unexplored? If so much of the land was unexplored and open, why could it not be shared? I looked over to Nate.

As much as I hated to admit it, perhaps the future was airship travel. It would have been much safer for us at any rate.

The men now stood at a table, poring over a large tome of maps the ticketing agent provided. The agent glared at them, leaning on the counter as though he suspected they would suddenly make off with his book of maps and disappear into the street.

The ticketing agent recognized me and finally came over. "Your Indian friends, who are they?" He eyed them suspiciously.

"They're Sioux. She is my maid, and the rest are coming to do some work on my estate." It was the only other tribe name I could remember. I hoped I was thinking correctly. Hired hands drew very little notice back home in England, and I hoped the same was true here.

He waved his hand dismissively. "Ahh, who can keep them all straight anymore? There's so many of them damn Indians. Just be sure you have their papers in order, and make sure you have enough good, proper white folk to keep them in line. Put them babies in a good Christian school as soon as you can to teach them to be Christians. It's our responsibility."

I nodded, doing my best to look like I agreed. "Of course, it is our duty." My duty was to get Chelan and her family as far from this ignorant cur and others like him as possible. I could not get them home to their kin and the people who loved them fast enough.

"Hope you didn't pay much for the squaw, with a baby, they don't work so hard," the ticketing agent continued. "And you can't sell the babies until they're about five. Well, you can, but no one wants 'em."

I wanted to hit him. Righteous anger burned through me and, for a moment, I felt blood pounding in my ears. It was a heated, angry pulse. My hands were itchy and hot. My chest was tight. If I could breathe fire, I would. I would slice him with my fangs, I would spear him with horns.

A train rumbled into the station, the whistle a dragon's scream. I wanted to answer with a roaring challenge of my own. I opened my mouth.

"Viv, are you ready to go?"

Nate.

Startled, I turned and looked at him.

"I—Yes." I blinked, trying to remember where I was. I took a deep breath to steady myself. I still wanted to bite the ticketing agent, to breathe fire into his face, to watch him twist and writhe. I wanted to turn his hateful words, his spewed hatred, into a poison meant for his flesh and burn him alive.

I exhaled a shaking breath. *Now where had that come from?* I was holding the ruby in my pocket. I forced myself to let go, and took Nate's hand instead.

We decided to leave our possessions behind in the HeadHouse. Other than Joseph Carey's clothes, Nate needed a new change of clothes, so we took the stairs up to our room and filled our packs with clothing and our American dollars. I would not need my dresses, only my adventuring clothes, and I doubted that would change while we headed north. Then, we reunited with Chelan and her family. We had our small packs and my satchel of healing supplies, while Chelan had a bundle of clothes for each of her children. In addition, Chameli carried a small parcel of bread, some tea, and other assorted foodstuffs. Haimovi and Nacto had saddlebags and bedrolls tossed over their shoulders. In all, they were small and pitiful bundles for what looked to be a long journey by rail. I would have to do something.

"Nate, how much cash do we have?"

"Some," he admitted and handed me a few of our folded dollars.

I took the money and pocketed it. According to the clock on the wall, we had nearly forty minutes before our train boarded. I rushed out to the street and spied what I was looking for: a general store.

The scent of the place hit me like a wave. Cheese and sauerkraut, eggs that probably should have been sold long ago, pickles, paint on new wooden toys, onions and molasses, and beneath it all, the scent of kerosene.

The kerosene brought to mind all the men, the chaos, and death caused by the wendigo on the Carey farm. I shook the memory away.

I swept through the store like a woman possessed. I had the man at the counter set aside two large cheeses, a box of crackers, a dozen cans of vegetables, and four cans of fruit. I added a box of tea, a box of matches, a bar of soap, a packet of dried beef and another of dried fish. When the counter man rang up the purchases, there was enough in my pocket for two more packages of crackers, so I had those added to the crate, paid, and dashed back with the heavy wooden box in my arms. Well, dash was an overstatement, waddled was a better description.

Nate was pacing anxiously when I returned. He jerked the box from my hands. "Where have you *been?*"

I opened my mouth to answer.

"Never mind." He glanced in the box, hoisted it up on his shoulder, and we boarded the train into a private car. We immediately drew the shade, isolating ourselves from the rest of the passengers.

SOS

Hours passed, and the miles flew by, speeding us to Chelan's home. Meturato sat near the window, his face plastered to the glass. For a moment, he was a young boy enchanted with the world. Chelan smiled at him. Not for the first time on this journey, I wished for an airship, but not only for myself; I would love to see the look on Meturato's face as he sailed through the sky. He was so like my Nate.

"How long since you have been home?" I asked Chelan.

"It has been a lifetime," Chelan said with a small smile. Her broken teeth must cause her pain, but she smiled the small, secret smile of one who hasn't smiled in a long time. "My children have never been home."

"Why were you in St. Louis?"

She turned to look at me. Her black hair was caught back in a single braid, and her dark skin glowed in the sunlight. I had never seen her more radiant, never more beautiful. I had to know. She turned to look out the window again. "For my people."

It was a horribly simple answer, but I wanted so much more. Yet, it was enough. It was the reason I had agreed to marry a man I had never really known. Before Nate, I was engaged to a boorish man from a prosperous family, yet with a good name. I did it for my family. It is what was expected of a woman. It is what I thought my own people had expected from me.

Chelan turned back to me. The smile had left her face. "My people are buried in that land. Their bones lay there. It was our home for generations. Now, it is not." She looked at the baby in her lap who cuddled close in sleep. Her smile returned, broken teeth and all. "So now we go home."

"We should switch trains several times." Nate said, "Every time there is a large station where several main lines meet."

Haimovi and Nacto were already bent over the maps again. Haimovi traced a line with a finger. "Crossing streams diffuses your scent."

Nacto looked at his sister and the children, "Once speed would serve us."

Nate nodded, "Speed looks guilty. But we need to do our best to stay out of sight if we can."

Haimovi rubbed his eyes, "We need speed and luck. We can still be removed to reservations, should white people have the mind to."

"Don't worry about being taken." Nate said. "Viv and I have a plan for that."

I sat up straighter in my seat. He must not have told Haimoi they were traveling as our servants. Haimovi did not strike me as the type that would accept the ruse, even temporarily. He gave Nate a questioning look.

I gave my most placating smile. "If anyone asks, we are getting off at Quincy Station and you are accompanying us to work for us for a time on our new property."

"Remember, the next station, Quincy, on the Illinois and Missouri border, is a hub—a huge station where many lines converge. We will get on the next train on the line, but if they are looking for us, they will be looking at the train we are leaving instead. Just in case."

"Will it still take us north?" Chelan gathered the baby's belongings into a sack. There was a tremor in her voice.

Haimovi turned to her, speaking in comforting tones. For the first time, I was glad I did not speak their language. Whatever words of comfort he spoke were for her, alone. She nodded.

Chameli held her bundle to her chest, wringing her fingers and nibbling on her lip as we waited for the train to pull into the station. Meturato took one last look at the landscape as it disappeared and became a city, crowded with people, and he returned to his regular, surly self. He glared at the world from beneath his shaggy hair, though looking a bit paler than usual.

Nacto met every eye with the same confidence and easy smile that I assumed was his armor. It struck me, not for the first time, how similar we all were. Societies had their rules, but the core was the same. Our rules protect us and hide our true selves, cover our naked, fragile selves so we can pretend we are not fragile. It was disarming, I wished the ticket agent or the rail workers or the other Americans could see it, to see how easily we could share this enormous land. Then again, maybe not. Father and son were mirrors of one another, and Haimovi also looked like a dog, ready to bite. I wished there was a way to put them at ease.

"The next train on this line will only take us as far as St. Paul, Minnesota." Nate said, pulling out a map. It was printed on thin paper, and had tiny lines tracing the paths of the railroads crossing America. Most of the stations were not labeled, but marked only with dots. The major hubs were labeled with neat lettering. We spread the map out between Nacto, Haimovi, and Chameli. Chelan held her younger son clear to keep him from tearing it with his kicking feet. "From St. Paul we head west on the Northern Pacific Railroad, and that line runs straight through several states and puts us into Montana."

Haimovi pointed to a small unnamed circle on the map. "The closest station on the rail to the reservation is here, Forbythe."

"How far is that?" Meturato asked.

"Four days." Nate folded the map. "Give or take. Barring any unexpected delays."

Chameli chewed her lower lip. The wheels were turning in the poor girl's brain. Unexpected delays could be anything. Trains broke down, passengers could attack them. Someone could happen upon Joseph Carey's body or the bodies of the mob that had come to arrest the adults and remove the children.

I gave her the brightest smile I could manage, but I was also clutching the ruby in my pocket. Nate and I needed to get them home, and safe, to have Chelan's mother assist us with a child of our own.

Haimovi put his hand on his son's shoulder, his mouth turned upward in a small smile, pleased beyond measure that he was able to touch the boy. I imagined their time together had been limited to Joseph Carey's absences, and too short by far. Chameli took up a lock of hair and braided it as she stared out the window.

The steam and coal sent clouds of gray smoke into the air. My chest was tight, and my skin felt pierced by a thousand needles. I felt like I was in the mists of China again surrounded by the gentle pines and the soft pat-pat-pat of the ever-present rains and the *huli jing* poisoning Nate's mind with promises of eternal life and power, if only he agreed to be his companion for all time. Looming in the darkness, in the mist and hidden from my sight, stalking us with breath of fire, fangs like swords, and horns that could impale a man or knock down trees was Xihuan-Lung, the bane of mankind that the archer God was forced to slay and therefore damn himself until the end of days.

The glass was cold under my fingers. I was haunted by the dragon. No matter what my reasons, I had desecrated the grave of a sacred being and I was cursed. I was the architect of my own nightmare.

Now we were hunted by the wendigo. My hand touched the stolen ruby. It made the magic within me strong, stronger than it had ever been before. As long as I had it, I could fight the wendigo. But, even as I held the ruby, I could believe Xihuan-Lung was out there, waiting for us in the mist. She would be crouching, her breath reeking of death, and seething in righteous anger at giving all to the world of men, only to be met with still more greed. She was a monument to betrayal hunted, forgotten, and left to rot, her bones a shrine to her might.

"Viv?" Nate took up his pack. "Are you coming?"

I released the ruby in my pocket. He took my hand, still warm and throbbing from the ruby's touch. If Xihuan-Lung was, in fact, out there, I would meet her. I would stand between her and my husband and I would stand between the horrible people we met and the Carey family. If I stood before the wendigo, I could stand before this evil, as well.

CHAPTER NINETEEN

WE CHANGED TRAINS three times as we traveled the main line. It turned out Nate was right, as always. With Chelan and her children, and Nacto and Haimovi traveling as our peons, we were given more advice than I cared to even count about how to keep our Indian servants under control and the proper way to keep them passive. Other than that, no one looked at them twice. I spent long hours with the ruby hidden in my hand pressed against my flesh. Keeping it close helped insure the world was safe from a deadly, vengeful creature. It made me powerful.

It also made me fight with the one person I loved more than anything in the world. And the knowledge of both truths was a suffocating weight.

Instead, I turned my attention to the one thing that did ease my soul. We insisted our "servants" were well fed. I asked for extra milk for my tea, then drank it plain and gave the milk to Chelan so she could soak crackers for the baby.

I spent most of our journey feeling more ill than I could ever remember being before. I hoped, more than once, that it was proof we were finally expecting a baby of our own, until my body proved me wrong. My head pounded and I touched the spaces where the Tarot had once lived below my skin. The skin itself was tender. I was missing the insulating symbols. I was alone and exposed to the world like raw, aching nerves. I wanted to cry, but instead I was numb. *The Chariot, The Lovers, The Sun, The Moon, The Star.* I would never use them, I would never read them again.

I sat for the long hours between meals in our private car, looking at my cards, the heirlooms from my family, tracing the symbols with one, pale finger. When meals came, I gave my food to our new friends. My clothing grew loose. The Tarot under my skin was wasting away, and so was I.

The train was nearly empty by the time we reached the Forbythe Station in Montana. We purposely waited until the last moment to leave the train. Chameli fidgeted, bouncing the bag of clothes in nervous, jittery motions. Meturato practiced the Cheyenne language under his breath, whispering the words again and again.

I could understand their nervousness; this was a home they had never visited. It was the land of their family, the land they would call home forevermore. So far, we had been lucky, other than murmurs and side glances at out strange indentured servants, Chelan's family had attracted little attention. Nate and I, on the other hand, were constantly harassed by the porters and the other passengers asking why we would take such unique peons into our service.

Nate had an answer for nearly everything as he explained their great, tireless value as hunters and trackers, and their beautiful handicrafts and diligence at housework.

We purchased a small cart and a mule to pull it. We had eaten through all the supplies I had gathered for the train journey, so I made my way to the Forbythe general store. I had no idea how long it might take us to travel to the actual reservation, but it would not do to arrive as beggars. I loaded the wagon with potatoes and oats, dried fruit and cheese, bread and bacon, dried meat and fish. They also had a small selection of canned goods. They were expensive, but I bought them out. I also included sugar and coffee, knowing how popular they were back home. There was no tea to be found.

The journey was a pleasant one, for the most part. The cart only got caught in the deepest ruts and the men had to help lift it from the holes while the donkey brayed and twitched his ears at us. It would haul the cart gladly but would refuse to help when it got stuck. The silly beast just knew when it was stuck and gave up. Thankfully, the men were more stubborn in their task than the mule.

We followed a worn track of dirt and stones. It must have been the only path in and out of the reservation. The pine trees were nothing like I had seen in England, standing like sentinels, looking over the land of tall, green grasses. The mountains stood purple and blue, and heavily powdered with snow at the top. Below us, a lake, clear as glass, reflected the mountains back at the sky, making a great spine where they met. In the foreground, cattle and sheep grazed in pens, while well-tended fields and gardens spread their bounty next to houses made of slabs of stacked sod.

I was enchanted. The cool breeze caressed us, welcomed us. Surely, as hard as it was for Chelan and her children to leave their home in Missouri, they would be happier here among their people.

Haimovi scowled at the sea of squat houses dotting the landscape. "Horrible, isn't it?"

I blinked. Clearly, we were not seeing the same thing. "Pardon me?"

"Once, we followed the animals as they roamed this great land. They followed the seasons. We lived in xamaevee'e, great skin tent lodges. Our grandfather's grandfathers lived in these pit houses dug into the earth, and only when the earth was sleeping and cold. Then, our people took to following the great herds. That is how it was meant to be. Until the white devils forced us off our land and into reservations. Now, we turn the grass under in the summer as well as in the winter. We force the animals into pens so they cannot run and be free. Their souls forget what they are. They are as caged as we are. We build pit houses to live in because if we move off our lands, the whites will steal our children or drive us like chattel, further and further from the bones of our people."

I didn't know what to say. Though I was overcome with loss for what his people suffered, I could not imagine a life where there was no tile roof and fine brick walls to come home to at the end of the day. As much as I loved adventure and travel, I could not deny a certain amount of pleasure that came from being able to hand my worn boots off to our boot boy to polish so I could sink into a hot bath and enjoy a glass of sherry and a nice roast duck. I suppose it was all what one was accustomed to.

I was stunned that he was so upset with the beautiful valley we were riding into. I had never seen anything so magnificent in all my life. Even the rising mists in China were no match for the gentle rolling sea of grasses in the shadow of the purple-blue mountains and the fragrant pines. I am sure it was far from the life they wished for, following the large game, but if this was the life left to them, it was hardly the prison I was led to believe their reservation was. There was a beauty to this life that I could not deny, and if he thought this life was awful, he would be horrified if he ever saw my home in the English countryside.

But America was a vast place. If Haimovi and his people once roamed across all of it, following the large game, riding their horses and dragging their skin tents, then maybe what he longed for was more than even this beautiful land could provide. He longed for more than the land, he wanted what I had so desperately needed before I met Nate: a sense of self in all the vastness. Freedom. "I don't know that it's disgusting, exactly. Sad, maybe."

Haimovi gave me a peculiar sideways look. Then he nodded. "Sad, yes. I think you understand. You and Nate are our brother and sister, after all."

They had been gone a long time from their home. We were a long way from our home.

Nate was their brother. Nacto and Haimovi were *Hotamétaneo'o*, dog soldiers, great warriors of their people, protectors and defenders of those who needed their protection. They watched over the bones of their people where they lay in the earth and over the living that still walked the land. Nate was a warrior of the land, who looked over the people who needed him, namely me, my family, and our tenants. They were symbolic dogs, embodying the noble side of man, the protective, loyal side. Nate was more the literal side and, yet, they were the same. Man was both God and dog, powerful and gentle, loyal and protective.

I wasn't so sure I was a warrior any more. Nate may be their brother, but my only means of defending us was vanishing. The Tarot marks that had been burned away sent a phantom ache through me. I did not belong here.

CHAPTER TWENTY

NATE MADE A gift of the cart and mule to the men, along with the unused supplies to the Cheyenne people. While they were engaged with their new treasures and the mule was enjoying all the attention, Chelan handed her baby off to Chameli and she had me follow her.

Chelan led me to a cabin partially set into the side of the hill, with a roof covered in sod. It was warm, living earth, connecting it to the land. Windows had been cut into the front and covered with wooden shutters. It had a good feel. I immediately felt at peace. I hoped the Cheyenne people would eventually find happiness, despite being forced to remain here.

A woman sat outside, carefully separating the thorns and leaves from a purple flower. She rose, and mother and daughter embraced, both weeping and speaking in their beautiful language. I stood apart respectfully, trying not to intrude.

I had expected He'heeno to be older. Her black hair was streaked with a touch of silver, but she wore a dress made of leather with tiny little shells sewn in and woven bands of blue and red. Her hair was caught in two braids. She wore a small round pouch around her neck, decorated with hawk feathers, and flat disks of abalone hung from her ears. A red, gingham apron hung from her hips. She shifted and wrapped a heavy dark fur she had been sitting on around her shoulders. "What brings you to me, daughter?"

It took a moment for me to realize she was addressing me. She blinked at me, her fine, delicate features waiting with an inviting smile.

"I, um—" I suddenly didn't know what to say. He'heeno was not a magician able to grant a wish. What had I expected? I wanted my Tarot symbols whole and usable. I wanted justice for the people Geiger and the wendigo had murdered. I wanted justice for her and her family. I wanted a baby in my arms. I wanted to hold the ruby in my pocket.

Chelan touched my arm. She spoke to her mother. He'heeno watched my eyes, gentle, merciful, patient, kind. She was a mother and everything that implied.

Finally, He'heeno rose and looked me over. "The Great Chief is the mightiest of all hunters. His command of good medicine protects all his people and all the hunts. It is his great wisdom that grants the ceremonies of renewal for all the people of this land. It is his great medicine that will help you, and heal you."

"What sort of medicine? A tincture or an infusion? Or something else entirely?"

Chelan smiled. "Medicine is the cure of the spirit. It is all that sustains us. It is the prayers of the spirit and the blessings of life. It is all that makes us what we are. It is…" she paused, searching for another word.

"Divine magic?" I offered.

Chelan looked pleased. "Joseph called it devilry. He forbade me to teach it to the children, but it is their birthright. For my children, it is as natural as the breath they draw or the water they drink. It is as natural as the sun rising in the east and the wind in their hair. We are one with the land. The medicine is part of the land."

The medicine may be a part of this land, but I was not. I bit the inside of my cheek. "Why would the Great Chief help me? I'm not like you. Not Cheyenne, I mean."

"The Great Chief hears all prayers, he hears all things, he is in all things. He watches over all prayers, all hunts, all songs. All one must do is ask."

I swallowed hard. I needed a miracle. "I wronged a great being on the other side of the world. I thought it was the right thing to do." I stopped. "No, it was the right thing to do. If she was freed, she would spread her wrath across the world. She was an evil beyond redemption. Even an ancient Chinese archer god thought so. It was a terrible choice. Would he fix me, your Great Chief, I mean?"

He'heeno looked at me, head to toe. Finally, she nodded. "He might, but he does not do these things blindly. For a great gift he asks us to make an offering of ourselves and our faith. Our faith in the order of things. Our faith in the people."

"What sort of medicine? A tincture or an infusion? Or something else, entirely?"

Chelan smiled. "Medicine is the cure of the spirit. It is all that sustains us. It is the prayers of the spirit and the blessings of life. It is all that makes us what we are. It is…" she paused, searching for another word.

"Divine magic?" I offered.

Chelan looked pleased. "Joseph called it devilry. He forbade me to teach it to the children, but it is their birthright. For my children, it is as natural as the breath they draw or the water they drink. It is as natural as the sun rising in the east and the wind in their hair. We are one with the land. The medicine is part of the land."

The medicine may be a part of this land, but I was not. I bit the inside of my cheek. "Why would the Great Chief help me? I'm not like you. Not Cheyenne, I mean."

"The Great Chief hears all prayers, he hears all things, he is in all things. He watches over all prayers, all hunts, all songs. All one must do is ask."

I swallowed hard. I needed a miracle. "I wronged a great being on the other side of the world. I thought it was the right thing to do." I stopped. "No, it was the right thing to do. If she was freed, she would spread her wrath across the world. She was an evil beyond redemption. Even an ancient Chinese archer god thought so. It was a terrible choice. Would he fix me, your Great Chief, I mean?"

He'heeno looked at me, head to toe. Finally, she nodded. "He might, but he does not do these things blindly. For a great gift he asks us to make an offering of ourselves and our faith. Our faith in the order of things. Our faith in the people."

Chelan patted my shoulder. "Do not be afraid, you are a friend. Maheo sees the hearts of all people and judges them by their spirits. That is how you will be judged. But you must journey to the great camp and plead your case before him, so he may judge your spirit for himself."

He'heeno took both my hands within hers and looked over the marks of my half-healed burns. "Spirits have been wronged by your actions, but your heart is pure, and you have done my family a great kindness. It is not my place to ask Maheo to intervene on your behalf. That is something you must do yourself."

I steeled myself with a heavy breath. "So how do we speak to Maheo?"

"Follow the smoke," she said, as though it was obvious.

"The smoke?"

She pointed to where smoke wafted gently up toward the clouds. "Maheo's great camp is above us. He oversees all that is, all that was, and all that shall be. And in his great camp is where people meet in the afterlife, and hunt and feast and live in peace and harmony with nature, forever. If you wish to regain your harmony with the spirits of the land and with those you have wronged, there is where you must go. Only Maheo can help you set things right."

I looked away. "Won't you ask him for his help?"

"I would, but this is a journey you must make yourself. Think of it as a journey both within and without. It is more than mere prayer. Prayer without belief is nothing. You must truly want the answers and the forgiveness you seek."

I chewed my lip. "I didn't mean that I wasn't sincere."

"I understand. But the journey is so much more than the destination. You could have sent my daughter and her children to me. Instead, you accompanied them, you and your husband ensured their safety. This journey is now yours. You must walk the path of Seana to the sacred camp and speak to Maheo. Why would you entrust something as precious as your fate to me?"

She was right. But, I was so tired of journeys. I just wanted to rest. I wanted whatever chasm had grown between Nate and myself to heal itself and for us to just go home. Then again, being on another grand adventure had done us a world of good. Guardianship of an estate and the people that called it home had all the appeal of a slimy, lukewarm eel pie in a warm, stuffy room for my dear Nate. It was liable to suffocate him where he stood.

"No, I would not." The moment I said it, I knew it was right. The safety of our home, though it held appeal only in its steadfastness, was the very thing that had led to our isolation. We had escorted Chelan and her children for their own safety, never mind that Nacto and Haimovi were more than capable warriors in their own right. "I will walk the path of Seana and visit with the Great Chief Maheo. With luck, he will understand why I acted as I did and he will see I was not being selfish. He may even protect us from the wendigo and end my curse."

The Great Hunter would see it. He would have to. I wasn't acting selfishly. Well, not entirely. Xihuan-Lung would not have stopped with murdering only Mr. Barrett and Charlotte and the rest of them, or even with Nate and me. Instead, she would have turned her murderous rage against the entire world. Hou Yi, the archer of ancient Chinese legend who was forced to slay the dragon did so for the good of mankind.

It occurred to me that Hou Yi had been an archer, a hunter. Maheo was the Great Hunter. I had only seen the silver casting of Hou Yi in the key to Xihuan-Lung's eternal resting place. Could Hou Yi and Maheo be related?

It was an intriguing thought, to be sure. They were on opposite sides of the world, and the people were so different, but I had never heard of Great Hunters before now.

We moved inside the sod house. He'heeno knelt and gathered dried herbs from various, tied bundles. I recognized some of the herbs as she moved between the bundles, dried and hanging from every available rack, frame, and niche in the walls. As I watched her, something even more interesting than herbs drew my attention. There were paintings, beautiful paintings, all over the walls, painted on leather which had been stretched in wooden frames.

"Is that an angel?"

Chelan shook her head. "That is the Thunderbird. Nonoma is a sacred force of nature, bringer of summer, the great thunder, and the banisher of the winter winds. Strong enough to banish the water monster, Menhe, and a powerful guardian of the people. Nonoma can carry the great monster of the sea in his talons like an eagle carries a fish. And, most importantly, Nonoma protects the worthy."

The paintings were beautiful in their simplistic design, all in stark colors. At first glance they appeared primitive, but that made them even more stirring. There was nothing gentle about their beauty. The power of them pierced the heart, with no backgrounds to confuse the eye, no flowers or mountains, no clouds, or birds. These were sacred figures. The Thunderbird with its beautiful white body had wings of red and yellow. He hung in the sunlight, making the wings of the summer bird shine.

Another painting hung in shadow. A forgotten spirit maybe? One to be approached with caution or fear? The figure rose and fell like a mountain range, like a snake in blue paint, with large red horns, jutting from a wide forehead, an open maw with curving black teeth and a forked tongue.

The blood in my ears throbbed so loudly a single thought beat against my brain in time with my pounding blood. *Xihuan-Lung. Xihuan-Lung. Xihuan-Lung.* I touched the wall for support. Bits of dried plants crumbled beneath my fumbling hand releasing their earthy scent. I swallowed hard, felt my breakfast at the back of my throat. *Breathe. Breathe.* I turned. "Who is that one?" *Please, no!*

"That is Mehne, the horned serpent," Chelan said.

I felt faint.

He'heeno shook her head. "One must use care when dealing with Mehne. She rests in rivers and lakes. She can bestow great gifts upon those she favors but can also eat men; it depends upon how she feels at the time. It is best to leave gifts to Mehne before asking for a favor." He'heeno looked up from where she sat grinding a mix of herbs into a fine powder. "Mehne distresses you. Come sit beside me."

I sat.

"My daughter tells me she sees a striped cougar that haunts you. It stalks you. It hunts your children."

I chewed my lip. "I have no children."

"Your children are trapped, they are prevented from joining you in this world. They cannot cross over to join you in this world."

"Where are they trapped?"

"The living exist in one world. The spirits exist in another. If you seek to free them, you must walk a dangerous path. All the wild spirits bend to the will of the Great Hunter. They do as he pleases. Maheo is the Great Chief of all that walks and crawls and swims and flies. He leads us all in harmony and wisdom. You must journey to his great camp and ask for his guidance. If he judges your actions to be fair, then he may command the cougar spirit to release the spirits of your children to your care."

"And if he does not?" I closed my eyes. If I could not be pardoned, then what?

"There is more to the value of women than their ability to bear children," He'heeno said, her hand on my shoulder. "There is great power in you, and great love. Motherhood does not define women. The medicine that empowers our spirits as women is strong in so many other ways."

I released the breath I didn't even know I was holding. "I-I want—" I swallowed hard. "In England—in my country, women are judged by the ability to bear children. We need to have them to pass our land and our possessions to when we die. We need someone to care for us when we are old."

"Your people will not care for you?" she asked.

"No, they will not." It never struck me before how strange that would sound to an outsider. These people would not have debtors' prisons. They would share food and cures with others, they would share work, they were one, large family.

"That is a poor measure of a woman's worth," He'heeno said.

"Yes, yes, it is," I agreed.

"Does your husband share that poor, unenlightened view?"

My Nate, how dearly he wanted a child to spread life and joy through our home, but he also wanted my happiness. He shared our home with Lum and his children. He welcomed those in need. He had said several times he didn't care about children, he cared about me. I had no reason to doubt him. A great weight suddenly lifted from my shoulders. "No. I don't believe he does."

He'heeno nodded. "I thought not. A man who would help bring my daughter and my grandchildren to me is no common man of the age. There is great power in you and to bring children to this world you must have a great power. But, there is something in you greater still."

I felt foolish, but I would have traded that power right then for the power other women wielded. He'heeno was right, women should not be defined by the ability to bear children, but it was still something I wanted, more than anything in the world, for myself and for Nate.

CHAPTER TWENTY-ONE

CHELAN INFORMED ME that Nate would be eating with the men. It was a great honor. I was happy to spend time with Chelan and her mother. Their knowledge of medicines and cures was impressive but, more importantly, they were telling me of our journey ahead.

"Along the path you will meet those wronged by the creature and wronged by the man that summoned him. They will be unable to find peace or complete their journey. They are ghosts that need to be heard. A medicine woman of great power can help them." Chelan offered me a flat bread that had been baked in a pan and a bowl of a rich, hearty mash of squash and corn, as well as half a fish, as wide as my hand, with charred skin and light, flaky flesh with a mild and smoked flavor. I took a few bites.

"Will they harm us?" I asked.

He'heeno accepted a bowl from her daughter. "No, the wronged dead do not wish to harm the innocent. They only need someone to listen to them. They long for someone to hear them, to tell their wrongs to. Once they are heard, they can leave the path and return to the camp of the honored dead, where they will join the Great Chief in hunting and rejoicing and rejoin their ancestors. There will be much feasting and the great spirits will never allow them illness or pain, again. They may look to you to help them. The Great Spirit looks favorably upon those that aid others."

I immediately resolved to help any spirit that approached us, especially if Geiger's monster was involved. He was a monster, and though not one of our making, I did feel a connection to his victims. "He'heeno, not everyone the creature harmed was Cheyenne. Many of them were white people, Americans."

She laughed. "Do you believe the afterlife is only for Cheyenne? We call the great maker our chief. Our name for him is Maheo. Your missionaries come speaking of a great God who also lives in the sky, able to make the dead walk, and who has a great camp in the sky larger than any other camp known or seen called Heaven, and his son Jesus. The missionaries tell of great monsters, demons that steal the life and spirits from the faithless."

"The devil?" I asked.

He'heeno nodded. "They say we worship false gods and accepting Jesus was all that would save us from the De-vil. If the life-drinker, the monster that devours men's reason and poisons their minds, is turned away by Jesus, he is not turned away by the crying of that most sacred name."

"Don't let my husband hear you say that," I said, half to myself.

"He believes in the power Jesus's name has?" Chelan smiled.

She was not challenging me. "He believes in the power of his faith," I explained.

"Ahh," He'heeno said. "Faith is a powerful thing. It is more powerful than a name."

Yes, we understood one another. Faith mattered more than a mere word. Faith sustained people. Faith sustained her people. Faith sustained Nate. Faith sustained me, for a time.

He'heeno shook her head. "That is why the white man fails when they steal our children and place them in their church homes. They can cut their hair, they can take them from their people, but their souls are still Cheyenne. They will always long to be with their people. They will always long to hunt on sacred lands with the buffalo and the deer, to sing down the sun, to breathe the holy smoke, and to sing the songs of their people. And they will do these things, in this life or the next."

The Cheyenne, no matter if they were moved or not, would always be Cheyenne. It was like, whether here or in London, I would always belong to England. I would always be my mama and papa's daughter whether they were living or not. Even before I met Nate, I was his. Even before I started my first grand adventure aboard the *Lightning Aura*, I was an adventurer. I just didn't know it at the time.

Of course, this was a pale comparison to having my culture and identity stripped away, but I could understand not being allowed to be what I knew in my heart I was destined to be. I looked away.

I was supposed to read the Tarot. I was supposed to wield its power for the good of those I loved. Or was I? Several of my beloved symbols had burned away. I was no longer sure that my faith was enough to sustain me. My blind faith in God was shaken when creatures like the Lamia and the dead men of Molten Cay were allowed on this earth. Father Henri was a priest and an educated man. His faith sustained him. But I struggled to reconcile faith in God and the power of the Tarot and all the monsters and otherworldly creatures Nate and I had encountered together.

How did that strengthen Nate's faith and weaken mine?

He'heeno reached for me, her hand warm on my shoulder. "There are those who use our wisdom bestowed by the Great Chief for good, and those who use that wisdom for evil. For all the whites that cause us harm, I do not believe you ever will. If I can help you, I will."

"Thank you." I said, "I don't have anything I can offer you in return."

"You brought my grandchildren and my daughter safely to us. That is a kindness. Kindness offered is enough."

CHAPTER TWENTY-TWO

THE NEXT MORNING, we planned to start our journey.

We had more of the flat bread, thick with honey after dinner. The great bear was the sacred keeper of dreams, and our bodies would need sleep and the blessing of honey to keep us strong while our spirits journeyed. The bee was a special friend to bear, so honey was a special, holy food for this ritual.

It made as much sense as anything else, so Nate and I ate as much as we were able to hold.

We followed He'heeno into her home. Wooden shutters covered the windows, and thick blankets and furs lay on the floor. The cabin was quiet, aside from the occasional pops from a small fire.

"You both need to understand what will happen. The striped cat that hunts your spirit does so because of a wrong done to the spirit world. You must ask the Great Hunter to calm the spirit of the striped cat so it will allow your babies to come to you."

Nate nodded. He had a mission. He operated best when he had a concrete goal.

He'heeno turned to me. "Remember the paintings. Our gods are not so different from yours. They wish to protect man. They wish to aid man, but some require gifts before you can receive their help. If you encounter the horned serpent, you must appease her before you can pass."

I swallowed hard. The horned serpent. I could only think of one horned serpent. The one I had wronged by desecrating her holy resting site by breaking apart her skeleton where she lay in the sleep of death, the arrow of Hou Yi forever in her side.

I had done it to keep an unstoppable killing machine from slaughtering all the world, a tiny voice in my head reminded me. I pressed the voice aside. A sin, no matter for what reason it was done, is still a sin. We had no good choices. Just because I did it to save the world from Xihuan-Lung doesn't mean her spirit wasn't angered by my action.

He'heeno continued. "In order to appease the striped cat, you must speak to its spirit in its own realm. And, of course, ask the Great Hunter for his forgiveness."

"So, we have to travel to the spirit realm." Nate nodded to himself.

"You do," He'heeno said. "You must walk the path the dead take to the afterlife. It follows the path of the stars, the bright band that stretches across the night sky to the camp of the dead."

"How do we get there?" I asked. "I know you said, 'follow the smoke.'"

"I can set you on the path to the underworld," He'heeno said. "It is a long journey, and not a safe one."

"We understand," Nate said.

"No, you do not," she said. "You are trying to understand, but if you do not return in time your body will die and you will be trapped in the place between worlds. Seana will not take you and you cannot return to the world of the living. You will be a shade, trapped between worlds for all time."

Trapped for all time. She suddenly had my full attention again. "What is Seana?" It was not the first time she had said the word.

Chelan touched my hand. "The Camp of the Dead. You would call it Heaven. It is the place we all go when we die; it is the afterworld. It is the place where we all must go someday, but trying to cheat the journey can trap you in a place man is not meant to be. A place meant only for the spirits."

"Is that where the wendigo is?" Nate asked.

He'heeno shrugged. "Sometimes. It is a place that is neither good nor evil. It is a path. The pathway is just a way of taking the journey. But a journey is not a destination, and it is certainly not a place for anyone of the living world."

"How long will we have?" I asked.

He'heeno reached for my waistcoat and started unfastening it. "If you cannot return from the sacred path through the stars in three days your spirit will never find its way back from the path and your body will become confused. Your body cannot live without a spirit. Without a true death your spirit cannot make the journey across the stars to Seana. You will be trapped between worlds forever, until forever ends."

"Do people last less than three days?" Ever practical Nate had to know.

"Yes. If someone from the living world dies upon the journey they are lost forever. They cannot return to the land of the living and they cannot resume the journey to Seana. They are lost forever among the stars." He'heeno piled my belt and weapons off to the side and added my waistcoat to the pile.

Nate took off his own belt and weapons and waistcoat as well.

He'heeno had us lay down before the fire on the floor. The wood planking was hard beneath the striped woven blankets. "Do not be afraid."

Nate shrugged, an awkward looking motion from where he lay across from me. "How can I die if I am already dead?"

"You will not be truly dead; your spirit will be removed from your body. It is a sort of dead. If you do not wish to make the journey, I understand. You will find guidance. The spirits will not leave you to flounder alone. It is not their way."

I took a shuddering breath, "How will we know what we are looking for?"

"Do not worry, what you are searching for is the striped cat. The striped cat will find you."

The striped cat. I felt a little shiver. My mama called the sensation a goose walking over your grave. Mr. Quinn said the Chinese curse was a tiger stalking my shadow. The *tiger* would find me once I crossed into the underworld. I wondered if the dragon, Xihuan-Lung, would find me, too. After all, it was Xihuan-Lung I had offended when I disturbed her grave. If that was the case, once we crossed into the spirit world both a tiger and Xihuan-Lung would come after me. If I was killed there, I would be unable to go to Heaven. It mattered to me because that was where Nate would end up, lost to the path or not, he was a good man of faith. He would be saved.

But if I failed, I would be separated from him. Striped cat or no, dragon or no, I was going. I only hoped the spirit of an angry, wronged dragon could be reasoned with.

"Remember," He'heeno said. "I can only set you on the path. I cannot take you there."

I put my hand upon Nate's shoulder. He was tired, we both were. Our nerves were frazzled after being harried by the wendigo and the possibility of being stalked by Geiger. I wanted to go home, but I knew that if we did there would be no baby for Nate. Not now, maybe not ever. No matter what he said, even if it didn't matter today, it would matter soon.

We had to try. I was losing my mind. I could not continue to see these phantoms forever. And, if the wendigo was truly chasing us, then returning to England would not stop it. If anyone knew how to fight it, let alone defeat it, it would be here.

Nate, my champion, was nearly useless against the wendigo. It seemed to pull the very life from him. While that was better than turning him into a killer, it was only marginally better. I was not about to stand by and watch the wendigo chase us across the world, wearing us down until we had no way left to fight him, watching it murder those we loved, or turn them into murderers, before it finally killed us.

No, we needed any guidance He'heeno could offer, even if it was just to point us down a path she could not follow. "I understand."

He'heeno nodded sagely. "You are in need of healing."

I caught my lower lip between my teeth. "I am."

She started chanting. The words were gentle, flowing water, soothing and beautiful and hypnotic. They lulled me into the kind of senselessness that came just before sleep, when you knew you were dropping off and moving was too much effort. A rich, herbal scent floated on the air, mingling with the earthy smoke, filling my lungs. It was intoxicating, and I floated between the smoke and the chanting. All that anchored me to this world was Nate's hand, warm and sure in mine. I fought to make my muscles respond. Finally, I gave him a squeeze. Thankfully, he gave me a reassuring squeeze back.

I was not alone.

Suddenly, it was difficult to breathe. It was as though a heavy weight had settled upon my chest. My pulse raced. I was being squeezed, strangled. He'heeno had said we would be removed from our bodies.

I could not breathe. The pressure on my chest became stronger, it crushed the life out of me. I needed He'heeno to stop, now! This was going too far. My blood pounded in my ears. I couldn't move. I felt Nate's hand in mine, but he was so far away, like a chasm had opened between us, growing wider by the moment. The scent of herbs and smoke strangled me.

I got a flash of a card. A figure, pierced in the back with one, two, three, four…no ten swords, straight in the back. The figure lay on his stomach, draped in a red cape. *The Ten of Swords*—defeat, crisis, sudden endings, loss. I squinted. Everything went dark.

Oh, God! I recognized the cape! It was my coat, not red but wine-colored, and the waistcoat was my own brown corset cover. The dark hair was lost under the shadows cast by the swords. It wasn't a man. The stabbed figure was me.

I was dying.

CHAPTER TWENTY-THREE

IT WAS DARK. The sky was warm, smoky, and orange. A soft haze had settled across the land. The ground was a beautiful slate gray, with flecks of dark, shimmering blue. The sky made these colors. It was like I was walking in the sky itself, on the far side, not the side you see looking up, but the side God would see when he looks down upon man.

"Beautiful, isn't it?"

I wheeled around.

It was Nate. I rushed to his arms. He looked different here, wherever here was. He was taller...no, not taller, his chin hit the same place on the top of my head. Here he was just more. More imposing, more radiant, stronger, more charismatic. His dark hair ruffled as though an unfelt breeze taunted and teased him. His skin was radiant, the rough stubble of unshaven beard a stark contrast on his pale skin. He looked moments away from transfiguring into his canithrope self, but showed no sign of the colic that generally accompanied the transformation. Here, he was fierce. Here, he was a true force of nature.

Whatever He'heeno had done to me, to us, we were together.

There were no trees, no grass, no mountains, no animals. I could not hear any birds, just the soft, deafening silence. My boots scuffed the ground. The sound they made was instantly muffled, but I was reassured that my ears worked.

I felt Nate just as much as I could hear him. "Where are we?"

I did not have to look around. "I assume we are on the path."

"To Seana?"

"I suppose so."

Nate released me with a frown. "Then we have three days to find your tiger."

I searched his face to make sure he was not mocking me. He looked resigned, nothing more. My back ached as though I had actually been pierced by the ten swords. Well, just as the *Death* card did not represent a real death, only the figurative death of a way of thinking, I supposed the *Ten of Swords* might represent pain that evolves into something new.

"You are right, you have to let go to grow."

I knew that voice. I never expected to hear it again. I turned, afraid of what I might see.

Papa. He stood, waiting for me. He was thinner than the last time I had seen him. Whatever disease had taken him from me was gone now. He stood straight and tall, no trace of fatigue haunting his steps. There was no bluish tint to his skin, no hollow in his eyes, no sickly pallor.

"Papa!" I couldn't help it, I ran to him, my boots a faint pat on the slate ground.

He welcomed me into his arms. I felt the warmth of his body, the fresh herbal scent he always carried, licorice and sage and yarrow, the scent of an apothecary. No matter how many times he washed, the scent of healing herbs never left him.

Nate greeted him with a hearty handshake. "It's good to see you again, sir." Every eye was wet with tears. This couldn't be real.

Finally, I had to ask. "How are you here?"

Papa smiled. "I am guiding you both."

Nate's smile faded. "Sir, I have to ask: Are you real? Are you here, I mean?"

Papa's cocked his head and the smile faded, it no longer reached his eyes. He made a small clucking sound, like he wasn't sure what to say. Finally, he spoke. "I am, and I'm not. I am your father, Vivian. I am more, so much more. But I love you, more than anything, and that is the most important thing I can tell you."

I nodded, everything in its own time with Papa. "How did you know what I was thinking?"

"Ahh." He touched his nose. "I am dead, Vivian. This is the place of the dead. The rules are different here."

For some reason I found that extremely unsatisfying. "Oh."

He smiled at me. "And you are my daughter." Papa chuckled. "Oh Vivian, your mother reads the Tarot. She never had the magical gifts you have but she is more than a bit intuitive with the cards and she knows all their meanings inside and out. She could read them in her sleep. If you think for a moment that I do not watch over my only child as often as I am able, then you underestimate the love a father has for his child. Being dead allows me some privileges. Your thinking is quite transparent at times."

I wasn't sure what to think. It was a comfort to know he watched over me. It was also bothersome to know he may have seen some of my intimate moments with my husband.

"How do we find the striped cat?"

SAS

I wasn't sure how long I could walk the path the dead took to reach Seana, the camp of the afterlife. The hard, slate-gray ground kept playing tricks on my mind. It glittered in places like the sun on snow on a bright winter morning. But, as beautiful as it was, it was also disorienting. It was just uneven enough to require us to focus on putting one foot in front of the other, just flat enough that the orange sky seemed to stretch out forever. I felt as though I could see the very curve of the land and sky itself, much like when riding in an airship.

It was neither hot nor cold, but the air itself shimmered the way the air over a hot stove dances, distorting everything. When I turned quickly, I felt as though I caught glimmers of something four-legged stalking us, but I was never able to catch a good look. The vastness and emptiness of this place left me feeling stupid and sleepy.

"Papa, how will we find the tiger?"

He paused. "The tiger?"

Nate froze mid-stride, dragging me to a stop with him. "We are here for the tiger. Vivian saw it."

"Actually," I said slowly. "I never saw a tiger. Mr. Quinn told me a tiger would haunt my shadow. I have to set things right with the dragon I wronged."

Nate stared at me. "The dragon in China? That we cannot get to since the key is broken and lost? You seek to make things right with the dragon from China whose ruby you kept?"

America had been a mistake for us. Nate discovering that I had kept the ruby from him, participating in the death of Mr. Carey, finding out Geiger was still alive and working a new scheme, and that we were being hunted by a terrifying monster he had brought forth, and now knowing I hadn't been entirely forthcoming about why we were journeying into the underworld. I had assumed he knew, or he had figured it out, or that Nacto and Haimovi had told him. If I was being honest with myself, I had not been good at communicating with my husband, lately. A great distance had opened between us, and I would give anything to close it. I just didn't know how.

"I see the dragon in all things," I said. "I see Xihuan-Lung. I see her in the fire, and I see her in my dreams. I see her in the steam and smoke when the trains rumble by. Her roar is in the scream of their whistles. But most of all, Nate, I see her in the blood each and every month I don't give us a baby of our own to hold."

He opened his mouth to protest.

"I see you want one, I know you do. I do, too. You want the family you never had. I see it when you watch Lum's children play, or when you visit our tenants. I want a child to hold and love and teach the art of herbalism. Most lords, most landed men, will never give up a bit of their wealth to see their people fed. I know you don't see it, Nate, but most men would rather watch their tenants starve than lose rents. That's why they don't know how to respond to you. You weren't born to lord over men, Nate, but you are doing a wonderful job looking after the tenants."

Nate shrugged. "Dogs are loyal."

I kissed him. "It's more than that. You are noble. You are so much more than just a dog. It's easy for you to hide behind that. I may have believed that once, but you are so much more than that."

"Would you give up on finding the tiger and making amends with the dragon if we were to adopt lost children to raise as our own?" Nate asked.

There was true hope in his voice. He had been one of the children lost and forgotten. It was a worthwhile goal and one I could agree to.

"Unfortunately, that will not cure all that ails my daughter," Papa said sadly. "We are healers. We aid those that need our help. The dead need your assistance to rest, Vivian."

I put my hand in the pocket of my long coat. There was still a bit of fine powdery ash from the rubbery, fast-growing plant that had grown over the tracks and then burned away with the rising sun. The dead needed assistance, indeed. They called for help in the only way they could; by burning away the rails that had caused them to be murdered and burned, showing how they were cruelly cast aside and burned away.

§§§

We walked for hours. My feet hurt, my legs ached, and my lower back jolted with every step. "How long will it take us to get to Seana?"

Nate squinted into the distance, using his hand to try to focus his vision, not an attempt to shield his eyes from the sun, for there was no actual sun. There was light, the orange light, the color of glowing coals or sunsets, but the light didn't seem to come from anywhere, nor did it cast shadows over the land. "Hopefully less than three days," he muttered.

I had to agree. If it took too long, we would never leave this place.

Papa marched alongside me. The trek along the uneven ground didn't bother him in the least. He wasn't puffing, he wasn't sweating. He didn't struggle. In fact, he was the halest I had seen of him in years. "Oh, my darling. From what you told me, an airship is a fantastically wonderful way to travel but even the fastest travel of the age is not instant. There is still the journey to consider."

"This journey is a journey the dead take to the afterlife, Papa," I said.

"There is so much more than merely the destination, dove."

I was in no mood for his gentle wisdom now. "Papa, if we cannot reach the destination in three days, we shall be dead."

"You would not be walking it if you were not meant to be here," he said with an indulgent smile. "If you were meant to be there, you would be there. It seems to me we are not making much headway."

Nate and I exchanged a glance. As much as it irritated me, Papa was right. No matter how long we marched, the landscape never changed. We could walk forever without moving beyond this place. Three days or three hundred days, we would never make progress without, well, making progress.

"Tell me, Papa," I said, "what am I to learn here?"

Papa stopped and turned to face me. "Why did you keep the ruby?"

I turned. "The world is safe if I keep it."

"You, alone, can keep the world safe?"

"I couldn't let Xihuan-Lung out of her prison."

"You, *alone*?"

I blinked at him.

"Why did you not tell your husband?"

I looked away. Nate was pointedly not looking at me. He scanned the horizon, his shoulders stiff, his mouth a grim line.

"I-I-I don't know." I looked down at my tired feet. "I was trying to—" I couldn't finish.

Papa gave me an indulgent smile. "To protect him? Your heart is in the right place, but does he look like a man in need of your protection?"

My canithrope husband, strong and powerful. Though he was doing his best to ignore the conversation, he was biting the inside of his cheeks. No, he did not need my protection. Maybe he did from the wendigo, once. But he is my partner, in all things. I should never have hidden it from him.

"There is so much more to you. You are an adventuress, a wife, a partner. That is what he loves about you," Papa said. "That is all you need to be." He gave me a knowing look.

He knew we were here for my baby. Our baby.

I had never asked if it was something Nate needed. He wanted children as I did, but he had come for me.

"I have something for you," Papa said. "Something you may need more than I." He pulled the dragon's tooth from his vest pocket.

I took it. "Nate."

My husband turned.

"Here." I handed him the tooth. My partner in all things, he deserved to be my partner in this, too. He looked at it for a long moment then folded my hand back around it. I tucked the tooth into my pocket.

"Your time here will only be enough if you open your eyes," Papa said. "You cannot fight this monster forever. The monster is not of this world. It's like fighting death. There are some things even the most skilled of us cannot fight. Especially alone."

"She's not alone," Nate said.

"No, she is not alone. But just as the destination is not always all that matters, winning is not always the aim of a battle." Papa took my hand in his. "Why does a healer serve?"

"To help people. To ease their suffering," I answered automatically.

"Not to stop death?" he asked me slyly.

"You cannot stop death," I said.

"Vivian, you cannot stop this. This monster is death. It is evil."

"Nacto said it could be sent away," I argued.

"Sent away, but not defeated. Death can be delayed, people can be fortified, disease can be stopped for a time. You have tried to banish the wendigo before."

He was not looking at me, rather he was looking through me.

In this landscape of orange and red and gray stone, a hulking black mass appeared, blurring in the uneven wavering air. It was Geiger's monster. Just speaking its name may have summoned it to us. It was joined by a second figure.

"How fitting to find you here. The path of the dead," it sneered.

Geiger.

I moved between the monster and my papa.

Nate growled low in his throat, his shadow grew longer and taller, expanding into a monster to equal the monsters that stood before us.

The wendigo stared. It had beaten Nate before. It planned to do so again.

"How are you here?" I demanded.

Geiger gave us a smile. "Amazing what can happen when you apply enough pressure."

Then I knew that he had forced He'heeno to cast the same charm she had used on us so that he could also travel along the path to Seana.

"Kill them," Geiger said to his monster.

The wendigo slammed into Nate with a bone-rattling thud.

I did not hesitate. I had seen what the wendigo could do. I threw myself into Geiger. For a moment he was too stunned to fight back. My shoulder hit his stomach and we both crashed into the stone. Just the touch of him made me feel ill, but I choked back the revulsion.

Nate battled the monster.

Geiger rolled, trapping me under him. I pushed up with my hips as hard as I could. I needed a weapon but there was nothing for me to seize. I slammed my hand into the side of his face, raking my nails at him, catching his jaw. It unnerved him enough so that I could swing my elbow into his face. He shifted his weight and dug his knee into my ribs. His metal hand grabbed my wrist. I twisted to fight free, but his grip was too strong.

Behind me, bone splintered and there was a yowl.

I jerked my other hand free and slammed my palm into Geiger's mouth. I tried to roll away, but he locked a leg around mine. I pushed against his chest, but he was too strong. His natural fist slammed into my face. Dots exploded in my vision. I tried to gulp for air as my body screamed for breath. His arm was around my neck. I don't even know how that happened.

I felt a hand reaching for my trousers, searching through them, intimately, violently. I felt a choking sob tear through me. I thrust forward with my hands, tearing at scar tissue from the burns, slick and tough like old beef. I managed to jam my fingers into his eye and he let go of my thigh to bend my fingers back. I expected it, and I made a fist. I punched him in the groin as hard as I could. He doubled over and crumpled into the stone. The pressure against my waist and throat abruptly relented. I rolled away from him.

Gasping and bleeding from the scratches on his mangled face, he glared as only a man consumed with hatred could. I turned to see Nate straddling the wendigo, raining a flurry of blows down on his foe with canithrope claws, releasing bits of fur and shattered pieces of sun-bleached bone into the air.

It was a wrenching, cracking, grinding battle, but it was a strong, dark caramel form that stood from the fray, shoulders heaving, fangs drooling, snarling breath coming in hot, sharp pants. The wendigo was violently reduced to splinters, the moth-eaten, bedraggled pelt tattered shapeless.

Geiger stared. I took a step toward my husband. The wendigo was able to force Nate away from his canithrope form in the land of the living, but here Nate was stronger. Here Nate's mystical side was more than a man imbued with magical energy. Here, he was a force to be reckoned with.

Nate roared a challenge to Geiger.

I turned, had my papa seen this? But he was gone.

Nate straightened and slid back into his natural configuration. I had seen him transfigure countless times but this one had a unique feature. He struggled to remain standing, the bones of his face shifted away, but as I was used to seeing his dark caramel pelt fall away to be reclaimed by the earth, for it was the earth magic that supported his change and returned him to a man, instead of nude, pale flesh, his body was once again clothed in what he had been wearing before, from his boots to his waistcoat and his long coat. He wiped his mouth on his sleeve. If he was as stunned as I was by retaining his possessions, he didn't show it.

Geiger stared at his monster, defeated at our feet. His eye was swollen, and blood from the tears my nails made in his burned face was streaking down his cheek.

He was clearly furious we had defeated his monster.

There was a *crack*. The very land around us snapped. The battle had cost us precious time. We had to move on.

"You lost," I yelled between gasps. "Your monster is gone."

"Are you so sure?" Geiger said. "The rules for magic are different for everyone here, girl."

Nate grabbed my arm.

"Old world monsters or new, makes no difference here," Geiger taunted, spitting blood.

At our feet, the shattered pieces of bone from the wendigo shifted. There was another crack. It was a sound heard as well as felt, a sound that resonated in the soul and shivered the spine.

The shards of bleached bone shivered and trembled, and the pelt moved. Long bony arms reached out, splintered and broken. The air swirled, gathering the splinters of bone, calling to them like a foul wind. Broken horns reformed, hollow eyes, colorless orbs flashed.

Geiger smiled. "The wendigo comes for you."

"Run," Nate whispered.

We ran. We needed to put as much distance between us and it as possible, before it was fully formed. Run and think, fight with a plan.

We needed to find Papa. The camp of the dead had to be somewhere up ahead, but we had lost our way and the monster and the demon that controlled him chased us.

Nate dragged me along, our boots sounding like horse hooves on cobblestones. Geiger had been searching through my clothing for something. He had pinned me down. It was more than mere assault he had in mind, he wanted something I had.

We still had the dragon tooth, and despite Geiger's desperate searching I had the ruby. Its comforting lump dug into my thigh.

The ruby! The ruby had been a way to amplify my power to drive away the wendigo. He didn't have rape on the mind, he wanted the ruby. My hand clasped protectively over it. It wasn't just the ruby, I realized with sick certainty, it was the dragon. He had to have been the one who sought to reanimate the dragon in China! That was our proof beyond all doubt. Lot of good it did here, now.

"Nate, stop!" I gasped. I doubled over, I couldn't run anymore.

Nate stopped and doubled over, panting, staring back the way we had come, intermittently pacing in tight circles, one hand pressed against his side.

"You cannot kill the wendigo," my papa said, as if he had never disappeared.

For an instant, for one moment, I hated him, a vicious, irrational hate. He had left me to Geiger. He hadn't helped us. But the moment I hated him, it was gone. I was a child again, consumed with the same soul crushing loss as when we buried him.

"Papa," I sobbed. "Why didn't you help us?"

"I told you, that is not how you succeed here," he said sadly. "You cannot fight death. That is not the role of a healer."

"But—" I could barely breathe, I couldn't argue.

"You are a strong woman, Vivian," Papa said. "You are a smart woman. But once you get an idea in your head, you do not listen."

I stared at him.

"How does a healer serve others?" He touched my back as I leaned over, gasping. "What does a healer need?"

"Ruthlessness and compassion," I gasped, recalling his early lessons.

"A healer needs to do what must be done. A healer needs to act with compassion."

Papa was still my teacher in all things. Dealing with injuries required a certain measure of resistance to the unpleasantness. You had to harden your heart to the cries of pain while you set a bone or stitched a wound, drained a cyst or cleaned out a pus-filled wound, or told a family that a loved one would never recover. You also had to have compassion to those in need.

Compassion, like caring for those who could not pay, administering care to the wounded and dying, or to the sick when they needed help. Giving food or forgiving rent when you could.

"How can compassion defeat this monster?" I asked. "Injuries and illnesses don't care one bit if I approach with kindness or with mighty magic."

"I do not know, darling," Papa said. "You are linked to these people in a profound way. But I believe they are representative of all those seeking salvation. They need to be heard. They need peace. And it is our job to give peace when we can to everyone we are connected to. Our actions affect everything around us in ways we will never fully understand."

He was right, of course. I turned away and looked out across the land. We stood in a place where no living souls were meant to be, walking along a path the dead took to reach the afterlife. We traveled to ask the Great Hunter, the lord of all beasts, to make the tiger, or the striped cat, stop stealing our babies. If this was not an act of faith, I didn't know what was.

I folded my arms. Nate's hand was on my back. I had sinned against an immortal creature, and I saw her in all things. Nate and I were both paying for it. I needed to atone by apologizing. I should not have kept the ruby a secret from Nate.

There was a gurgle and a gulp. I turned. The wendigo was there, fully regenerated, fully restored.

The monster held Papa in its fist. The wendigo's bony fingers were wrapped around his throat, holding him off the ground.

I screamed. Nate's eyes opened wide as he turned.

Nate leapt for the wendigo's hand. I searched for Geiger. If the monster was here, Geiger could not be far behind. But, for the moment, it appeared he was gone. Nate had his seax in hand and chopped at the monster with heavy blows. The weapon could cut logs, but it did nothing to the wendigo.

I could not move the arm, it was a metal vise clamped around Papa's throat. I didn't have a choice. It had my papa! I had to use the ruby again. Immediately I felt my right shoulder burn. The King of Cups waited upon his throne of stone, overlooking the majesty of the ocean stretched out before him. But where there is beauty in the ocean, there is also immense power. Like my papa, the ocean is deep, and though it can be gentle, it is a force of nature. The Magician gave me strength as he united the elements, I needed his help to harness the power.

The harnessed power was a punch to the gut, but my aim was true. "Be gone!" I screamed, my voice cracking under the strain.

It caught the wendigo in the sun-bleached skull. It dropped my papa, who crumpled to the gray stone.

My knees buckled and I hit the ground hard. The impact brought tears to my eyes.

The ruby was so hot here. It fell from my hand and clattered across the gray slate.

In the brilliant red-white flash, the wendigo grabbed for the ruby.

Nate moved to intercept it. His booted heel slammed into the weakened wendigo and pushed it back. Nate slid the ruby to me. I dove on top of it.

The power channeling through the ruby burned my hands, a searing pain with a terrible throbbing, like a heartbeat, echoed through my entire being.

A skeletal hand with long thin fingers gripped my collar. I grabbed the hand, tearing at it, my fingers slipping between the fleshless bones. I kicked and struggled. The bones wrenched my fingers apart like furnace tongs. I gasped but pushed back.

My other hand got tangled in its foul-smelling, black pelt, clumps of the moth-eaten fur coming off in my hand. It carried the musty scent of improperly cured skins.

The throbbing pulse of the stone took over my vision and everything turned hot and red. I slammed my knee into the creature. Dry bones snapped and moved beneath my knee, but it was as if I had kicked a great stack of firewood, and was about as effective.

It jerked me into the air, away from the ruby. I released the bone arm and snatched the ruby up in my other hand.

The world turned alarmingly to one side. Nate wrapped his arm around the wendigo's neck and hammered several heavy punches into the side of the monster's fleshless head.

Sharp coyote teeth gnashed inches from my face as the wendigo opened its mouth. Inside was an endless void within which all light disappeared. I trembled with dread and jammed my fist beneath its chin to force the gaping maw away. Nate wrenched the head back by the antlers.

The wendigo dropped me onto my back.

The wendigo's bones made a cracking sound as it turned, slamming into Nate, hammering him as hard as it could. Nate blocked the punches, throwing them aside, but he was bound to miss one eventually, and the wendigo was frighteningly strong. Nate switched tactics and slammed his foot into the wendigo's side with immense force, then again, higher. The wendigo shifted with each blow.

I clutched the stone to my chest and kicked as hard as I could.

Nate dodged and aimed his next kick into the monster's other side. More bones splintered and cracked. Nate jerked me to my feet.

The wendigo wanted the ruby. Geiger wanted the ruby. I held it before me, the only talisman I had that could do it harm. The wendigo looked at us, its broken and malformed bones cracking and crunching as they returned into their correct alignment.

My papa lay on the ground. I dove for him. "Papa!" He was diminished, paler, a ghost of his former self.

"I cannot guide you anymore," he said. "You and Nate need to continue on now."

"I cannot," I said. I'd already had to say goodbye once, I didn't want to do it again.

"You can," he said, "and you will. I will see you again a long time from now. Tell your mother I love her."

He slowly regained his feet.

"Take her and go now, son," he said to Nate, who took my arm. I tried to jerk away, but my husband's grip was iron.

Papa stood between us and the wendigo. "Compassion, Vivian," he said,

"The only thing stronger than hate is love. It makes us strong when all else is lost."

"We have to go," Nate said.

"No," I said, still trying to jerk myself free.

"He is dead, he belongs here, we don't. He is safe here. The monster cannot harm him, not forever. He is protecting us."

"I have the ruby, Nate! I can protect him!" I cried.

"You can't! I don't think it's supposed to work like that," Nate said. He dragged me along, and we ran down the path away from the monster and my papa faced each other.

"Stop, stop," I gasped. "Can't run...anymore." My lungs felt like they were going to burst from my chest. "Have...to stop."

He swallowed hard. "It's killing you, Viv!"

"It's not!" My throat was raw.

"Your hands are burned." He gasped. "The marks you use to fight it are gone, scarred over." He pressed his hand to his side.

He groaned and paced in a small circle, trying to catch his breath. "You can't fight it," Nate said.

As much as I hated to admit it, nothing we did seemed to have any lasting effect against the monster. We were running out of options. I was running out of Tarot symbols. And, worse, we were running out of time.

CHAPTER TWENTY-FOUR

ROCKY PILLARS CAME hazily into view. I was tired, so tired, and all I wanted to do was rest.

No matter what we believed, we were all the same. I had been looking at it all wrong. I assumed the Cheyenne were being mistreated and, though unfortunate, it was not anything I could help with and that the affairs of the Americans—any of the Americans, white or African or Native—were not our affair. I was wrong. If this monster, this wendigo, could be stopped by appeasing the spirits of the wronged and we could calm the tiger, or the striped cat, and Mehne, or the dragon, then it was our duty to do so. We might not be able to help the plight of all the Cheyenne people, but for these people, for Chelan and her children, we could help.

My head was a jumble. Nothing made sense anymore. The only thing I was sure of was that we helped bring Chelan to her people and Geiger had followed us into the spirit realm. We had brought this evil to their door, and we needed to help fight it. Anyone with the means to help had a duty to do so.

The endlessness of the land left me disoriented. I struggled to keep moving. My legs were heavy. My shoulders slumped. Our baby, we had to find our baby, and the dragon, and the tiger. I looked down at my hands, blistered and burned. At least they didn't hurt here, not really. There was only a dull ache, like a sore tooth. Papa was gone. So many Tarot symbols were gone. I needed my husband and my baby now. I had to keep going.

My ears yearned for sound in this muted place. Then, as if by a miracle, my straining ears heard the kind of sobbing that Lum's daughter, little Mary Catherine, would make when crying for her absent mother.

I spun around, looking for the source of the sound. It cut through me. A child! Nate heard it and looked around, too. As if in response to our searching, the shivering, shimmering landscape shifted, and rocky terrain with boulders larger than a man seemed to materialize from nowhere.

"Didn't He'heeno say we would meet those the monster wronged?" I didn't want to see those wronged. I was afraid of what we might find.

Nate nodded. He continued to search the landscape, shading his eyes his hand, his mouth slightly down-turned.

I swallowed hard. "Hello?" I called. "Where are you?"

"Viv?" Nate raised a hand, warning me.

The wendigo made mocking sounds before, it lured like a child's cries, but I could not ignore this sound. "It's a child, Nate. I know it is. We have to help it."

He nodded. There was a muted clomp from his booted feet as he leapt onto another bit of rock.

The rocks shifted, wavering into a dark shape, before revealing a small human form. A little girl, no more than three or four crouched, holding a doll blackened and scorched by flames. Her feet were bare, blackened by dirt and soot. Her ragged hair hung loose, a dirty blond curtain. She sobbed and cuddled her doll.

"Mama?"

"Did the monster do this?" Nate asked.

"I want my mommy."

I knelt by her side. "Please, did the monster harm you?"

"I want my mommy."

Her skin was covered in ash, the edges black and peeling and raw red underneath. The fire had blistered her beautiful, fragile skin. I carefully took her in my arms, and was surprised that she weighed nearly nothing. Her limbs were rail thin, and the tiny bones beneath her skin were fragile and sharp like a bird's. She coughed and her breath smelled of smoke.

"What is your name?" I asked.

"Rose."

"Rose, I'm Vivian. My husband and I will find your mommy. What does she look like?"

Rose coughed again. "She's very pretty."

"Well, of course. She would have to be." Rose was here, she had been murdered by the monster. There had been children at the Tate family farm. She must be one of them. We would have to set her to rights. Hopefully, her mama was here, somewhere.

Hers were the tiny, fragile bones. Oh God. She would have been teething about a year or two ago, enough for toothmarks in wood to still be discolored. A child this size would cower from a fire in a small corner. I gulped hard. My vision clouded with tears.

I could see the bones, twisted and terrified, shrinking away as fire raged through their home. A fire set to cover a murder.

"Do you need me to carry her?" Nate asked. His hand was warm on the small of my back. "Is she heavy?"

I swallowed past the hard lump in my throat. "Horribly heavy."

He nodded. He understood and let me carry her without offering to take her again.

For just a moment, I was glad we did not have any children. The pain of being unable to protect the innocent girl even though I was not present for her death was the heaviest weight I ever carried. If we stopped Geiger years ago she would be alive. I would carry her with me until I died, if nothing else so she was remembered as a treasure that was lost too soon.

Ahead of us stood a woman, gaunt from lack of good food and from too much hard work. She had long, dark blonde hair that hung down her back in a messy braid. Most of her apron and dress was discolored with a dark blood stain. I could not tell the exact nature of the injury, but it felt like it would be exceptionally intrusive to stare while trying to determine what had happened.

She tucked a wisp of hair behind her ear. She was searching, looking far off into the distance, staring through the rocks and boulders as though they were not even there. I knew without knowing how I knew: She was *The Queen of Pentacles*, a woman in red and blue robes seated on a throne, lovingly holding a disc in her arms; the picture of a mother looking for a child. I could see translucent flowers sprout along the path where she walked, and as fast as they grew they were gone, so quickly there and gone I might have imagined it. She was a mother. And I had her child, whose breath smelled of smoke, in my arms.

"Mother," I called. "I have your child!"

Suddenly, she could see me, she could hear me.

She turned and ran to us, the blood flowing from her stomach, her dress, dripping down her legs and onto her feet.

Whatever had killed her was deep; a slash to the stomach. She would have been the one with a scored spine. She was murdered with vicious hatred.

"Mommy!" Rose struggled to get free.

I set her down. Her doll dropped to the slate and mother and child rushed to one another.

"Please," I begged in a whisper. "Can you tell us what happened?"

Nate touched my back. His hand moved gently down my arm and took my hand. I didn't want them to answer. I knew what had happened. I turned to Nate and set my damp cheek against his waistcoat.

"It is a monster," Papa said.

I wheeled. So, he was back. But he didn't quite *feel* right.

"Can you name the monster, Vivian?" he asked me.

"Hate?" Nate guessed.

"Yes," Papa said, "and no. The one that murdered them did not merely hate them. The one who murdered them saw them as less than human. She was below him. Unworthy of him."

It wasn't that something was wrong with him, he was just incomplete. He was there and yet not.

"How can you hate a child? A mother?" I remembered the body so burned that all I could find was a set of deep cuts along the inside of the spine. Everything else had been burned away. How could another human being be reduced to nothing but scored bone? Or perhaps what I should be asking is what could create such a horrible wound that would tear through a woman so deeply it would tear her apart and scrape the bones on the far side? How could that be anything but hate?

"That is too horrible a wound to be anything but hate," Nate growled. That came from the dog in him. The part of him that abhors those who bully and those who hurt the innocent or vulnerable. That part of him was offended. So was I.

"It is more than hate," Papa said sadly. He was also brighter than I remembered; he was glowing from within.

"The monster," I concluded. "Nate, you saw what it did to the men at the Carey home. It turned them into something else. It was the wendigo."

"The monster came later." The mother had her child in her arms, the girl's tiny head cupped to her shoulder.

"Who did this?" Nate asked through gritted teeth.

"The man," she said, distracted. There was blood in her mouth, as she spoke I could see her mouth was wet with it. It bubbled against her lips.

"What. Man?" Nate asked slowly. It was the voice of a lord.

I looked at him. We knew who it was. Why would he ask?

Nate's mouth was a thin line. It wasn't that he didn't believe. It was the pain of a man who would hear the name of his enemy spoken.

"Silver arm."

"Silver arm. Geiger."

We would have to face him. It would be him or us.

Nate nodded quickly. "I will make him pay." He was strong enough to bear witness to her murder. He would see justice done for her and her child and her family that was murdered and burned.

"Nate, honey." I felt cold. "She has what she wants. Her daughter."

The woman and her daughter slowly began to fade away. The shimmering mist reclaimed them. There was peace. Whatever had kept them on the path from the afterlife was gone.

But the peace was replaced with a nameless dread. Something awful was coming. The very air itself was warning us, and it was something I was not sure I could fight. Whatever it was setting these people to rest was making the air itself very, very angry.

More than merely angry, it was blood-rage. We had wounded it, not through magic channeled, but through compassion. It would not toy with us any longer.

Now, we were mighty. We had a true weapon that could wound this monster. It was greater than the sins of man that called the monster. I took a shuddering breath. "We can fight it, Nate. That's what Papa meant. We can defeat it through ruthless compassion."

The doll was gone. Gone was the tiny girl and her charred lungs, gone was her smoky breath, gone was her mother, gutted and broken, left to bleed and burn. But the Tate family farm had many more victims, and Silver Arm had left no one alive in his rampage.

I still felt the weight of her in my arms. No, more than the weight of her, the heavy burden. It was no accident that these poor people were harmed. Geiger did this. He was the only man with a silver arm. He believed he could use lightning and fire, use immense power to push the engines, to drive them harder, move them faster with less coal to make the Pennsylvania Railroad a grand power driven by electric lines.

In doing so, he had murdered this family. And how many others?

There was laughter, heartless and cruel. It surrounded us, but was impossible to locate.

CHAPTER TWENTY-FIVE

WE NEEDED A better ground to battle on, and we needed a plan. We had run out of room to flee. The ground before us changed. Instead of the usual, uneven gray slate, there was a great, dark void. The ground opened itself up, revealing a lake of inky black waters. It was so deep, it had no bottom.

I turned to find the monster that mocked us and our journey. Figures made their way toward us. More murdered victims of Geiger and his hate, hunched over and crawling along, begging for our help, I guessed.

No, these were stalking, crawling along in graceful motions, hips and shoulders rolling in perfect feline movement.

I stepped backward, and my feet slipped on the edge of the chasm. I could not look way from the cougars before me. If I did, I was sure they would pounce. Massive cougars, their tawny bodies heavily striped with soot, painted in ethereal symbols of both respect for the mighty spirit and fear of the hunter. They spread out to split our attention, to back us up to the void. One screamed. I thought of the baby that I desperately wanted in my arms and my husband at my back, standing by me, doing his best to keep me from falling into the ooze.

I was a wife. I wanted to be a mother, but I would not sacrifice the family I had for the one I wanted. If facing these cougars and atoning for my sins against the dragon would make things right again then I would have them both!

"No!" I screamed, "You will not take what is mine!" I shook.

My outburst made them pause. They stopped, their bellies nearly touching the ground as they stared at me, taking my measure.

If where we walked was the land, then the void behind us was the great river of this land. We could go no further without crossing. I reached down and touched the great void. It was sticky and cool, like black mud from the banks of the Thames.

Papa was right. Our destination did not matter, we were on a journey. We had to transition from one place to another. I was afraid I knew that lay below. I had seen the monster the Cheyenne were wary of deep in the waters. We would have to be allowed passage. I turned my back on the cougars. Whatever harm they could do to me was already being done. They were keeping my babies from me.

My heart grew cold and I felt squeezed so tightly, I couldn't breathe. I fell to my knees. The cats behind us, the void before us, and somewhere in all the emptiness waited Geiger—the devil—and his monster and all the people they had murdered. My skin felt as if it was being pierced all over by tiny needles, while my mind was being stabbed by daggers. I struggled to breathe and the stony ground dug into my knees, while the ruby in my pocket dragged me toward the cold, black emptiness in front of me.

The black ooze bubbled and frothed. Waves from the center caused the level to rise and move toward us. I scrambled backward but there was nowhere to go. Two sets of horns broke the surface, one set jutting forward, straight like spears, the other set curved back like a ram's, over two sets of eyes. It was a great serpent rising from the dark void. It was the monster from the painting from He'heeno's cabin. It was Mehne, but that was not all I saw, it also bore an uncanny resemblance to Xihuan-Lung, the dragon from China.

Of all the spirits painted on stretched hides in her cabin, Mehne, the water-serpent, filled me with dread. The others were helpers of men, but this one had a fickle nature. The monsters were never painted, to do so would attract their attention. Mehne's nature was as tempestuous as the waters. She could bless or curse you as she pleased.

A shape slowly materialized in the air around us and with it came a horrible sound. Screaming. So much screaming. The screaming grew to a piercing crescendo and, though it was feminine, there was also something distinctly inhuman about their cry, something warped and twisted, crying in rage and pain.

"Wendigo," I called to the monster, "I know you for what you are."

It stopped, the skeletal head cocked to one side, staring at me.

"Kill her!" Geiger commanded.

The wendigo continued to look at me, clearly intrigued. It stepped forward, bobbing, stalking, drawing ever closer. A part of me wanted to run, but I had to control my fear. Fear was what it wanted. Fear was what the monster fed upon.

I could not win it over. I could not hope to make it understand. Such creatures are not for understanding. Such monsters are beyond understanding. One cannot hope to explain compassion to a shark, or to a snake. The concept is beyond them. But the failing is not with them, it is merely a flaw in man to try to force that which makes us human upon inhuman things.

No, this was not even a tool of the devil, as I once believed.

The devil is a fallen angel, created by God, and therefore blessed with all the knowledge of what he is and what he lacks. An angel, even one hurled from Heaven, is a true higher being, able to feel pity, able to feel sorrow, able to love, able to hate.

The wendigo was merely a monster. As a monster, it can only feel pleasure and pain, but what it delights in the most is the hunt. When it hunts, it feeds. The consumer of flesh, life-taker, both a murderer and a destroyer of lives, its names were so fitting. The cold, empty eyes watched me, waiting to see if I would run. For an instant, I wanted to. My heart leapt like a hare starting from the brush. The wendigo sensed it. The empty eyes kindled, flashing the way a coyote's eyes did when caught by firelight.

I forced my fear down. I grew calm, and so did the monster. Interesting.

Geiger needed a strong body he could offer to the wendigo. One like my husband's. But Nate had a good heart. He would not be turned by this monster's evil taint. So long as good men remained, then evil could not find a home.

There was definitely a shortage of good men. The world of man is a sinful place and when good men were gone, it would grow darker still.

The eyes rekindled. A buffet of prey was laid out before it. All it needed was a body that could not be turned by the goodness, the spirit, of man.

The monster must have read my thoughts. It laughed.

Then, as soon as the horrific noise had come, it was gone. Madness. The wendigo made the sounds of madness if madness had a voice. I needed several breaths before I could speak again. My hands shook from fear.

"Your master has given us the key to your undoing," I challenged. "You thrive on fear. You are banished through love."

"I have no master!" it said, using many murdered voices that echoed together in a horrible cacophony of noise.

Nate took a step toward the wendigo. It turned and snarled at him with its fleshless face, its fangs bared in malice, the sound spewing forth filled with pure hatred. It slammed its bone hands into Nate, throwing him to the ground.

Nate may have distracted the wendigo, but had I struck a nerve.

"Mr. Geiger believes he is your master." I forced a singsong tone to my voice. Just how far could one mock a monster? "Geiger struck a bargain with you and he has the upper hand."

"The bitch lies!" Geiger snarled. "Kill her!"

"See how he commands you, 'kill her.' Are you not your own master? How long were you your own master before he dared call you to him with the promise of a new form?" I taunted.

"Kill her!" Geiger said again.

Nate rose and threw himself at Geiger. The two of them tumbled to the ground.

I scanned the landscape. We were on the wrong side of a scorched orange sky, on a flat colorless land. There was no cover.

We needed faith. We needed to ask for compassion to see this through to the end. We needed forgiveness. I needed forgiveness.

"Nate. I'm sorry I kept the ruby from you. I thought I was doing what was right."

I turned to Mehne. She rose up from the black waters.

He'heeno said Mehne's favor could be bought with offerings. What did I have that the water-serpent might be interested in? I had my wedding ring and the ruby. We would need the ruby to fight the wendigo again. I could not part with. Then I realized I did have a gift, an offering that meant more to me than anything else. I had given it away to the most important man in my life before I had met Nate. It was in my pocket now. I had set it in my papa's pocket before we buried him, and Papa had returned it to me here. He knew we would have need of it before the end of our journey.

Three inches long and slightly curved. A dragon's tooth.

"Mehne," I said in a voice stronger than I felt. "I give you the greatest gift I have. A piece of a dragon, a serpent long turned to stone." I pulled the tooth from my pocket. She turned her attention to me. For a brief moment, it was not Mehne but Xihuan-Lung; the Chinese dragon readied herself and took a deep breath. Her fire would melt Nate and me. It would murder us where we stood. If we were lost here, we were lost for all eternity, He'heeno had promised as much.

Mehne looked down at us. She growled, baring her stiff reptile lips. There was a gap in her teeth, behind a lower fang. *Mehne was missing a tooth.* I felt the tooth in my hand. It did not feel like stone any more but warm bone with a pearly covering of enamel where the tooth would erupt from the serpent's jaw. I stared.

With trembling hands, I held it out. The tooth rose from my palm and up toward the water-serpent. It was driven, called by its mistress. It floated into her jaw and settled in her mouth in the empty socket behind the lower fang.

Tears clouded my vision. I had cursed us by desecrating the grave of Xihuan-Lung. I hugged myself, feeling the same ache that had nearly crippled me, reminding me each month that there would be no baby to bless our marriage. These tigers, these striped cats, they were not in my head, Chelan had seen them. He'heeno had seen them, too. We needed to beg a favor of the Great Hunter. He was the master of all the beasts of the world. He could command them away.

"I am sorry. I am sorry for the wrong I did you." I didn't have the strength to cry. "You killed him. I mean when you—she—the Xihuan-Lung—" I didn't know how to explain myself. "Please, what can I call you?"

The dragon stared at me.

I licked my dry lips, my words barely more than a whisper. "Xihuan-Lung killed Nate when the arrow was moved. I broke the skeleton apart to save him. I would say it was to protect all the world, but that is a lie. I did it for my husband. I love him, and the truth is, I would do it again. I would not do it to save the world. I would do it to save Nate. The world already took my papa. It will take my mama. It won't let me have a baby. The world is a horribly cruel and unfair place. If I am to be damned for saving the one person I cannot live without, then I accept that I am cursed for my role in it."

I couldn't stand anymore. If the wendigo was going to come for us here, it would find us and the horned serpent. "I never meant to harm you. And I never meant to keep the ruby. I didn't want anyone else to find the key and let Xihuan-Lung loose upon the world. She—I mean, you —would consume it and turn it to a graveyard. The only way I could keep Nate and the world safe from Xihuan-Lung was to keep this." I held the ruby out.

"A dragon that has fallen out of balance is a terrifying monster indeed." Mehne's voice filled my mind, comforting and warm.

"I have had my fill of terrifying monsters," I said crossly.

"Hou Yi understood this. He was a mighty hunter. The ancient dynasty of Xia understood this. The Great Chief of the Cheyenne understood this. It is the burden of the mighty hunters to cull the strong, legendary beasts from the land as their coming foretells great and terrible events. The people call them fools. The people call them prophets. The people call them heroes. In time, they become myths or legends. We forget they were once mortals with lives of their own.

"Then, in time, new heroes arise," the dragon continued. "Do you know why the ruby is the center of the key to Xihuan-Lung's grave?"

Its beauty could not be the true reason despite its obvious appearance. I did not have the stomach to be witty with a god, so I let it pass.

"A key and lock are strongest when it is formed from pieces of a whole. The physical remains of the dragon, Xihuan-Lung, is set apart from the rest of the world of men, locked away. The only way to access it is with a part of her."

I instantly knew what the ruby must be. The ruby made my Tarot spells more powerful, it throbbed in my touch, it made me feel strong and brave and I was loath to part with it for even an instant. According to MeiLin, Xihuan-Lung fell out of balance giving of herself to men. She loved them too much. The ruby itself tried to pull me to the earth, pull me to the core of the land. A ruby, red as blood. A ruby that made my magic strong and seemed to pulse in my hands. I could use it to drive a creature of hatred away. What was stronger than hate? Love. "The ruby is a piece of her broken heart."

The dragon nodded her massive horned head. "She and I, we are one."

My voice cracked and broke several times. "Then I would return to you what was stolen. Mankind was not ready for and not worthy of such a gift. We love deeply but our love is rarely that perfect."

"I see true love before me," she said. "It is rare, but mortals are capable."

I thought I was too exhausted to cry. I was wrong. A hot tear of joy slid down my cheek.

The oppressive weight of the ruby eased, and I no longer felt pressed to the earth, drawn ever toward the center of the world. Mehne raised herself up, exposing her chest. Her breast gleamed. I slipped into the inky black, sticky waters. The waters came to my waist. I approached her chest, and like a giant magnet, the ruby drew me into her. I waded in, letting the power of the ruby pull me to her chest.

I pressed the stone to her breast and it faded from view. For a moment, the dragon's eyes glowed, then faded. I took a deep breath, the first I could remember in a very long time. I was glad to be rid of the crushing feeling in my chest.

Geiger screamed in rage.

Nate gave me a smile, warm but welcome across his pale face. At least this would no longer be between us.

"You have made my heart whole again," the dragon said, "and so I will do the same for you. The cat will hunt you no more. But you are in a place you do not belong."

I turned. The cat that had stalked us all through this place with unceasing measured steps, bowed. The cat was a spirit. It was a servant. Mehne was a god. The spirit that had haunted my steps and denied me my heart's desire took her leave; the tiger that had hunted my shadow disappeared like smoke on the wind.

Mehne was right. We did not belong here.

We still had to fight to get home.

But there was still one obstacle in our way: the devil and his monster. At least her heart was now beyond his reach.

CHAPTER TWENTY-SIX

I TURNED TOWARD the nameless dread that surrounded us.

"How did you come to be here?" I demanded.

Laughter, menacing and mocking, surrounded us. I raised my chin. Geiger, through his monster, had murdered too many people. I was not afraid of him, anymore. I had seen too much.

The air shimmered. He was not afraid of me either. Geiger, tall and dark, square shouldered and polished on one side, solidified in the distance. In this place, his silver arm had an ethereal quality, gleaming with an otherworldly radiance. Anything else glowing this way would seem holy, sacred; this was obscene.

Geiger had been a handsome man once, before hate and indifference turned him and poisoned him. "Like everything else in this world, foolish wagtail, it is all about leverage."

I should have been offended he called me a whore. Though, honestly, if that was all he could think of to insult me, it was laughable.

"You made one of the Cheyenne set you on the path," Nate surmised.

"My pet can be quite persuasive," Geiger hissed.

So Geiger *had* forced He'heeno to send him here with the wendigo. He must have threatened her family, or her people. There was too much truth in him for it to be otherwise: too much pride and arrogance in his words.

"How?" Nate demanded.

"We have come to an arrangement, that is all you need to know," Geiger said.

"Why would a creature like that make a pact with you?" Nate scoffed.

He sneered at us. "Because 'a creature like that' is a monster from the old world. It is ready to enter into the new, but it needs a little assistance in making the transition. Don't worry, it is a matter you are not ready to understand."

"Geiger," I said, "believe me, old world demons are nothing to be trifled with," I said, remembering the Lamia and her flute made of a human thigh bone that called dead men from their graves. "They are more powerful than you can possibly imagine."

"As I remember, you are afraid of men seeking power," he said.

"I have no fear of powerful men," I said.

"Close your mouth!" Geiger was beside himself that I dared to speak to him.

"You have no idea what you're doing." Nate's voice was rough and dangerous.

"No, *you* have no idea who you're dealing with!" Geiger said. "I am the master of the wendigo. I can give him a body, eternal and lasting in the real world. I have the only thing he wants."

The air behind him wavered, dark and ominous. A dark chill coiled around me, cold and palpable, making my palms sweat. We were too close to the wendigo to run. It would catch us in a flash. Too many tattoo symbols on my flesh were still burned away and unusable after I had channeled power through them against the wendigo.

My mind raced. What could I use to burn him and force him away again? Before *The Sun, The Moon,* and *The Star* had forced the wendigo from the Tate home. Outside the Carey home, *The Lovers* and *The Chariot* had worked, but only because Nate had been in mortal danger.

Could I command him away by using *The Emperor,* by forcing my will upon the wendigo and, by virtue of authority alone, compel him to depart? I chewed my lip and decided probably not. I wasn't willing take that gamble, even if I added *Strength* to it for courage and control.

Whatever we were going to do, we needed to do it now. The figure forming behind Geiger was indeed the wendigo. The longer we delayed, the more solid its smoky, wavering form became. It took a bobbing step toward us, its hollow, gleaming eyes staring at us, amused, hungry, hunting like a cat waiting for the mouse to run.

Nate was not going to wait another moment. Transfiguring into another form was uncomfortable, no matter which form he chose, because both bone and flesh had to reorder themselves into either dog or canithrope. He generally groaned, doubled over from the colic-like pain of it but, this time, rage and maybe fear drove him.

Here, on the path to Seana, he was more. There were no words to describe it accurately. The canithrope form was larger, but back in our world it always had a shaggy, unkempt quality to it. Here, his fur was darker, sleeker, and shinier. The form underneath was stronger, more sinewy. Nate crouched, snarling at the skeletal monster.

CHAPTER TWENTY-SEVEN

NATE CHARGED INTO the wendigo, his massive claws flying, littering the ground with bits of shattered bone and rotting black fur. This may be the domain of the wendigo, but it was also a place of great magic, where spirits had sway, and whatever linked Nate and his dog, Ranger, was just as powerful as the evil of the wendigo. The soul-drinker had no power over Nate here. They were evenly matched.

The wendigo was stunned, if such a creature of evil could be stunned, and Nate was all too happy to take advantage of its hesitation. He struck a flurry of vicious blows, an avenging force for all those whom the wendigo and Geiger had murdered.

Geiger stood, similarly stunned, that his monster was ineffective against Nate. But there was no way I was about to let the sinner that held this monster's chain escape. He had me to contend with.

"Mr. Geiger!"

He tore his eyes from the battle before him with great difficulty. "Miss Harper."

I raised my chin. He may have banished my papa, but he would not banish me. "It is Mrs. Valentine now."

"Of course." Mr. Geiger smiled. The light caught his pockmarked face, casting shadows over his features, making him look moth-eaten and hollow.

"Leave now," I commanded. I was proud my voice didn't shake.

"Stupid girl, if all you want to do is talk, ask me 'why'?" Geiger said.

No, I knew why. He believed we ruined him, and in a way, he was right. Whatever plans he had had for the machine beneath Sterling's factory, for the leywell, we had ruined. Whatever he had planned for Xihuan-Lung's bones or the arrow that Hou Yi shot to slay the mighty dragon, we had ruined. Whatever he had promised Mr. Cassatt of the Pennsylvania Railroad, it was either an empty promise or one he had never intended to deliver.

"No," I said. "You are a murderer."

He laughed. A deep laugh that chilled me. "I am that, and more. But come, one more will be a small thing." He pulled his hand back, drawing on some foul power within him, twisted his body, and wound himself like a great spring. He whipped forward, his silver arm suddenly glowing hot, as a great gout of flame shot out.

I dodged. Barely. *What was that?*

There was no reasoning with a monster. There was no reasoning with the devil.

There was no Tarot card I could draw to mind that could act as a shield.

Dodging again would buy me nothing, and it would only take one slip-up for me to end up dead. If I died here, I was dead forever. I dove for him and we collided with a *thud*. If I could not win one way, it was time to get creative.

In our free time on the estate, Nate had taught me pugilism. And I was nothing, if not an earnest student.

My foot shot out and I caught Geiger at the side of the knee. He went down hard. His metal arm clubbed me in the chest, knocking the wind from me. I struggled to stand. I was an easy target now, and he knew it. Geiger knelt over me, his metal arm ready to conjure more fire, and at this distance, he could not miss. I was frantic. How had he learned to conjure fire?

Then it hit me! He managed to get inside his machine as the factory was burning and the machine was enveloped with leywell magic. He harnessed fire through the magic we had exposed him to.

I would have to fight with my heart. I closed my eyes and forced a slow breath into my body. *The Wheel of Fortune.* Everything has its turn. I was not done yet.

I forced another breath into my lungs; I would not die this way.

Geiger hovered over me. I was still on my back. I could feel my seax digging into my back. I rolled up on my side and stabbed it hard into his bent thigh. He howled and fell backward. The conjured fire blasted away, high above us, like a signal flare.

He screamed in rage and jerked the blade free.

I conjured up the image of *The Tower,* huge and crumbling, as the lightning strike of unexpected circumstance sent the people at the top scrambling. It wasn't much, but it was shelter.

A pillar of rock shot up between us, nearly taking my head off, immediately creating a barrier between Geiger and myself.

There was no way it should have worked like that, but a tower it was, made of shimmering slate like the stone beneath my feet, with shadowed depressions along the sides, squared and evenly placed. Those would be the windows, affording a commanding view of the land around it.

The symbol for *The Tower* on my torso was suddenly hot. Maybe here it did work like this. Suddenly, this was a fight I *could* win. I smiled.

Towers fell, that was the nature of change, the nature of control. *The Magician* unites all four elements to bridge the world between the spirit and the world of humanity. Concentration, resourcefulness, control. There were typically so many meanings but, right now, a literal meaning was best: balance and focus. In this place of amplified magic, I could unite elements and bend them to my will. I was the magician, here.

Geiger gave a scream of rage. The stone tower shuddered as he attacked it from the other side. He would tear the tower down to get to me.

I glanced over to Nate. He and the wendigo were locked in a battle of furious blows. Nate, in his canithrope skin, snarled, thick slaver dripping from his snarling maw, his ears pinned back in canine fury. They circled each other, sizing one another up. Then they crashed into one another in a bedlam of fur and hammering claws and teeth. Nate could handle himself. I needed to worry about Geiger.

A mad giggle escaped my lips. *Oh, was that all?* I had only to defeat a maniac consumed with hate, wielding fire, and with a monster at his beck and call. *Focus, Vivian!*

I didn't have the ruby anymore, so focusing great blasts of fire or light to just blast Geiger into oblivion was beyond me now. I doubted using fire against him would work, in any case.

Could I be more literal? *The Magician* united elemental forces to create magic. In fact, it was one of the most basic lessons of druidic magic. The minor arcana, the suits of the Tarot, were deliberately aligned with the elements. Pentacles were earth, swords air, wands fire, cups water, and the suit of cups lay beneath the skin of my right arm, all of them from *The King of Cups* at my shoulder to the *Ace* in my palm. It was worth a shot.

My tower of gleaming stone finally had all the punishment it could take. With a mighty crack, not unlike the lightning in the card's image, the stone yielded to Geiger's assault and came tumbling down. My tower threw no cloud of dust. It was not natural stone.

In this flat slate landscape under the orange sky, there was nowhere to go.

Geiger panted as he stepped through the rubble. "You. Stupid. Bitch."

I backed up a step, I couldn't help it. He radiated such raw hatred that it was frightening, even with a plan. His metal arm glowed, and in its menacing light the sweat on his face gave him a demonic glow that was almost as threatening than the wendigo.

He stalked toward me, one measured step after another, his metal fist glowing. I swallowed hard. I was running out of space. I did not want to run into the black lake where Mehne had disappeared. I changed direction and lured him to follow me.

Let this work. Let this work. Let this work. The thought repeated in my brain. I took a deep calming breath. I imagined water, clear and cold, flowing over rocks from a sacred spring. Water, warm and wonderful from a hot tap in a bath. Water, hot from a kettle. Water in a bucket from the wells of the earth, water flooding the streets and gutters of London, trickling off the leaves and plants as the earth welcomed the deluge of the weather. All these things were the power of the water, the comfort, and the majesty. I brought all the imagery I could think of to mind. My palm grew wet, as though I held an overflowing cup.

It was a wonderful start, but I needed more.

I closed my eyes. I forgot Geiger. I forced Nate and the wendigo from my mind, difficult as it was. Water was more than a gentle thing. Water was the power of a roaring river, it was creativity, it was fantasy, and it was all the mind could imagine. Water was emotion. It was hate, but it was also love. Love is the most powerful emotion, certainly more powerful than hate. I took a deep breath. If I couldn't stop Geiger, he would kill me. He would kill Nate.

I felt it. Deep, flowing through me in waves, moving with me like my heartbeat. I opened my eyes and turned to face him head-on. I needed to face him with my full heart. I raised my right arm to my chest. This power did not consume me as the ruby had. This was from within me; this would not harm me.

My arm burned as all the cups were suddenly thrust to the surface at once. They united and glowed blue, as water emerged from the elemental world and channeled to this place. It flowed through my own body with such force that I was bent forward. I tried to dig my toes into the slick slate to keep my footing. One foot slid backward. I stubbornly held on.

Geiger took the full blast of the water in the chest. It threw him backward, flinging him into the rubble of the shattered tower. He gave a strangled cry, his arm steaming in the water, growing into a lake that spread out across the slate. It looked just like the night sky, punctuated with tiny stars, beautiful and hypnotic.

I was pleased with myself.

The water shimmered, it was no longer the still night sky. Geiger, like some demon newly risen from hell, struggled to his feet. Battered and bruised, he bled from a gash that ran down the left side of his face. The blood mingled with the water, creating red rivulets. He whipped from one side to the other, thrashing like a wounded boar.

My mouth grew dry. The water had been my best weapon, and it hadn't been enough.

If I could alter the rules of this world, then Geiger could, too. A bolt of fire crashed into me like a great spear. I did not have time to think as my world exploded into a bloom of pain and fire. My face. My hair. My skin. I rolled, desperately beating at the flames. I tried not to scream. I needed to breathe, but I could not risk sucking in flames. All I was able to do was exhale. I heard myself scream, high and thin, a scream that did not sound anything like my own voice. The world spun; I lost focus.

Be strong, said a voice I had never heard before. *The High Priestess*, a gracious guardian of the unconscious sitting at the veil of awareness and all that separates us from the real and the world of intuition, the world of things we can sense but not always see. I rarely drew this card in readings; I rarely encountered her in life. She was always a herald of some great power, for good or ill. When last I encountered her, she was inverse and Nate and I were about to meet a creature intent on regaining her stolen power, even if it meant burning the world to nothing. Now she stood, radiant and warm, upright and welcoming. A promise of the light to come.

The High Priestess spread wide her robes and when she let them fall four women, motherly and loving, dark and fair, stood with her.

Four women. Did I conjure them or were they part of a dream? A nightmare?

A sword, a staff, a cup, a coin. One held a cup to my lips that muted my pain, eased the burning. The mother with the coin stood before me as it spun and spun. I was so dizzy, I could not breathe or I would vomit. As it slowed, it became a pentagram, the elements, balanced. All things in harmony; earth, air, water, and even fire with the spirit. Each could consume, if out of balance. The mother handed the staff to me. I needed to rise. I used it to regain my feet. The last mother handed me the sword, but it was not yet time to lay down the sword, my battle was not done.

The fires would not consume me.

I stood. My face was in agony, and I could not remember anything hurting so badly before. I could not see out of my right eye, so everything seemed strangely off-center. I raised my right hand and touched my face. It was sticky and bloody, my hair and clothing, my skin, probably more had melted away.

It was no matter. My bloody seax lay on the ground. It was only a seax, but it looked as big as a sword. In this place where there was no shadow, it was the silhouette of holy light that could vanquish darkness. *Courage and Victory*. For those without a victory. For those who could not fight this monster and win.

The wendigo had become mangled and diminished under the relentless battering from my husband. Nate was bleeding from dozens of minor wounds, and the ground was littered with splatters of blood, bits of bone and tufts of fur.

"Geiger!"

The madman turned and paled at what he saw. I had to look quite the horror, burned and mangled, but I was still standing. More than that, I was still ready to face him.

"You are a surprise, Mrs. Valentine."

I did not waste my time in talking.

He closed the distance between us quickly. He was determined to finish what he had started. I swung my seax. He caught it in his metal fist, twisting it in his grip, trying to force it back toward me. He was stronger, but I would not be pushed aside. I sidestepped, quick as a cat, and jerked my blade free. Geiger stumbled forward and I caught him in a wide slash across the back. He hissed. Geiger spun, swiping at me. His metal fist caught me in the kidney. It hurt. I let the blow push me a few feet away as I turned with the blow. I tried slashing at him with my seax as I went.

The *Five of Swords*. Win at all costs. I focused all of my energy upon my left arm, specifically my forearm, where the suit of Swords lay beneath my skin. The *Five of Swords* grew dark. Five stone pillars sprang up, hemming Geiger in, cutting off his retreat. They were thin and tapered, sword blades, symbolizing defeat.

Geiger turned back to me. For the first time, I saw uncertainty in his eyes. His mouth formed an ugly sneer. He was not about to give in that easily. His metal fist grew red-hot, then burst into flames. He reached out to grab at me. If he managed to get hold of me, it was over. I dove out of the way, my shoulder banging painfully into a rock. Hate burned in his eyes.

A deep snarl rumbled behind me—I knew that sound. To me it was comforting and it settled my nerves as much as it unhinged Geiger. His eyes grew wide at the sound. Nate had finished with his opponent. He stood behind me. Ready to assist.

I held up my hand to stop him. I would not lay down the sword. This was my fight, for the mother, for the child, for those who had been unable to stand against Geiger. He had murdered the Tate family and countless others because they stood in the way of his personal progress. Their deaths demanded justice. To take a life was a great and grievous sin. It marked a person, harmed them. This was justice.

Geiger reached out for me again with his flaming hand.

I let him.

He took hold of me. His burning hand closed around my throat. The flames licked at my skin. I could feel it charring, blistering, burning. I plunged my holy sword, the *Ace of Swords*, deep into his heart.

His eyes flickered with hate. The flames died. I closed my eyes and fell.

SŞS

Falling. Falling and burning. First pain, then cold. Then nothing.

Nate sobbed. The soft, shameless tears of a broken heart.

I fought to open my eyes—my eye. My right eye was blind, milky, painful, sticky, and cold. I could not imagine what I looked like now. The world was watery and wavery. Nate, wonderful, beautiful, loving Nate, cradled me in his arms, rocking me. I had moved beyond pain now. It was cold, a soul-melting cold that had sunk into my bones. I shivered.

Beyond him, Geiger lay crumpled in a heap, my seax buried deep in his chest. His metal arm was cold and still. The wendigo shuddered. The heap of fur and bone swirled as though caught in a gentle wind. The bits of shattered bone pulled itself together, reforming the horror back into the life-taker that awakened the secret sins of man.

My last eye leaked tears. We could not defeat this demon. We were going to die here. There was nothing left. I could not defend Nate and I didn't have the strength to call upon anything else to protect us.

Nate ignored it. Maybe he didn't see it. I'm not sure he cared. The ground around us had changed. For the last three days and nights it had been solid, like slate, with a beautiful, shiny sheen. The ground had grown soft. He'heeno had explained that the path to Seana was what the astronomers called the Milky Way, a bright path of stars in the night sky. We had been walking on God's side of the sky. And now I lay upon it, unable to move, as Nate held me. We would not leave this place. A heavy weight pressed against my chest, a smoke, stealing the air from my lungs, that settled upon me and I could not rise above. But Nate could. He needed to rise and move on to the camp. People needed him at home, too many lives depended upon him.

"Nate, I can't," I gasped. "I can't go any further." I was too broken to go on.

We had been here for a long while, but never before had it felt cold. My hands were weak, as though my limbs were lead. Nate hauled me into his arms, the massive canithrope strength bulging his muscles, nearly tearing his flesh as he dragged me along. We made it one step at a time. There would be no fighting the wendigo this time. There would be no tricking it with words. It would find us and, when it did, we would be doomed here for all time. We were not even supposed to be here. We only had been allowed three days before our bodies realized we were no longer within and passed.

Three days.

I looked at Nate.

I didn't have to explain, he already knew. We had failed. We were dying. We had been here too long. We had not completed the path to the great camp, or Heaven, or whatever the destination was. She had warned us the journey would consume us if we could not complete it, that we would become one with the sky for all eternity.

Was the ground we had walked upon the spirits of those who never completed the journey? Was it just God's view of the sky? Whatever it was, it was consuming us. I struggled in Nate's arms. He needed to run. If he could get to Seana maybe the Great Chief would send him back. He might have a chance.

But he didn't seem to notice he was sinking.

Finally, he sank down beside me. It was as though he was sitting on a beach as the tide came in and made the sand soft. Nearly an inch of his seat was already in the ground.

"Run." My voice was rough.

He turned to watch the wendigo. It had finished reforming and turned its exposed skull and glowing dead eyes upon Geiger. For the first time there was no interest, no play, only hate, tense, fierce, and vicious.

It apparently no longer had interest in us. The wendigo crept to Geiger's body, where my seax lay embedded deep in his chest. One long-fingered, skeletal hand pulled the blade free and examined the knife with great interest. The monster seemed to sniff the blood with its nose-less face, brought the blade to its mouth and licked it with a tongue-less mouth.

A shudder cut through me I knew had nothing to do with the cold. I swear the monster smiled. The wendigo took another bobbing step forward, throwing its shaggy, black body wide, and, like a great vulture, crouched over its prey.

My stomach clenched.

Flesh tore, bones shattered. The monster fed.

Nate turned his back upon the horrific scene and held me tighter. "I'm not going to run."

I closed my eye, letting my body fall deeper into the void. I didn't have the strength for anything else. He thought I wanted him to run from the wendigo. I couldn't summon my voice to tell him to run to the camp, not just from the wendigo, but for his immortal soul. I was not sure the wendigo wanted to catch him, anyway. And, I had to admit, it was a comfort to not be alone.

God help us now.

Judgment. The wendigo was passing its own form of horrible punishment. Geiger had made a deal with the devil and lost. But judgment was for all, and when we died, we would be judged for our deeds. In the Tarot, *Judgment* is an Angel, probably Gabriel, coming down with a great horn to judge the dead for their deeds in life, and to either welcome them to heaven or send them elsewhere. The dead are rising from their tombs, their hands raised in supplication, in trust. God would do what was just.

In the Tarot, *Judgment* represented judgment and rebirth but, most of all, absolution, a formal release of guilt or punishment. *Let this work.*

I slid deeper into the ground. Even Nate felt it now. He held me closer, his arms clasped tightly around my torso, but I was sinking. Even if he didn't understand what was happening, I finally did: I was dying. If he didn't let go, I was going to pull him down with me.

I summoned the strength I had left. I needed this to work. I shook then suddenly, possessed with vigor I could not name, *I demand judgment upon myself and Nate! Let all that he has done on my behalf pass to me, for good and for ill.*

The Tarot mark on my chest grew hot and sharp. I could not breathe, and the ground swallowed me up. The world screamed like a hawk, like an eagle. Like a glorious trumpet. Then silence.

CHAPTER TWENTY-EIGHT

IT WAS DARK. I had not seen the dark in what felt like an age.

My throat hurt. My back ached, and I was shaking. I didn't want to move. I hurt so badly, I worried that my flesh might just slough off and my bones lift right out. Tears dripped down my cheeks and I tasted salt and smoke. My papa was gone. I fought and burned and fell through the sky and I could not feel my husband by my side. All I wanted was for him to hold me.

Suddenly, hands were on me, peeling my eyes open. The world was blurry, but at least it wasn't the orange sky and gray slate ground. Somebody jerked me upright, painfully by the underarms, and then honeyed water trickled down my throat.

The sod house was dark and smoky.

"Rest," Chelan said. "Your spirit returned to your body just in time. Your body learned your spirit had left it behind. There was nothing we could do. You were dying. You both were."

I was so hoarse I could barely speak. "My husband?"

"He is strong. The thunderbird carried you both on his mighty wings."

I forced my eyes open. "Thunderbird? Does the thunderbird sound like a hawk?"

"Nonoma gives a mighty victory cry, calling the storms and banishing evil spirits. To some, Nonoma sounds like the thunder. To some, it is the cry of the eagle or the scream of a hunting hawk."

"Or a trumpet?" I asked

Chelan blinked at me. "I have not heard Nonoma's cry compared to a horn before. Why do you ask? But you must rest now. Your body is weak. It is good your spirit is strong. It is fortunate for the both of you. Your spirits were nearly gone for too long."

I looked over at Nate. He lay, covered in a woven blanket with colors too dark for me to see clearly.

The ruby was gone. I had grown used to where it always pressed into my hip in the pocket beneath my trousers. It had been my only weapon against a monster that made men tear themselves apart.

I was overcome with the need to feel something, anything. We were alive and whole. My shoulders hurt so badly, I could barely lift my arms. Though I knew I had been lying right here the entire time, it was the same pain I had experienced when Nate desperately held me as I was slipping from his grasp, falling though the wrong side of the sky, my soul dying.

I reached out and squeezed his hand in mine. He squeezed back. He was not sleeping, he was staring at me. The firelight made his eyes warm and welcoming. I did not think he ever stopped looking at me that way, but I didn't remember him looking at me that way in months. Then again, I didn't remember actually looking.

My hips, my thighs, my shoulders, everything, hurt. It was a deep, bone-weary ache that settled into me like I had been battered upon the rocks of the world and left washed up on the shore. I had lost so much. I would not lose my husband.

My corset lay with our boots, coats, and packs, all thrown together in one comfortable, untidy lump. We were so different here, not an esquire and a lady but a man and a woman, tempered by fire and magic. The rest could just fall away. And for the moment, this moment, everything was right again.

I crawled over to him and set my head on his chest. He must have felt like I did, weak and tired and, yet, wanting more than food, more than rest. We had traveled to the land where no mortals dwell. We had battled monsters and demons. I had striven to defend him with my life, while trying to keep my very soul. He trusted me with his sacred self. It was only fitting I remind him I would share my body with him.

We snuggled in a blanket, sharing small touches. Though we had never been physically apart, there had been a chasm between us for so long. The ruby had created a distance between us as I tried to shield him from the doom of the world. It had not been mine to bear alone. We were together, in all things, now and forever, Nate reminded me with a touch. His hands flexed on my hips. Beneath the blankets, his hands were warm. His touch was soothing.

The dragon, Mehne, took back the dragon's heart, and it no longer drew me into the earth. And perhaps it was just my imagination, but whatever else had conspired to keep Nate and me divided, it was no longer present.

Nate's fingers ran lightly across my skin, touching where the symbols should lay, searching for the raised marks of the burned-out Tarot symbols. They no longer hurt. Healed or gone, they no longer pained me. I returned the favor, tracing the scars left by the Lamia during our first adventure together.

I lay on top of him, letting our bodies match up, my knees resting to either side of his waist. It was the warmth of life, a purifying, loving heat, nothing so forceful or crude as mere fire. It was Nate, in all that made him powerful and masculine. It was the man I had lost in the ever-expanding responsibilities of running an estate. I never realized, until that moment, how much I had missed him.

§§§

Later, we lay with our limbs tangled under a warm blanket. I listened to his heartbeat slowly return to normal. I still ached, a delightfully wonderful fatigue of hard-won battle.

All was right in the world.

The monster—the real monster—was gone, as was his pet. The key was now and forever broken. With the ruby beyond the reach of men, locked in the otherworld and back in the possession of the dragon, it could never be used as the center of a key. My Nate was safe. The rest of the world was safe. I rolled to my side to ease the pressure from my hip. My husband lay with me, mated up like matching teaspoons in the silver drawer, his hand casually resting below my navel in familiar, comfortable ease.

CHAPTER TWENTY-NINE

I LAY WRAPPED in my husband's arms, listening to him breathe. I was home for the first time in what felt like an eternity. No matter that we were thousands of miles from our bed in England, this was home, beside Nate, this was where I was meant to be. Moments as wonderful as that do not last forever. We dressed and left the smoky comfort of the cabin.

My eyes blurred in the bright sunlight, I had not encountered actual sunshine in days. The village that greeted us was unnaturally quiet. Nate swept me behind him and glared at the sea of suspicious faces.

It was kindly meant, but I had just faced the wendigo and Geiger and made demands of a god. I was hardly going to be afraid now. "What's going on?"

A heavyset woman, missing several teeth but with a friendly smile, waddled over to us. She locked eyes with me once, twice, then again. She touched her beaded necklace, and beckoned for me to follow her with short fingers with cracked skin from heavy work, stained dark. We followed a few feet behind her.

She led us to several racks where a root I could not identify was twisted and laid out on frames to dry in the sun, past racks of reeking hides that had been scraped and set out for tanning. She pinched the roots, testing their elastic feel, and then motioned with her head to several horses that stood, snorting and rolling their eyes.

These were not Cheyenne horses. These horses were unpainted, and their manes were undecorated.

For one thing, they had what I come to recognize as western saddles, they were not the riding saddles I was used to from back home and they were not the saddles the Indians used for their own horses. These saddles had large horns for roping. The most telling thing was the gear they carried, not just saddlebags and bedrolls, but special pouches designed for rifles. The Cheyenne were not allowed to own firearms of any kind.

The woman snapped off a piece of the twisted roots and squeezed one to taste the juice that oozed out. "Haimovi and Nacto are meeting with their brothers to battle several of the devil's men. They hold He'heeno as their prisoner."

"How is such a thing possible?" Nate demanded.

"The devil and his men brought many guns."

Guns. The devil brought guns. The Cheyenne would be outgunned, literally. Nacto had told me his people were not allowed to own guns, either on or off their land. His people were forced to hunt with spears and arrows. But that would not matter to the men Geiger brought. I doubted they would leave without a fight. Geiger was dead, and whatever they were promised for their aid would go unfulfilled. They would be looking for something as payment. I looked up. The sun was still rising but nearly at its peak.

Was Geiger still up there being consumed in ravenous bites by the vengeful wendigo? If the devil was true evil then Geiger had been the devil, while the wendigo had merely been his latest tool. I had never seen a man so consumed by his own selfishness, his own desire to achieve, and with a willingness to harm anyone to reach his goals. The wendigo was a monster, a terrible one, but a monster that merely followed its nature. The true evil was in the man's soul.

Geiger would be here somewhere, or at least his body would be lying somewhere, watched over by his men.

He'heeno warned us that if we died there, we could never return to our living bodies. We would be lost along the spirit path for all time.

Geiger's men might not realize he was not returning to his body. "We have to do something before they realize Geiger is dead."

Nate nodded.

I pushed aside my fatigue.

§§§

I counted nine horses. That should mean Geiger and eight of his men. I was sure one of them would be Mr. Massey. We needed a plan. I was not willing to risk He'heeno's safety while trying to rid the Cheyenne of Geiger's men.

"Little Dog, you will come now," Haimovi said, grabbing Nate's shoulder.

Nacto waited with another warrior. Both men wore white feathers in their hair and painted black stripes down their noses and across their eyes. I had seen similar paint before—Chelan had painted Haimovi in a similar pattern before he went out to the Carey yard after the wendigo attack to protect him from the monster's sight.

The warrior touched his chest. "Tahopa."

My husband touched his chest. "Nate."

Both men were satisfied with the introduction. Tahopa was convinced we were not with Geiger and his band, and Nate was convinced Tahopa was an ally.

Haimovi pulled his knife from his side. "Tahopa has other warriors looking for more of the men that came north with the devil man."

"There will be about nine of them," Nate said.

"There are four in He'heeno's house," Nacto said. "They forced her to let him follow you. Great men make great enemies."

Nate smiled. "Then the Cheyenne are great men."

Haimovi gave Nate a hard, genial smack on the shoulder and the flash of a smile.

Nate and I led the way to He'heeno's home. Shadows moved within. The only windows were at the front of the house, shuttered against the sun and the elements. I had been in that home before. It was set in the side of the hill like the rest of the homes. While it protected the people from the elements and kept the homes from becoming either too warm or too cold, it also made sneaking up on the people within impossible. The only way in or out was through the front door.

Nate was unconcerned. He burst through the door and into two men. One knee slammed into a man, leaving him winded and sucking air with a wheezing gasp. Nate threw another man, Mr. Massey, into the log wall with a bone rattling thud. Nacto moved in on his heels, and pinned one man's arm behind his back, dislocating it with a pop. I knocked over the last man, one of the rail worker crew we had met. He blinked stupidly as he rolled, trying not to roll into the fire. He'heeno darted past us and into Tahopa's care.

He'heeno was free.

Near the fire, lay Geiger. I could stab him here. I could roll him into the fire. I could strangle him. I trembled. Hysterical laughter bubbled up. My lips trembled, and my chin did, too. On one hand, I saw myself dissolving into a fit of hysteria, while on the other, I thought I should check the man for signs of life. I had to. I had to be sure he was finally dead.

I swallowed hard. The last time we had touched, Geiger had been burning me, melting my flesh and turning my hair to ash. I had driven a sword through his chest, felt his hot blood wash over my hand and over my fingers, then down my arm in an evil flood of hate and greed.

I could taste the fire, hot and metallic, like an English penny pressed painfully into my palate until the oily taste of it made me retch. My fingers twitched, aching for the phantom weight of the *Ace of Swords*. The card was victory, crowned, and it was justice. I had found justice for those murdered by Geiger's bloodlust.

I knelt next to Geiger. My hands shook. I could not see his chest rising and falling with breath. *Please, please be dead.* His pulse was thready and weak, his skin cold and stiff. He was not yet dead, but I doubted he was truly alive.

His jaw twitched. I nearly leapt out of my skin.

Geiger's eyes snapped open.

I stumbled backward into two men. Mr. Massey cursed.

Geiger shuddered and regained his feet slowly, shoving Mr. Massey aside. He had never been a tall man, but now something about him was huge.

He cocked his head at me, it was a strange turn of the head, a motion no man would make. Papa's birds would watch us like that, first through one eye then the other, head tilted forward, bobbing to look down his strong Roman nose. One might expect an animal to stare that way down a beak or a muzzle. It was the look of a predator or a scavenger—the look of one that fed on the misery of mankind.

He strode past us as though we were not there and went out into the square where the Cheyenne warriors were gathered, painted for war in white and black, with white feathers in their hair and dots of sacred red. They were gathered around He'heeno, Tahopa, and Chelan, ready to fight.

I stepped back, stumbling into Nate. He released Mr. Massey and thrust me behind him. It was a futile gesture. Of the assembled warriors, only Nacto and Haimovi knew what he could do, and the last thing we needed was for the warriors to assume that we were aligned with Geiger and his men. He'heeno and Chelan might be willing to speak on our behalf, but if that wasn't enough we might be caught in violence against all who were not Cheyenne.

But it was not Geiger, it couldn't be. As arrogant as Geiger always looked, as cold as he was, there had been an underlying rage to him. The way he was moving now was more like the monster he had called forth, but confused by its very essence. It understood hatred, pain, and sin, but the wendigo was confused by love. It was angered by the compassion we showed Geiger's victims.

"Stay back!" I shouted. If they touched his skin they would be consumed by the wendigo's evil. They would turn upon each other.

I searched the crowd. Chameli held her baby brother in her arms. He would not be spared by Geiger. Haimovi stood beside her, ready to protect her. Meturato wore his hair untamed, still short as Mr. Carey demanded, but it was now wild. He had a spear in his hand, ready to stand and fight.

I tried to swallow, but my throat was dry. Geiger had died on the path beyond the stars, and still that wasn't enough to stop evil. Here he was, standing before us. I felt cold and every bit of me ached.

The Cheyenne warriors were not about to listen to me. They had no reason to. They knew what traveled their lands.

The men were ready for battle.

Haimovi carried a spear heavily decorated with fur and feathers. He led a group of warriors ready to stand against this demon. He hadn't been able to see the wendigo before because he lacked a connection to the magical and spiritual realm, but the wendigo now occupied a man's body; at least for now.

Nacto held a club with a heavy, shiny head. Beads and shells rattled with every step he took. Several warriors followed him.

Tahopa carried two hatchets, each with long shafts and ax heads the size of a man's hand. They were painted with ashy paint and the hafts had been wrapped with leather, which had been cut into a long fringe that swayed as he walked.

My hand flew to my pocket, searching for the ruby that was no longer there. I was willing to burn away more symbols to banish this monster yet again. Even though it would not grant us a permanent victory, it would buy us time. Fighting him here would guarantee death. Nacto, Haimovi, Tahopa, even Meturato bearing a spear like his father—men would bleed, men would die. I looked at my husband. He rolled his shoulders, readying himself to rush into battle in his canithrope form.

If God and dog are both opposite sides of man, then Nate was firmly between them, a man of power and loyalty ready to protect those he loved by virtue of a noble heart. Or die trying.

Nate snarled a challenge. The other men let out whoops. The wendigo watched us unconcerned, waiting.

My husband ran forward, his face contorted with pain, his jaw stretching and lengthening, his teeth turning into fierce, canine fangs.

There was a flash of recognition in the wendigo's face. Did he remember us from the path above? Did he recognize what could harm him?

The wendigo grabbed Nate's throat. My husband made a strangled sound, but kept driving forward. They pushed against one another, neither giving ground.

Nacto's club slammed into the back of the wendigo's knee. Haimovi's spear punched into its chest, jutting out the back and breaking the monster's hold, but the wendigo's spell had already affected Nate, and his transformation had been incomplete. His face returned to its normal color, his skull returned to normal human dimensions, his ears shifted back down, his shoulders shrank to a human width, and his jaw receded. Nate collapsed, panting.

It slammed its fist into Nate, two punishing blows that left Nate gasping for breath. There was no way I was about to let the wendigo continue to harm him. I grabbed the nearest thing I could find, a burning log from a fire under meat set to dry, and swung it with all my might. It connected with the monster at the waist, just above the hips, sending up a shower of sparks and knocking him to one knee. Nate took the opportunity to roll backward and out of reach.

Though my blow with the firebrand was well-placed, it was hardly effective. It turned and growled at me, showing teeth yellowed with tobacco and tea stains. I realized Geiger, intentionally or no, had transfigured himself into a pyromancer when he meddled with the leymagic at the factory in Sterling's Emporium. He had become a master of fire. Through my own skill with the Tarot, and the manipulation of it from a symbolic to a very literal form, I had been quite impressive in combating this magical monster in the realm of the unliving. With Geiger and his monster fused into a single, deadly form, Nate and I were grossly outmatched here.

It glared, eyes wide, as fierce and pale as the moon, as it reached for the firebrand. No matter that it was out of reach, it was the fire itself it called. It manipulated the fire, causing the embers to burst into a leaping, crackling, hungry monster, intent upon my flesh. I dropped my burning club.

The monster took on a ruddy glow, the flesh had a wet sheen, then it began to darken and peel. Geiger's face began to peel from the edge of the wendigo's skull.

The Cheyenne warriors were more than ready to fight this evil. They stood with grim faces, prepared to meet Geiger's men and the demon they had brought. Tahopa slashed the wendigo twice with his hatchets. I waited for the blood to flow and stain the earth.

The wendigo may be a new-world monster, but now the demon and Geiger were one. Geiger's flesh grew hot, deforming around the edges and splitting from the temple to the jaw. The flesh slid and fell, bouncing to the ground. The lupine skull was revealed beneath, and white, bleached bone and fleshless sockets glared at us. The body was still that of a man, with long, muscular limbs, one natural and one metal, with the entire form smoldering as though it would burst into flames at any moment. The metal arm glowed hotly, nearly molten.

He'heeno stepped out of her home, carrying an arrow. Tattered, ancient feathers floated in the waves of heat. Painted and decorated, she carried it aloft like a sacred object. She called to it in Cheyenne, raising it above her head, rallying her people. She was their medicine woman, their spiritual center, and they looked to her for guidance.

I did not understand the language, but the meaning was clear. *Stand, stand strong! This monster means us harm. Stand brothers, stand sisters. We are stronger than this evil!*

I stood with them. One of the warriors darted in with a spear, slamming it into the wendigo's knee. The monster's blood did not flow. Black smoke billowed from the wounds, gaping like mouths that screamed obscenely, longing to bite us.

The demon wheeled, and a gout of flame shot out from its upraised fist into the crowd. People shrieked and tried to run away. One man's clothes burst into flames. He dove at the monster with his knife, stabbing as he fell. He gasped and cried as the unnatural flames stole his voice, leaving him smoking and still. One of his friends grabbed his arm and jerked him free. A woman smothered the flames with a woven blanket of blue and yellow.

The Cheyenne set upon the monster, battering and slamming the great demon with their weapons as one great army, jabbing with their spears and smashing with their clubs. For a moment, I thought I saw Meturato slashing and crying out against the monster with his father and the other warriors, but then I lost sight of him. He was nearly a man, not quite a boy any longer, but I offered maternal prayers for his safety.

Still, the monster fought on, his metal fist burning and beating, the warriors' blood hissing like grease in a skillet wherever it touched.

Recovered, Nate joined them. I quickly lost track of him in the great orgy of violence before me.

The scream of the horses startled me, drawing my attention from the splatters of blood, the cries, the burning. A flash of motion off to one side made me turn around, my pistol in my hand.

Mr. Massey was having none of this. With wide, terrified eyes, he had sprinted for the nearest horse and vaulted himself into the saddle. The Cheyenne were unwilling to let even one of their foes escape. Two men fired arrows at Mr. Massey. The first shot went wide but the second struck home. Massey rocked violently in the saddle, but managed to retain his seat as he galloped away. He leaned low over the horse's neck, an arrow jutting from his right side, and quickly faded into the distance.

Several of Geiger's other men also used the chaos of the moment to cover their own escape. The Cheyenne called to their people. Mr. Massey was beyond their reach, but his fellows were not. One man managed to escape, but two others fell from their saddles while one never made it to his mount.

Warriors gathered to pursue the strangers who had fled.

The wendigo shattered the Cheyenne with his molten metal arm, cutting through them with a firebrand in the other hand. He grabbed one Cheyenne to toss him into his fellows. The man's eyes dulled. Would he start turning against the others like outside the Carey house?

The warrior's friends helped him up and they again set against the monster.

I blinked hard. How had they withstood the monster's corruption? Was it because they were Cheyenne? Was it because the monster was within Geiger rather than just the wendigo spirit? Was it something else? I had no time to ponder it. I needed to help them now. Men lay mangled in pools of blood, bleeding and dying.

We all needed help. We needed more help than I could provide with any Tarot spell I could envision. We needed more help than anybody here could provide.

He'heeno and I locked eyes from across the fray. We ran toward one another. Her people needed help. My husband needed help. Our presence had brought this monster here, as well as the man that had called it. Her arms locked around mine. Chelan appeared with her. He'heeno glowed with earned wisdom. She could lead us through this ancient moment, a cry to something greater than ourselves, our counsel, their counsel in this moment of need. She raised her voice in wordless song. Chelan, a mother who did everything out of love for her children and those children in in her care, raised her voice in pure harmony.

I stood with them. I was not a mother, or a woman of age and experience. I was a huntress, a woman of sensuality and power, something I never believed I could become. I blocked the battle from my ears and recalled the one Tarot card that might help us: *The Hierophant*, leader of the church, spiritual guide, and uniter. I surrendered to the deep community here. I let the voice in my throat, in my heart, come from deep within me, surrounded by my sisters. In this moment, we were all sisters and brothers facing a terrible evil.

And, from within us, our song transformed into something else. It was a cry, a trumpet, an eagle, a thunderbird. I became blind to the battle around me. The sounds of men fighting, the cries of pain, the thuds of flesh on flesh, the snap of bones, the slice of skin and muscle, all faded away. I was surrounded by wings, soft and gentle. A powerful bird with lustrous dark brown wings, a radiant white head, and a shining golden beak stood over us. A spider enveloped us with her web. A snake wound herself around our feet. A wolf trotted around us, her tail gently tickling the backs of our thighs. The scent of sage and sweetgrass overtook the scent of blood and fire. The circle we created extended to the land we watched over, so everyone and everything was strong and safe.

We were united and strong. The wendigo was weak. It would fall. Our song prayers raised their spirits. The people—the Cheyenne and my husband—battled this monster with renewed vigor.

Geiger had tried to make this circle when he called the monster. His circle had been smoky, salty, and incomplete. He had used charms to defend against the evil he called. We needed no such clumsy magic. Chelan and He'heeno chanted. I knew no such words. I breathed in the sweetgrass and sage. My body transformed it with all the Tarot magic I still contained, and I breathed out the magic, strengthening their prayer. Nate and I were not one of them, but we were welcomed as worthy allies. The Tarot symbols did not burn away, but instead glowed within me, gently enveloping me with a warm, golden sacred light like a blanket. I wept with joy.

I fell to my knees, and the sounds of battle came rushing back. Grunts and cries, the meaty sound of flesh on flesh as men and monster battled in the dirt. He'heeno and Chelan were beside me, our hands still joined. Our breathing was heavy, we were exhausted, but our job was done, we had bolstered our people.

The wendigo was on its knees, smoldering in a heap of half-melted flesh and bone. The man or the monster could take no more. Great gouts of smoke billowed from it and the Geiger-wendigo collapsed. Blood suddenly gushed from the ruined mass. The melted face was now a heap of ruined muscle and exposed bone. The tears in his flesh made by spears and knives leaked blood and were no longer gaping mouths of horrible black, but terrible wounds in very human muscle. Bones that had been shattered by clubs were now the pulpy remains of pulverized skeleton and flesh.

The Cheyenne, who had battled so bravely, darted in and out, challenging their fallen foe. Panting, Nacto and Haimovi waved them back.

Nate took one step forward. His hand shook as he pressed his fingers into Geiger's shattered neck. He looked over to me.

There was only one force on earth that could make me touch that thing again: Nate. I shook as I got closer.

Geiger stunk like rotten meat.

I turned and retched. Being dead, really and truly dead, had not improved the man one whit.

CHAPTER THIRTY

THE WOUNDED WERE a horrific sight to see. So many had been burned, battered, crushed, and mangled. Too many had been hurt. The Cheyenne would take a long time to recover from this tragedy.

Men lay on makeshift beds and spread out blankets, crying in pain. Their wounds were something I had never seen before. They were foul and rotten, deep and sharp, as if from a razor, but the edges were burned and dark like old wounds left to fester. These were caused not by a man but a demon. They needed a form of healing that was beyond my skill. Their bodies needed healing, but so did their souls. It would take medicines I did not possess to help everyone here.

I set to work doing what I could, while Chelan and He'heeno moved among them, saying prayers and wafting fragrant smoke, touching them with feathers and rattles and blessing their spirits to keep them strong. I did my best to treat their physical bodies, all wounded by the monster and by the hate it brought. I wished I could do more. My presence caused alarm in some of those I tried to treat. I was just as pale as those who had brought the devil to their peaceful home. I looked just like those who had forced them to live here. More than once, Chelan or He'heeno had to calm my patient.

Though I had experienced this before, being a woman in a field where men were more respected, I had never experienced fear and hate because of the color of my skin. My cheeks burned with shame. This was how they were treated. I would cry for them later, but for now I had to harden my heart. I was busy doing battle against the wounds the wendigo had caused.

The medicines I had at my disposal were woefully inadequate. The body was so strong, but the spirit was where the worth of the man was measured.

I recalled the conversations He'heeno and I had had over the herbs. She and had I sprinted to her home, where the bundles hung, waiting to be used. We snatched them up by the handful and threw them into my long coat, using it as a makeshift blanket to bring back a load.

She talked me through their application as we worked, and I learned as quickly as I could. It was both humbling and exciting to be an apprentice again. Prickly pear pads split open could make poultices to clean wounds, and so would yarrow, wild garlic, and piñon pine sap. Stiff goldenrod would control bleeding when bound to the wounds, with devil's claw for numbing and willow for pain. At least I knew about willow bark on my own.

I cleaned wounds and tried to neaten up the edges as best I could before sewing them shut. There was no shortage of clean water and garlic and goldenseal to boil for a paste, but I would have given anything for laudanum and carbolic soap.

Nate held hands for support and held men down when needed. His gift for languages allowed him to quickly pick up bolstering words of encouragement. He hauled water for us and ground herbs.

Soon, my eyes ached from the pain of battling death for the young men and women over the lives of these people. The smoke from the fires made my eyes sting, the steam from the boiling water I doused my needles in again and again before sewing wounds closed made my hands clumsy. Still, I worked.

The Geiger-wendigo was an evil monster. It had harmed and murdered so many. He'heeno and Chelan sang and touched the victims. They blew holy smoke into faces and waved smoldering fumes of sage and sweetgrass over their wounds. When their time passed, they had Haimovi, Nacto and Nate help lay out the dead.

SS

The funeral was the following day.

He'heeno raised the sacred arrow above her head, facing the structures, invoking a blessing to the homes that were missing beloved occupants. She turned to the bodies lying before her, stretched out in two neat rows, all dressed in their finest clothes, beautiful combinations of leather, decorated with beads and shells and paint, feathers and fur and clean, modern clothing from stores.

Great care had been taken to cover the wounds that had caused their deaths. I knew because I had covered many of them myself, binding them in linen, snugly, but not too tightly. I knew they were beyond caring but, for the living, comforting the dead still mattered. They almost appeared to be sleeping.

He'heeno said a prayer over the dead, and the arrow she held over her head shook from the effort. Nate's hand touched my back in mute support. His touch released something in me. Geiger was dead. The monster he had summoned was gone. I felt the true absence of it as surely as I knew the people lying before me were really gone. But the cost was high and I was so tired. Silent tears rolled down my cheeks.

I would have given so much to do more. I thought of *The Four of Swords*, where the knight slept below the earth in healing repose, attended by the four queens waiting to recover from great wounds until they were ready to rise again. I would gladly burn the Tarot mark away to give such peace to these people, and return them to their loved ones.

Nate's hand found mine, calloused and bruised, nails torn, and knuckles bloodied from battle and from moving the dead. Nothing felt more comforting. And still, my heart bled.

S§S

To all who called those people uncivilized or inhuman, I would challenge them to attend a village in mourning that has lost people to violent battle. The warriors valiantly rallied around the monster in their midst and bravely battled, striking it away.

The women who lost loved ones wailed their grief, crying to the sky. They cut their hair short and gashed their legs with sharpened stones until the blood ran down their calves and they walked barefoot through the center of their village where their beloved dead were laid out in neat rows.

The men unbound their hair, taking out their long, beautiful braids and leaving their hair loose around their shoulders, tangled seas of midnight, quiet, stoic, and falling down to proclaim their grief.

A part of me was stunned at even more blood spilled into the dirt, but it was a quiet, hushed part of me, silenced by the horror of the last few days. I wanted to dress these new wounds, treat them for pain, ensure against infection, and yet…there was a strange beauty to their shared mourning. These dead warriors had shed their blood to protect their loved ones. Those that remained behind shed blood in their honor. I took comfort in knowing that their healers would see to their hurts when the time was right.

On the fourth sunset, the moon rose, and the sky was clear. The ribbon of stars was bright, disappearing behind the dark mountain range. The souls of the dead would have finished their journey and would be in the camp of the Great Chief.

He'heeno oversaw the placement of the bodies, dressed in their finery, placed in a communal grave in the shadow of a great tree. They were all carried on litters of hides stretched between long branches. Then, by the light of the moon and stars, the grave was filled in and the mound of earth covered by stones to keep animals away from bodies of the honored dead.

He'heeno addressed her people. "Our loved ones are gone, but we must remember *Hestanováhe*, the life taker, is not gone from this world. It becomes strong when we are weak. We must love one another and keep goodness in our hearts. It is misdeeds against our brothers and sisters the monster craves and fear is what it feeds upon. That is why it was called by that devil."

The Cheyenne nodded in agreement. Their battles, their victories, their shared sorrows renewed their bonds to each other. They each reached out to their families in comfort.

Chelan stood by her mother, watching over their people. "We offer our hair and our blood to the creator for the safe passage of their spirits. Our beloved lost were great warriors for our people. They gave all for us. We give a part of us for their safekeeping."

It made as much sense as anything else. It was a sacrifice. It was giving all for someone they loved. I would give no less for Nate should the situation arise. I had burned my Tarot symbols away for my husband. I asked for the knife and without another thought I hacked my own long brown hair, grown rich auburn from our adventures in the sun, off at the shoulder, adding it to the pile of cut hair on the graves of the dead. They deserved my offering and my gratitude. We had brought this evil to their door. We had done our best to set it right. I stood in an ocean of misery.

He'heeno turned to us, her eyes wet. "We are strong. Remain with us until you are strong as well."

"You did not do this." He'heeno said. "The monster, Geiger, sought old evils that feed on the bad medicine in men's hearts. There is good in men's hearts but, in some, there is bad, too." She motioned to the smoke rising from a dozen small fires set around the bodies. "When you call an evil thing by its name, you draw its attention. That is never a safe place to be. You can be master of the darkness for a time, but never master of evil for long. The only way to master evil is to banish it from your heart and never let it infect you."

"How do we banish the w—the creature?" I asked. "Geiger promised it a body, one that is not dependent on the greed and sin of man. That will only grow."

"We realize our sins and forgive." He'heeno said, "We do our best to practice peace when we can, and when we cannot, we are swift and sure in heart."

Nate put his arm around my shoulder. He gave a small appraising glance at my newly cropped hair. He had bled for them, fought for and with them. We had burned their enemy, for it was also our enemy. We burned it with fire and, when fire was not enough, we tore the flesh from its bones and crushed them to nothing. I gave of myself. We are human, same as them and, yet, our loss was nothing in comparison to theirs.

CHAPTER THIRTY-ONE

HE'HEENO SAT WITH her people, sheltering and leading them through their long grief. It was another week before we were strong enough to leave. Our long battles and journeys had taken their toll, but I found that without the ruby, my mind was clear again. With a clear mind, the color returned to the earth and, with it, I found I could eat again.

I helped He'heeno and Chelan replace their stores of herbs and medicines and Nate helped hunt and fish. With many of their hunters dead, they needed every hand possible. At night, we slept like the dead, our bodies intertwined.

Finally, one morning, Chelan came and sat with me. "I will have my brother return you to the train station. You may return home."

Return home. Return to the land of the white people that were forcing her people into this little corner of the mountains. Haimovi was right. It was a prison. It was a tragedy. A cage with beautiful walls was still a cage. The Cheyenne were safe here, but only if they remained here.

As much as I longed for my home outside of London, I would be miserable if I was never allowed to leave. Nate would be beside himself and would rail violently against the very idea of incarceration, no matter how large his prison. Freedom was the idea that drove him to airships.

But this was not our place. We did not belong here.

We said our goodbyes. I embraced and kissed He'heeno, Chelan, Chameli, and the baby. Meturato came to see us off, glaring from beneath his shaggy hair and several pimples. I thought I saw him give Nate and me a small smile. It was as friendly as I had ever seen him. Haimovi and Nate exchanged back-pounding hugs. I was sure the goal was to break ribs.

I closed my eyes and said a prayer for the Cheyenne. I hoped they would find peace but, more than that, I hoped the Americans would grow to understand their brothers and live in peace with them.

Nacto hitched the cart we had given them to a strong horse, and we rode with him to the train station in Forbythe. I watched the houses and farms and animal pens disappear behind us as we left the valley. The mountains looked over the land, purple and proud. The dark pines were sentinels, watching over the people that had once been free to come and go, following the herds of animals that fed the Cheyenne, and giving them their wonderful houses of tanned skins. The lake was a cruel mirror. It showed beauty in a prison. It was a beautiful place they were never allowed to leave safely, unless they had specific business, and even that carried risk. The ocean of grass waved goodbye to me. I knew I would never see this place again.

At Forbythe, we bid Nacto goodbye. I could not help it, so I gave him a hug. He froze in shock before returning my embrace. He and Nate shook hands before Nacto headed off with a pile of hides to trade at the general store for goods they did not have on the reservation.

Nate and I went into the train station. It was strange to see so many people like us. They stared at my trousers and my short hair. We paid for tickets back to St. Louis, found our seats on the train, and collapsed in the car.

I felt the call of *The High Priestess* again. She was insistent but gentle. The symbol on my side was warm and inviting. I closed my eyes and drew the image to my mind. Positioned between pillars of darkness and light, sitting before the tree of knowledge with the moon at her feet and the crown of the triple goddess upon her brow. She is the gate keeper of great mysteries and the protector of faith and secrets. She keeps sacred text within the blue robes of truth that cover her body, she conceals and reveals much.

I always loved the card. As the keeper of sacred mysteries, *The High Priestess* used her great knowledge to teach rather than control others. I couldn't help but think her sudden appearance in my life as I battled Geiger and the wendigo meant she had wisdom to share. I just wished I knew what she was trying to teach me. Had she just come to me with all four of the great queens of the Tarot to help me rally, or was there something more?

I had more than enough time to ponder this mystery. The return trip would take us just over a week to return to Pennsylvania, by way of St. Louis to collect our belongings, barring any significant delays. It would also have us switching trains three different times to different lines.

Watching the country race by filled me with a profound sadness. This land was immense. We had traveled for days on end and we had not even seen the other end of America. Days would pass before we would see the lights of another town, before we would see signs of another human. And still, there was not enough land to share. The Cheyenne, and the other Native peoples, the Cherokee, Sioux, Cree, Pawnee, Navajo, Arapahoe, Crow, Ute, so many more people cast off and pushed aside because they were in the way. The people from the south, the Mexicans, were murdered and forced away from their homes in the name of progress. There was also a great number of people, descendants of slaves stolen from their homes in Africa and other nations, whose freed descendants were now sharecroppers, a legal form of slavery. The people were free in name but were treated little better.

America was supposed to be the land of opportunity. America was supposed to be the land where a man willing to work could make a life for himself and for his family. Instead, it was the same as in England. The poor were cast aside for the convenience of the rich. Their lives were worthless. We were not the wealthy who were careless with the lives of others, but we were gaining wealth by a system built on their backs. I hated it. I also hated that I could not see a way to change it.

Nate sat across from me in our private train car, sipping tea. I was so fortunate to have married such a man. Perhaps his humble beginnings made him care more about our tenants. Perhaps it was the sudden responsibility for the welfare of others. Either way, I was grateful. Nate would not cast others aside.

To truly love was to honor the truths of another and to try to understand. It was not love to force others to see the world as you do. The Cheyenne sons gave their lives to protect the people from this demon so, in turn, the people honored their dead with gifts of their bodies, their blood and their hair. God gave us angels. Maheo gave the people the thunderbird, Nonoma, to protect them from harm.

The Chinese Dragon was a creature of immense power that loved man and gave great gifts, but was corrupted through failing to maintain balance. She gave too much of herself for her love of man.

Devils and demons fed on the sins of mankind, causing their fall from grace or drawn to their failings. It was that way in the oldest place I had been, China, in the place I was born, England, and the new world I was now in, America.

No, there was only one logical conclusion. There is one united truth. All people are one, we merely call our gods by different names.

Gods, Angels, Demons, Devils.

We are all united. We are all one.

I felt faint, and set my forehead against the cool glass window of the train. The rocking was soothing. When I opened my eyes, I stared out across the darkening landscape.

Four women stood at the doorway of our car, looking at my reflection. I turned in my seat. They must have the wrong car.

The door was closed; Nate and I were alone. He was asleep, his arms folded, head bowed, the rocking had lulled him senseless.

I turned back to the window. The four women were still in the window, watching me.

Blonde, brunette, scarlet, and raven-haired, I knew these women, they were queens, the great queens of the Tarot, powerful and wise.

I had called upon the Tarot many times before, I had used the cards and the power they represented, but I only twice demanded the cards serve my will. The first time was to separate Prince Qixiang from his twin sister, for he used her for his own selfish ends and my sense of justice was offended. That was not love, but abuse. My throat still ached from the lash I received for exerting my will against the fate of another. I had paid for my arrogance.

The only other time I forced my will upon them was my demand for justice. I demanded judgment be brought upon myself for my crimes and to absolve Nate for the sins he had committed on my behalf. He did it out of love for me. Anyone with eyes could see that. If God could not absolve

Nate for all he did for love, then I would not owe God my faith. A God loved. A dragon loved. A man loved. A dog loved. We all loved, fiercely. That love raised us and forced us to act rashly.

If these great queens were here to punish me for my arrogance, I would already be suffering their wrath.

The Queen of Cups was beautiful and shapely. Her blonde hair fell elegantly over her shoulders, her blue eyes twinkled. Her gown was covered in silver scallop shells and at her throat was a silver trout. She held a golden cup in her hands offering her support.

The Queen of Pentacles stood next to her. They were night and day. She was a vision of night, the beautiful dark color of the African women. Her hair was short and curly, her features strong and proud. She wore robes decorated in patterns of vines and fruit, and in her hand, she held a bowl with a pentacle engraved in the bottom, full of bread.

The Queen of Swords had the beautiful skin of the women from China and Asia. Her eyes were a beautiful almond shape, her hair was thin and fine but dark brown, nearly black, and straight. She was lean and well-muscled, and in her hand, she carried a sword, the promise of justice for all in her path. There was a kindness in her eyes, a sort of mercy but also a fierce intellect.

The Queen of Wands was dressed in robes the color of sunsets decorated with lions. Her fierce green eyes watched me, her fiery auburn hair was caught up in beautiful coil of braids setting off her olive skin. A leather-wrapped book sat in one hand, a wooden staff in her other.

These queens, goddesses, spirits of all that women are and all that women could become, stared at me. And then, very slowly, as one, they reached out a welcoming hand.

I turned to Nate. He slept on.

The queens beckoned. Wands, Pentacles, Swords, Wands, the Tarot itself may indeed be a new construct, but it represented the elements that bound our understanding of the world. These were more than the suits, more than Queens, these were mothers. They were strength, passion, intellect, energy, possessions, and both the spiritual and physical worlds. They were all things. They were the things that bound everyone everywhere.

And then, as if they could read my thoughts, in unison, they each moved a hand protectively over their abdomens, cradling the sacred cauldron of life.

Sister.

We were sisters. They were women from across the world: mothers, healers, huntresses, warriors, lovers. Women had great strength within them, and we needed to support it in one another. We were so much more than a single, simple thing. I would become all these in time, or not. I was passing into a new role. I looked at my sleeping husband. He would be beside himself with joy but for now this was my secret.

I had spent my time following *The Hermit*, seeking to be led through the darkness to a greater truth and understanding. I had wanted someone to make sense of my grief and loss. I had to stumble through it myself.

The Magician is more than a man that bound the elements. It is a force, and women are a force of nature. We bind all things within us, as the sacred keepers of life, and we are mighty. As defenders, we are mighty, as lovers, we are mighty. We are mighty in all we do, and as a woman, I am mighty myself.

The knowledge was empowering. No matter what came next, I would face it well. I was *The Magician*, and my power was united in me.

CHAPTER THIRTY-TWO

MR. CASSATT DIDN'T bother to offer us coffee or tea. We had barely sat down before he spoke. "I understand you have been touring the railroads."

To his credit, Nate didn't appear rattled. He cocked an eyebrow at him, one leg crossed casually across the other. "We have."

"I see you were kept well apprised of our activities," I added.

Mr. Cassatt's clerk knocked and entered, juggling a tray of mugs and a coffee pot.

Mr. Cassatt nodded to Mr. Burris, who carefully poured the coffee into the mugs. The gentlemen took it black. I put sugar and cream into mine and carefully stirred it. I didn't really want it, my stomach felt off.

Mr. Cassatt took a sip, then set the cup down on his desk. "Mr. Valentine, I would appreciate your honesty in this matter."

I couldn't help myself. "And we would appreciate yours."

Mr. Cassatt pinched his mouth closed as though he tasted something he didn't care for.

Nate toyed with his cup, twisting it in his hands. "You heard her, Mr. Cassatt. You answer her questions, we will answer yours."

Mr. Cassatt glanced at me then looked at Nate again. "Mr. Valentine, you have to understand, the issue at the end of the line was—"

Nate held up his hand, cutting him off. "You will answer my wife's concerns, or I assure you our business is concluded."

It was a bluff. Most of our capital was tied to this railroad. Cutting our losses now would necessitate selling our remaining treasure from the Lamia's lair, our safety net. Thankfully, Mr. Cassatt didn't know that.

"You were employing a Mr. Newton Geiger," I said simply. I didn't think he would deny it.

Mr. Cassatt sucked his teeth. "I was."

"Why?"

"I suppose, since no one has seen him in more than a month, I can assume he has abandoned the special project. He assured me he could revolutionize locomotives so they would propel themselves across the track. It was our secret project to be announced later this year. Such a thing would have saved us hundreds on coal annually." He turned to Nate. "I'm sure I don't have to tell you, we could pass substantial profits on to our investors."

I cleared my throat, drawing his attention back. Whether he believed women were proper for business or not, he would hear me out. "I wonder, please enlighten me, Mr. Cassatt, how does the railroad expand when people with farms own the land the railroad wishes to move through?"

Mr. Cassatt gave me the indulgent smile one saves for precocious children. "You must not be familiar with the concept of eminent domain."

Nate poured himself another cup of coffee. "I'm afraid that power is reserved for the crown in England."

Mr. Cassatt turned to face Nate, happy to speak to him for a change. "The Pennsylvania Railroad achieved its charter in 1846, so it is quite old and respectable. Eminent domain is basically the power to take private property for public use following the payment or compensation to the owner of the property. We offer compensation—fair compensation—to encourage people to move."

I knew where this was going. "And if they won't move?"

Mr. Cassatt suddenly looked very uncomfortable. "We make several offers. If they refuse to move, we utilize the portion of land—as the railroad must—and pay them for that portion of the land. But it would be easier on everyone involved if they agree to move."

Nate and I exchanged a long glance. Finally, Nate set down his coffee cup and fixed Mr. Cassatt with a knowing look. Whatever silent communication men master with just a look, now passed between them. Neither flinched.

I hated to be left out of whatever passed between them as they stared each other down. "Mr. Cassatt, the Tate family is dead. Their land is the current terminus of your little railroad matter."

Mr. Cassatt turned to me. "Mrs. Valentine, I assure you, you are mistaken. My records in this matter are quite clear."

Nate didn't even blink. "Check."

Mr. Cassatt set down his cup and stood. "Mr. Burris, the file regarding westward expansion out of St. Louis, please. We made a payment to the Tate family."

"Outside of Maddenville," I added helpfully. Nate nodded.

"Outside of Maddenville," Mr. Cassatt hollered out to his clerk.

A moment later, the door opened, and the thin youth stuck his head in. "Of course, it will take a moment, but I will bring it right in."

I wondered how he would find anything in the mess he called his desk in a month, let alone a moment.

Mr. Cassatt turned to Nate, but then remembered that he was supposed to be dealing with the both of us and turned until he was facing both of us. "How do you know Mr. Geiger?"

To my great delight, Nate answered. "We have had the misfortune to deal with Mr. Geiger in the past. He will not be returning to finish the project."

Mr. Cassatt fixed us both with a steel-eyed glare. His mouth was a thin line. Were I not a woman he would be chomping at a cigar. I was sure only manners kept him from yelling at us both—well, manners and our investment in his railroad. Clearly, he was not impressed with being forced to speak to us both as equals.

Mr. Cassatt took a deep breath. "And why are you so sure he will not be returning to finish the project?"

How could I explain he was dead? His body lay buried on a Cheyenne reservation, but his soul had been murdered by a demon he could not control. Was that even believable to a man like Mr. Cassatt?

The clerk entered with a knock and a folder. "Mr. Augustus Tate took a payment in full for his land—quite an impressive sum, I might add—and left. Then we continued the line."

I reached out for the file "Mr. Burris, might I see that please?"

"What for?" Mr. Cassatt blinked at me.

I needed to know their names. The people Mr. Geiger thought were beneath him, disposable and worthless. More people worth crushing in the name of progress. "I wonder, do you have the names of the Tate family in your file? I was curious."

"We keep accurate records. It is part of the new census project, you see."

I nodded. "Of course." The file was a thin thing. A parcel number and survey coordinates for the land, a few sketches of the land, a map. A list of names:

> *August Tate*
> *Evelyn Tate*
> *Julia Tate*
> *Ian Tate*
> *Daniel Tate*
> *Rosie Tate*
> *Hattie Gates (colored maid)*
> *Clyde Gates (colored hired hand)*
> *Matthew Hancock (hired hand)*
> *Albert Booth (hired hand)*

There were ten names, we had found ten bodies in and around the Tate farmstead. I mourned them all the same but wondered which names belonged to the children. I had touched their bones. Hot tears welled in my eyes. Ten lives all wiped out for the land and money—and all that served as the record of their passing was this a sheaf of paper.

"And the payment?" Nate pressed.

Mr. Burris pounced upon a pitiful scrap of paper. "Ah, here it is, we paid Mr. Tate $11.36 per acre for his land. Quite a respectable sum considering the Pennsylvania Railroad holds the charter allowing eminent domain for seizure and use for the public good."

"Mr. Burris, how would that money have been paid out?"

"A cheque drawn against the railroad's funds, of course."

I already knew the answer, but I had to ask. "Would Mr. Geiger have delivered those cheques personally?"

"Why yes, he and Mr. Massey. Mr. Massey is one of our surveyors. That is over thirteen hundred dollars."

I had a hard time doing the conversion from pounds sterling in my head but even I knew that was quite a respectable sum. More than enough to tempt a less than moral man to commit misdeeds. "Excuse me, please."

I excused myself to the lavatory and was sick in the toilet. The sound of retching echoed off the clean white tile. It was much less impressive now. Murder for profit. Geiger was dead, Mr. Massey was probably dead or dying. The Carey family broken apart. Joseph Carey murdered, the mob murdered, and that was only what we knew of. Mr. Cassatt might not have done the crimes, but he had helped fund it. *We* helped fund it. We were not clean in this issue no matter our intentions.

Mr. Cassatt scowled when I came into the office again. "Mrs. Valentine, I was just about to bid your husband a good day. You know the terms regarding your investment and—"

"I'm afraid our terms will require further refinement," I said.

Mr. Cassatt looked from me to Nate as though he was pleading for him to do something about his outspoken wife.

"Mr. Geiger and Mr. Massey delivered the compensation to the Tate family themselves, didn't they?"

"They did."

Nate motioned me to continue. "Vivian."

I nodded. "Mr. Cassatt, we believe Mr. Massey and Mr. Geiger murdered the Tate family, and possibly others."

Mr. Cassatt's pen rolled noisily off his desk. "That is a very serious accusation, Mrs. Valentine."

"She would not say it if we were not serious," Nate said evenly.

Mr. Cassatt was silent. His pen had left an ink blot on the rich carpet. He was stiff, too stiff for this to be an entirely unexpected accusation. He clenched his jaw slightly, the actions of a man doing his best to hide anger at having a long-feared rumor being confirmed as true. The thumb of his right hand fiddled with the gold and ruby ring on his little finger.

"How much did Mr. Massey make in your employ?" Nate inquired.

"Sixteen dollars a week," Mr. Cassatt said evenly.

Nate shook his head. "Thirteen hundred dollars even split between the two men is a year's salary. It is not unthinkable. Unreasonable to murder for money, of course, but not unthinkable."

Mr. Cassatt was pale behind his mustache. "Mr. Burris, inform Mr. Massey that he is to report immediately to this office. Have Mr. Mullen send word to the western line."

I raised my eyebrows, at least we were being taken seriously now, "Oh, you will not find him there."

Nate nodded. "Yes, the last my wife and I saw of him, he was with Mr. Geiger in Montana intent upon harassing the Cheyenne peoples on their reservation. At the Tongue River Indian Reservation."

"Though Indians is a generic term. Those particular Indians are called Cheyenne," I amended. "Indians would be in India. If you had a map, we would be happy to show you. It is near China and Africa."

Mr. Cassatt gritted his teeth. I fought the urge to smile.

Nate, however, could not help himself. "There are many fine, lucrative investment opportunities there as well, and the Bombay Rail Company is looking for us to expand our stake in their railroad."

Mr. Cassatt was no longer amused. The red splotches on his cheeks belied a growing rage. "If you wish to withdraw your support from the Pennsylvania Railroad you are welcome to do so, Mr. Valentine. Understand, we will not be able to refund your initial investment. Our operating funds are currently lower than they were, but we are open to other ideas for expansion."

Nate leaned forward. "You wished innovation. You want to offer something no one has ever seen before?" Mr. Cassatt couldn't help it. He leaned forward an inch. "Mr. Geiger is not the way. All he brought you is scandal, angry investors, and lost profit in the form of wasted expensive steel. Such a shame."

Mr. Cassatt gave a slight nod. Yes, it is a shame, all that steel turned to rust, all those people, all that scandal, all that money paid to move people off their land—a land they couldn't even use.

Nate dropped his voice, forcing Mr. Cassatt to lean further in. "My wife and I visited the World's Fair in Buffalo, New York when we first arrived in America. So much is being accomplished with electricity. Electricity is the power of the future. Why not bring it to the people? We have seen electric streetcars. Why not expand the technology to run trains?"

Mr. Cassatt nodded, the great wheels of innovation turning in his brain. "There would be a cost to run the electric lines. But the price of coal is so high and the people in the large cities complain of the smell and smoke."

I did my best to be polite and agreeable. "Imagine the electric lines no longer soiling my clothes; the clear skies outside my windows."

Mr. Cassatt looked at Nate, the spell was suddenly broken. "I would need a new inventor."

My husband didn't miss a beat. "I can give you a name."

Mr. Cassatt stood and walked to the window looking over the streets of Philadelphia. He was quiet for a long moment. "It would have to be done in secret."

I was more than happy to change his mind about a woman's place in business affairs. "We can supply you with electricity in stable batteries for experimentation in secret until you are ready to unveil your great project to revolutionize travel."

He turned slowly to face me. His eyes flicked over to Nate. I was sure my husband was smiling at him. I was more than happy to let him set the hook in this whale. He was more than happy to let me reel him in.

"Very well, Mrs. Valentine. And what would you demand in compensation for this kind assistance to set the Pennsylvania Railroad above her competitors?"

"I am sure we can come to some sort of agreement," I said smoothly. Nate's hand found mine beneath the table. "Now, Mr. Cassatt. I'm sure you have heard of lightning hunters. There is a ship called The *Lightning Aura*. It is captained by the shrewd Captain Morgan, but the correct letters of recommendation will nearly guarantee his cooperation. Among his crew is a brilliant engineer named Eli Church."

SஆS

The train station did us the service of taking custody of our belongings during our meeting with Mr. Cassatt. I was glad to be headed home. We planned to realign our investments, we had the care of our tenants to consider and I had news to share with him. Our fortunes were improving.

"I was thinking, there are many places where the railroads are a fine investment. More importantly, we could make a fine, modest living by investing in our own tenants. If we help them replant their farms will yield more and their value will increase."

"We should also invest in airship futures." Nate gave me a sly look

"You win." I threw my hands up in mock exasperation. "We shall invest in the airships, my dashing pirate."

He grabbed me and swung me around in a big circle.

"Be gentle with me, Nate." I said, cuffing his shoulder. "For though you have a fondness for air travel, we shall be taking a transatlantic steamer ship journey home. I find myself disinclined to that brand of excitement given my *delicate condition.*"

Nate turned and gave me a look. I waited for the words to sink in.

"Delicate condition?"

I nodded.

"Are you sure?" He asked, squinting at me.

I thought of the Sisters on the train. The warm blanket of joy I had spent the last week wrapped in was better shared with him. His soft brown eyes crinkled and he swept me up in his arms.

"You shall be a wonderful mother, Vivian."

"You thought our lives were full of adventure before," I teased. "Just you wait!"

FIN

ACKNOWLEDGMENTS

SPECIAL THANKS to the friends and family who have given me their support, their love, their time, and their critiques as I ran down this path. It is all that I ever really wanted to be and thanks to you I am here. Special thank you to Rex, William, Colleen, Dani, Charlie, Aaron, Mia, Lou, Stant, and Ellie.

SßS

DISCLAIMER: Places, names, and titles are used in a fictitious manner. Much of the information presented was altered to be used in the framework of this fictional story. For more information on 19th century history, the good and the bad, please enjoy the research done by reputable sources. The history of humanity is an amazing topic that cannot be rightfully covered by a work of fiction.

The Tarot is an amazing divination tool used by many cultures for hundreds of years. Though an attempt has been made not to damage the traditions of the Tarot, much of the information presented is fictitious and should not be used for actual divination. For more information on the Tarot, please contact a reputable source.

The cards represented in this story are based pictorally upon the Rider-Waite Deck.

ABOUT THE AUTHOR

VENNESSA ROBERTSON is the author of the Arcane Adventuress series. She is also active in the writing and historic reenactment communities. She taught high school with dueling degrees in Colorado and Alaska until a traumatic brain injury in 2009. Now, she lives in rural Colorado. When she is not writing or homeschooling her two small children she is managing their ever-growing large and small animal rescue ranch.

SBS

ARCANE ADVENTURESS BOOK 1: CANITHROPE
ARCANE ADVENTURESS BOOK 2: THE CLOCKWORK EMPEROR
ARCANE ADVENTURESS BOOK 3: THE RAIL SPECTER

www.ingramcontent.com/pod-product-compliance
Lightning Source LLC
Chambersburg PA
CBHW060909250626
47159CB00008B/2931